Gifts from the Sea

A New Novel

by

Lew Trigg

About this Book:

After retiring, Gio Valducci purchased a condo in Southern California just a couple of blocks from the ocean. A small beagle hound shows up at his door and while they are walking the beach he sniffs something out that sends Gio on the adventure of his life.

Gio meets Sally, the woman of his dreams, and soon he moves into her ocean-side home. Suddenly his life comes alive with intrigue, as he is consumed with collecting one of the ocean's most treasured possessions: ambergris. It is a mysterious waxy chunk of flotsam expelled by whales that is used in the production of expensive perfume. The collection of this precious resource is not without risk and Gio is soon dodging a renegade thief, a Mexican crime cartel and aligning himself with local people of questionable character.

As Gio successfully sells his ambergris to a broker from Copenhagen, whose personal body guard, Alsace L. Wohljung, a retired Interpol officer still using his Interpol identity papers, befriends Gio and soon is asked to be best man at Gio and Sally's wedding. Amidst all this activity Gio sees something that makes him wonder if Sally's best friend, Marge, is also her lover.

As Gio and Sally leave for their honeymoon in Cabo San Lucas they believe a quiet life will follow, unaware that Ormando, a category four hurricane will bring devastation and death. Remarkably the Mexican cartel chief and his henchmen are in Cabo for a fishing tournament that Gio and Alsace are also participating in.

What more could happen to this ordinary man? How about narrowly avoiding death by a cartel hit man, being jailed in a Mexican prison on trumped-up charges and later unknowingly smuggling two dealer-sized bags of marijuana across the U. S. border.

About the author:

Lew Trigg still enjoys hiking through the hills of Missouri where he was born. An avid nature photographer, Lew often has new ideas for stories pop into his head while communing with nature. "When I get a story idea, most of the time I don't write much of it down until I have the characters clear in my mind. Then it is a matter of putting them in different situations and seeing how they respond. I doubt that any reader would think they recognize themselves in my writing; most of the characters are an amalgam of many people."

Lew is a resident of Alton, IL.

Lew wrote many short stories in his younger days and has published some of them as a Kindle book. You can also find essays and other stories on his blog at:
https://rewriter2014.wordpress.com/

Lew is a past winner of McKendree College's – McKendree Writers' Contest with a short story titled: "The System" – Printed in the publication, "Mermaid's Tales."

ISBN-13:978-1539984429
ISBN-10:1539984427
BISAC: Fiction / Action & Adventure

 ©

Definition:

Ambergris, pronounced amber-grease.

Sperm whales feed on squid deep in the ocean. Giant squid have a beak for a mouth similar to a parrot's beak. It is the only part of the squid that the whale cannot digest. The digestive system produces a coating around the beaks to protect the whales intestines. Eventually this substance is expelled into the ocean and can spend years floating around in the sea. It sometimes washes ashore and is collected for use as a fixative in expensive perfumes.

READ THIS!

There are some conventions in writing that are strictly adhered to by most high school English teachers. The minute a work of fiction defies these conventions and exhibits a better way to tell a story; well it is just all wrong, wrong, wrong, and the red ink flies to set that student straight.

So, if you are an English teacher, you may not feel comfortable reading this book. Having said that, I can tell you that there are many established authors who have adapted the exact method I have employed here to tell a good story.

Often in this book a scene is set-up as being past tense and then suddenly, often by dialogue, is brought alive to live in the present moment.

Perhaps you've seen movies where a narrator is telling of some past event:

"And there we were with our backs to the ocean, our ships having returned homeward to pick up more supplies and we were facing the foothills of a mountain range which completely concealed the deadly army we were to soon face. That morning as I walked down the beach......" And Walla! We see the narrator walking down the beach and we are there as it is happening.

I think you will find that once you get past the "high school English teacher mentality" you will find these segues nearly seamless and it will add to your enjoyment of an unfolding story. I have kept most of the chapters short and to the point. Thanks for picking this book up and sit back and please be entertained!

1

A Happy Man

Giovanni worked hard all his adult life as a baker. He often thought, God willing, I will retire some day with my small pension and social security and live near the ocean. He knew that living on the ocean was not an option for him since only the very rich could live there. Then one day he reached the ancient age of sixty-seven and would now get the maximum from social security and his baker's union pension. No one really knew why Giovanni never married but when he was young there were many young women that tried but could not capture him. This was his thinking: to get married was to be captured. Try if you like, but you will not find a 100% honest married man of retirement age that would not agree with him, after all, they have been caught!

Giovanni had saved his money his whole life and lived in a modest apartment less than a block from the bakery. The sum was large to him and he knew if he had two or three ex-wives and a tribe of offspring he would be retiring flat-broke. It would be hard to argue with this man who had figured things out for himself when he was young and he was resolute to these ideas his whole life.

So, a little while after he retired he visited some small cities near San Diego and found a nice ground floor condominium only two blocks from the ocean with a high enough elevation that even a tsunami could not ruin his new life. He had always planned to buy a bulldog after he retired so he would have someone to walk the beach with. On solitary vacations all through his life he had walked the beaches alone and always imagined walking a bulldog and he also knew why: everyone always said he, Giovanni, looked like a bulldog, which he considered to be a compliment when compared to all the possible alternatives.

Although his life, and now his retirement, had gone almost near plan-perfect, happenstance now began to creep in.

A few days after he was moved and settled a little beagle hound started following him around town. He had a collar that was engraved "Amber" and strangely no other information was given. Even stranger; what kind of a name was "Amber" for a male dog? At first he fed him outside his condo and then he started letting him come in a bit and before Giovanni knew it Amber was sleeping on the bedroom floor next to his bed. After buying a leash and taking Amber with him everywhere he went, he decided he should advertise in the lost & found, while equally hoping that someone would claim the hound and also hoping that he had himself a dog. He was pretty sure that Amber was a lot smarter than any bulldog could be and the vet said that he was probably less than a year old.

One day soon Giovanni had an idea that he thought would gain him attention from people, especially from kids. He liked being with children before they turned into dishonest grumbling teenagers. Soon after he thought of this new idea he started training Amber to do tricks. All the usual tricks dogs learn: sit, speak, roll over, play dead, come, and the less common; walking on their hind legs and then the front legs.

The change-up that would prove to delight both children and adults was the commands he gave. At first Giovanni had to make a list so that he didn't confuse himself:

Sit – means: play dead

Speak – means: walking on front legs

Roll over – Speak

Play dead – walking on hind legs

Come – sit

Walk on hind legs – roll over

Walk on front legs – come

When Giovanni was out walking and children stopped to pet Amber he would tell them Amber was very well trained. He then would proceed to tell Amber to sit and he played dead; then to speak and he walked on his front legs; and thus through the whole list of tricks and after each one Giovanni would pretend to be even more exasperated as the children laughed with glee at this dog that just wouldn't follow the owner's commands. For the finale Giovanni would sit on a nearby park bench or stoop down and say, "go away you silly dog." At which time Amber would run and jump on him and the dog's owner would praise him, "good dog Amber, good dog!" Everyone watching would have big smiles and a look of admiration that this man had trained his dog to entertain in this way.

Like most kids, as a child he had loved getting attention in one way or another. Somehow, having been single and leading a solitary life had kept that need in him throughout his life and it had accelerated in his later years.

Giovanni could not remember his father who had left town under a cloud of suspicion when Giovanni was four and one-half years old. His father's name was John Smith. Giovanni soon realized that Giovanni Smith was an odd name and although his friends and classmates called him Gio, when he was fourteen years old he had saved enough from his paper route to have his name legally changed to Giovanni Valducci, his new last name being his mother's maiden name. Then he thought it sounded pretty cool. "You mess wid Valducci, you mess wid da mob." As time went by with his new name he and his two best friends put the secret word out that Gio's missing father had been Mafioso and was gunned down by the F. B. I. A few kids believed it and it seemed to keep the bullies away.

Two of One

"I hate reporters," Bryan said. "Those assholes are going to ruin the market if they keep publishing World-wide that whale poop is one of the most valuable commodities on the face of the earth! I mean, look at this, here is the Nature's World website telling how a ten-year-old boy in Wales finds a funny looking rock on the beach and then he and his dad Google-it and identify it as Ambergris and as usual the fucking reporter exaggerates the value saying it weighs more than a half-pound and could be worth up to $80,000. Plus they show a picture of the mysterious rock. Where do they get this crap?" Bryan turned to his brother who was occupied with eating his breakfast cereal. "Did you see this?" Bryan asked. "This seems to be happening more and more and if enough people read it and start stalking the beaches, we'll have to find some other way to bag some cash." Bryan's brother Ryan shrugged his shoulders and continued eating his cereal. Bryan spoke again, "remember that time we bought that grisrock from that guy at the flea market for twenty bucks and he even told us where he found it? I think we eventually made about two hundred grand on that one? Do you remember?"

"Yeah, that was awesome but now the fucking guy would see it on the internet and cash-in for himself," Ryan stated.

Bryan laughs knowingly and they both shake their heads no and Ryan says, "not that old guy, I don't think he was into technology in any way, but they had it on the fucking national news last week. The reporter even told the whole fucking story of how sperm whales eat squid and can't digest their beaks and it turns into ambergris in their gut and when expelled, he actually said expelled, it bobs around in the ocean until someone maybe finds it on the shore. It was very fucking educational, like we need an educated public to ruin our latest gig."

"Yeah, yeah," Bryan said, "and they even gave the name of the perfume companies that buy it. Like the guy was just going to call them up and make a deal on the phone without going through the whole stupid process to get some cash."

"Yeah," Ryan replies, "but that was in England. The thing we really have going for us is that in the good ol' U. S. of A. it's against the law to traffic in it." Ryan pushes his lower lip out a little and says sarcastically, "although that never stops us."

"I wish I knew what happened to that dam beagle Jordan tried to train for us, at least he got lost before we paid for him," Bryan quipped.

"Yeah," Ryan replied, "unless he was really good at it and he sold him to someone else."

"Fuck," Bryan speculates, "I never thought of that. I wonder if Jordan is having any luck training that other hound to find meteorites?"

"I don't know," Ryan answers, "maybe we should pay him a visit and ask him a few questions."

"Good idea," Bryan agrees, "let's do that."

Bryan, the oldest by five minutes and Ryan, who came into the world next and both as identical twins were always an adventurous pair. The names their mom selected were thought "cute" by all but as they grew older it became a problem when shouting between different rooms of the house and on athletic fields and other public places. So their parents started calling them "R" for Ryan and "B" for Bryan. That worked pretty well and they insisted that they have separate teachers in grammar school to give their boys a separation experience not realizing that the boys often switched places without anyone being the wiser. So that identity became easier for those around them but more confusing for "R" and "B" who had to remember which one they were supposed to be in a given situation. Their humorous Uncle Jack called them Rhythm and Blues.

3

Cast Back Into The Sea

Two weeks to the day after Gio moved into his Condo he finally had the time and energy to go walk the beach. Amber seemed to really tug at the leash, as if he just couldn't wait to get there. That didn't seem at all unusual to Gio as he had always felt that way himself when near the beach. Gio wasn't up to any petting by strangers and he and Amber "doing their act." He simply wanted to walk the beach and see what was there. It was early morning and not too many folks were there which was perfect as far as Gio was concerned. He could come back later in the day and check out the babes in their skimpy bathing suits. He called them bikini bitches, as most of them would glare at him if he looked at them overtly or if he was caught covertly checking them out. He just figured that if they didn't want him to look at their pubescent parts hanging out they shouldn't have nearly dressed that way. But of course, most of them would be delighted if a Brad Pit type stared longingly, but never a human "bulldog."

There were mostly other beachcombers out in the bright sun and mist and quite a few fishermen had their rigs pointed at the ocean. Some were back up the beach a bit with their rods in holders and the taunt line high enough in the air that the beachcombers could walk under it unimpeded. The remaining anglers were standing in their wet suits with waves up to their waist surrounded by aged and lazy pelicans hoping to get a free handout. Somewhere along the way Amber tugged at the leash more than usual and pulled Gio to the water's edge and started sniffing a rock. Gio pulled hard to get Amber moving but to no avail. Gio looked closer at the rock and was almost afraid to touch it. It was a strange looking rock in an area void of rock outcroppings. The ocean had recently begun to "cough up" debris from the Fukushima, Japan tsunami. In a recent TV newscast the commentator had advised that the government was asking local citizens to become involved, "if you are walking along the coast and you see a piece of debris that you are able to move, pick it up and

15

move it above the high tide line, then call someone from the Fish and Game Department to report it."

Finally he picked it up and flung it back into the ocean and restrained Amber and got him moving again. His hands felt waxy and he washed them a little in the surf and dried them on his khaki pants. He then sniffed his hands and was both repelled and drawn to the odor. Jeez, he thinks, I've probably got Japanese nuclear waste or some other dreaded chemical on my hands. After a few minutes the two happy walkers turned back the way they came. When they reached the same area where the rock had been it was there again and again Amber was intent on sniffing it and this time he exhibited that ancient ritual of all dogs of rubbing his back on this odiferous hunk of something. Gio was tired of this floating rock and he took out some napkins from his khaki jacket and picked it up and walked up to the sand dunes and tossed it in the middle of a clump of sand and sea grass. "Good riddance," Gio exclaimed!

4

Miss Happenstance

It is a fine spring day and Gio is up early as usual and has breakfast on the terrace among the plantings and flowers with a resolute guard posted by his side anxiously awaiting a little taste of bacon. "O.K., O.K., kiddo here you go" and Gio pops a piece of bacon into Amber's mouth and then holds his empty hands out as Amber anxiously waits for more. "Hey, you old hound dog, you want to go for a walk? Hmm, want to take a walk on the beach?" Amber runs through the open patio door and comes back with his leash in his mouth and drops it at his master's feet and barks. Gio clips the leash onto the "Amber collar" and hooks the looped end of the leash over a nearby fence post, goes through the house, locks the patio door, grabs his jacket, locks the front door and walks around to his waiting pooch.

Gio had forgotten about the "smelly rock" from earlier in the week and was hopeful he could find a couple of seashells on their walk to display on his patio. He recognized several of the fishermen as he walked by and nodded and gave them all a hearty "good morning." Jeez, he thinks, how could life be any better than this? What a glorious day, retirement is everything I thought it would be! After a few minutes of walking Amber suddenly stopped. Gio was glad to hesitate for a moment as his enthusiasm for retirement had sped him up from their usual casual walk.

Amber starts sniffing the air and then moves up the beach and then stops. "What's the matter fella, are you O.K.?" Amber turns so quickly he wraps the leash around Gio's legs and nearly trips him over and Gio seems to have no choice but to follow. Then in the middle of the dunes and sea grass Gio spots the object of Amber's ambition: the rock; only not just "the rock" but another similar rock lying within a few feet. Amber is sniffing the rocks and just as excited as the last time. Gio was not a man to curse often, not even to himself, but he sat down hard on the sand and said aloud, "what the fuck?"

17

He was still leery of touching the rocks. What is going on? He asks himself. Did this thing reproduce itself in the last couple of days? It couldn't have washed up here, even at high tide. He stared at both rocks again trying to determine if it could have broken in half but he knew they were both too big for that theory and he didn't have a better one. He takes a protein bar from his jacket pocket and peels the wrapper and eats a little while he thinks it over again. Amber is excited about the food and Gio reaches into his other jacket pocket and gives Amber a dog biscuit and now they both think it over.

Soon a dog is growling and barking and Gio looks up and sees a woman walking toward them being pulled along by her stocky bull dog. Gio pulls himself up and brushes the sand off his pants and puts the food away and begins to walk on. But Amber thinks he has found a new friend and pulls him toward the bulldog. As the dogs do their ritual sniffing that dog etiquette demands the humans perform their ritual hellos and that's how Gio met Miss Happenstance, Sally Cruthird.

"So you found our mysterious rock?" Sally asks.

"Found two of them!" Gio replies.

"What?" Sally looks around and sees that there are indeed two rocks. "I threw that one up here yesterday; I couldn't get Wilma to move on. I think they have magical dog powers or at least some irresistible odor that dogs can't resist. I have a plastic shopping bag I brought to collect shells in, why don't we take one of these up to the house and see if we can find it on the internet?"

"How far is it?" Gio asks.

"Not far, just up the beach a little ways," Sally replies.

Gio also has a couple of bags in his jacket pocket and they work together to get one of the rocks covered with a bag from each side. Gio holds it in front of him with both hands and asks Sally to use the third bag to pick up the smaller rock and place it on top of the larger one so that he doesn't have to touch the exposed one. As Sally bends over to pick up the dog leashes Gio gets a good look at her bottom and feels a twinge go through his penis and both he and his penis like what they see. As they are walking along they each have difficulty thinking of something to say.

Soon, Sally asks, "so, are you retired?

"Well, retired or retarded, some days I'm not sure which," Gio laughs.

Sally chuckles and adds, "I know what you mean. I'm not quite old enough to retire officially in regard to Social Security and Medicare but I don't work. Are you married or single?

"Single."

"A widower?"

"Nope, never been married and don't go thinking I'm gay or something, just never met the right woman."

"I'm a widow, Howard passed away a little over a year ago. That's when I moved down here to the beach house. He would never have bought the beach house except to please me. He wasn't crazy about the ocean. But it's home to me now and I recently put the other house up for sale."

"How much are you asking?"

"They've got it at 3.3 million but I'm thinking if I can sell it for at least 2.9 I'll be happy with that. Guess I'll have an auction for most of the furniture and things. Do you live around here?"

"Yes, I'm up at the Windward condo complex, it's a couple of blocks up the hill, just moved there a few weeks ago. Amber started following me around and I haven't found the owner so I guess I've got myself a dog. He's a smart one.

Funny that you have a bulldog, that's what I intended to buy until Amber showed up."

"Isn't your dog a male?"

"Oh, you mean the name Amber. That's what his collar had on it and nothing else. You're right it seems a little odd for a boy dog to be named Amber. But I didn't try to change it in case I found the owner, so Amber it is. He does a lot of tricks; I'll have to show you sometime."

Soon, they arrive at Sally's beach house. As they turn up the beach and it is obvious that the glorious home belongs to Sally, Gio is thinking; holy mackerel, this woman is filthy rich!

5

Stripped

They took the Porsche. Since Bryan enjoyed driving he took the wheel and they headed into the countryside. R and B's dog training friend, Jordan, lived deep in the hinterlands where his father ran a chop-shop. The chop-shop specialized in luxury cars and sporty models. There was a steady stream of car thieves that found their way there. The thieves were mostly drug addicts and if they needed a fix and what addict doesn't? – Then Jordan's dad, Theo, would usually only give them a few hundred dollars for a sixty to seventy thousand dollar automobile. Each vehicle was then disassembled and the parts sold to shady parts dealers of which there was a network, as well organized as any cross-country auto supply business. If any of the drug addicts ever complained about Theo's compensation they risked being arrested and imprisoned as nearly all the county officials were on Theo's payroll. Theo would not accept a vehicle procured through carjacking or any violent crime. The man had his ethics and so did the bribed county officials. His staff's 24 hour monitoring of a police scanner assured that any vehicle stolen as a result of what Theo judged to be a criminal action was immediately turned over to the authorities and if possible the perpetrator of the crime as well. This was a great source for the county prosecutor and one of the benefits of "doing business" with Theo.

Although he would never tell anyone, Theo long ago realized his son, Jordan, was nearly useless. Jordan's strongest attribute was having never gotten into any trouble and he didn't use drugs. Well, at least he didn't do any hard drugs. Jordan's big thing was treasure hunting. Not that he ever actually found any, but he liked talking about it and hanging out with real treasure hunters. Most of all Jordan loved animals and he had dogs and cats and also some exotic animals that could only be obtained through smuggling operations. And that is how he got started in dealing in ambergris. The laws regarding protected species are very tough and do not permit ignorance to exclude an offender. If you are caught with a bald eagle's feather in your hat you will be prosecuted as if you had killed the eagle and plucked the feather from its corpse. The fact that you found the feather lying in a field is not relevant as there is no way of proving it and you will not be excused. Similarly sperm whales are protected as no one can determine if the ambergris was washed ashore or was removed from a harpooned whale's gut with a chain saw. That is the argument however the truth is that the longer a chunk of the commonly called "grisrock" is tossed about in the ocean the more the aging brings out its best qualities: not just its scent, which can be quite alluring, but its ability to act as a fragrance amplifier and fixative that binds the fragrance of perfumes to the human body.

It has been a while since Bryan has driven the Porsche out through the countryside and he is cruising at 85 mph and squealing the tires on the curves. Ryan buckles his seat belt which makes Bryan chuckle. The radio is playing loudly and the disc jockey has just spun a disc by The Comet Chasers, a song called "Why Are You So Cruel to Me?

Ryan says, "Bet I know what you are thinking about. Or should I say "who" you are thinking about or maybe the "things" you are thinking about." Both men laugh and simultaneously say, "Kimberley's humongous tits."

The song had been popular when the boys were in high school during the time they both had really hot girlfriends. Kimberley was Ryan's girl and Bryan's steady was Judy Maddress. It was quite prestigious to be dating those girls, both known for their beauty, cheerleading and Kim had a perfectly petite body with breasts way out of proportion to such a petite size. Many identical twin siblings do their best to be individualized by dressing differently and other distinguishing activities. The boys always dressed the same and switched identities so often that it became second nature. Kim had been a willing participant in many forms of sexual play and intercourse. Judy had made a pledge through her church youth group to remain a virgin until she was married. Naturally the boys took their turn with each girl, so much for feminine intuition. The competition R and B had going was to be the first one to steal Judy's virginity. She stayed true to her pledge but that didn't stop her from having oral and anal intercourse as the unknowing hormones coursed through her veins seeking unknown descendents.

Something happened in their junior year and it was the first time the twins had a serious outcome from their switching places. It had mostly been lots of fun up until that time: being able to study for just one subject and scoring high on the tests as they switched places; switching soccer teams to perhaps determine the outcome of a tournament. Yes, indeed, it was all fun and games until Kim became pregnant. There are consequences for identical twins when even their mother cannot be certain of identity. No moles, no difference of proportion on any bodily feature, same height, same weight, same personality, same, same, same and not even DNA tests can tell who fathered the baby. Just imagine being the parent of two teens facing paternity at the exact same time. It was a huge event and rumor mills coursed through the town and no matter how outrageous gossip can be the truth was even more scandalous. The twins and both families quickly righted themselves when Kim miscarried. Such a sad event to have promoted the happiness of so many and it proved to Judy that remaining a virgin did have its virtues even though everyone including her parents assumed she had "gone all the way" also, until her mother's gynecologist determined that a hymen did exist.

In order to enter the grounds of Theo's chop-shop, where Jordon's apartment was located, it was necessary to stop and talk into a squawk-box and then the electronic gate would be opened. When they arrived someone in front of them had already talked to someone and as the gate slid out of the way they drove around to the side of the huge warehouse type building and entered a side door. The twins looked at the tall shelving throughout the building where the auto parts were

23

filed as if Dewey himself had been here with his Decimal System with row after row of all the parts that it takes to create or repair high-end automobiles. The door to Jordan's apartment was open and the twins could hear a cacophony of jungle sounds coming from the various exotic animals in Jordan's collection. Bryan calls out their friends name but they hear no reply and begin looking around the apartment. When Bryan peers into the bedroom he sees that Jordan is in the middle of something. The "something" as they later discover is Tekeysia, Jordan's new Jamaican girl friend. While they wait for Jordan the twins are entertained by Soliloquy, Jordan's African Grey Parrot. "Jordan's gone, Jordan's gone," Soliloquy repeats many times. Then he says, "What the fuck do you want? Hmm? What the fuck do you want?"

Bryan says to Ryan, "yeah man, what the fuck do you want?"

Ryan answers, "I want my fucking dog, where is he?" They both laugh. A trip to Jordan's is always an adventure. In a few minutes Jordan comes out in an oversized robe and they all tap knuckles together as a hello greeting.

"It's been a while," Jordan says, "I hope you've brought me some grisrock."

"Haven't found any lately," answers Ryan, "We have been wondering what happened to the beagle?"

"It was worth it man, totally worth it. I went to Monk's Beach about a month ago with the idea to see if that hound dog could sniff-out some grisrock and I sat in the car when we arrived and smoked a huge joint. I'm not sure what was in that shit but it really tripped me out. After we walked the beach for a while I decided to let him go, thinking he might do better if I gave him free reign and that is when I saw Tekeysia, a beautiful Jamaican girl. She's back there in the bedroom now, and we started talking and she came back to the car with me and we smoked some more weed and came back here. I didn't think about the dog until the next morning and I went up there but I couldn't find him. So I'm going to have to start over, training a new one."

"What about the meteorite dog, is that working?" Bryan asks.

"I don't think it will," Jordan answers. "Meteorites only give-off the burnt residue for a few days, then, they are just another rock."

"Or if the meteorite hits the dog in the fucking head, then he would find it." Ryan quips.

"Yeah, hell yeah," Jordan responds, "then you would know!" The young men all laugh.

"So, bring that new Jamaican girl friend out here," Bryan requests. Ryan jumps in, "yeah Mon we'd like to check her, I mean we'd like to meet her." Everyone laughs again.

Bryan says, "I peaked around the corner and saw you guys in bed."

"So what," Jordan replies, "I've seen you two messin' around before."

"Yeah, but," Bryan replies, and then Ryan finishes the statement, "we're twins, for us it's the same as masturbation." Everyone laughs again.

Jordan tells the twins, "I'll try to get another dog and train him, but right now I have to take Tekeysia to pick up her shit, she's moving in with me. I'm going to have a party next Saturday night, so you guys come over and you can meet her then and we'll talk a little business. I also want you to meet some guy that might be helpful to us. He's a real Mexican, but over six feet tall with red hair, his fucking name is Fred McCallister and he knows a lot about the smuggling trade. Come early; say 8 o'clock, so we can talk business before we get fucked up."

In Bryan's best Jamaican voice, he says, "yeah Mon we be wearin' dreds an' smokin' beeg cigars o' the weed, yeah Mon."

Ryan tells Bryan, "You sound more like a fucking Irishman than a Rastafarian." They all laugh again, and then Jordan walks out the door of his apartment and out the warehouse door with the twins following.

Just outside the door Jordan asks, "Where's your fucking car?"

Bryan touches his pocket and doesn't feel his keys, "I left the keys in it."

"Oh, fuck," Jordan exclaims and starts running and the twins follow him as he rounds the corner of the building and enters into the warehouse through the overhead door opening and suddenly he stops.

They are all looking at the twin's Porsche, Theo's crew already has the doors off and the engine compartment lid up and Jordan yells, "stop!"

Squeeze Those Lemons

Before Gio, Sally, and the dogs entered her house she and Gio removed their shoes on the deck and she washed the dog's paws at the outdoor shower and dried them with a towel hanging on the rail. Sally chose not to give Gio a tour of the house as she was still wondering if bringing him here was a not-very-bright thing to do. She pushed the button to boot-up her desk-top computer and asked Gio if he would like something to drink. Having both decided on lemonade Sally poured it into tumblers and sat Gio's drink close to the desk-top computer and told him he could work there while she was getting her laptop to search for the mysterious "rocks" that they had left outside on the deck's railing. Sally thought the search would go faster with them both working and it also gave her a chance to get a good look at Gio while she was deciding why she would bring a strange man into her home after only meeting him minutes before.

She thought him a handsome man, especially for his age. She had been fantasizing lately that she would by chance meet someone but had decided it was just because she was "too lazy" to work at meeting someone by design. They each carried out their solitary quest without much conversation as the dogs romped throughout the house and finally had to rest from exhaustion.

As the time passed Gio was also sneaking glances at Sally and thought she was a beautiful woman with a petite body and a smile that would brighten anyone's day.

"I think I've got it! Gio says, as the printer springs to life. I want you to see this; I think we may have found some ambergris." Gio pronounces the last syllable just as it looks rather than the correct way, "grease." He removes the printed news article from the printer and moves to the sofa and sits next to Sally and says, "This is from a children's publication, but it explains it quite well."

Curiosity Leads a Fourteen Year Old to Riches, by Gloria
Nichols, Staff Reporter

How does a kid pick up a quick $75,000. Enough to
cover four years of tuition at some of the more reasonably
priced universities? That's just what Claude Hilliker did on a
trip to a West coast beach in New Zealand. Claude, being a
very inquisitive 14 year old, just couldn't agree with his father
that he found "just a rock." "It was quite smelly and felt waxy
to the touch. I wanted to take it home and see if I could find
out what it was."

And that's just what Claude did. Claude's father,
William, stated to reporters, "I told him to throw it back into
the sea. Luckily Claude thought it was something special."
Something special, indeed, as it turns out Claude's discovery
was a one-half pound chunk of ambergris.

Ambergris' great value comes from its ability to "fix a
scent to human skin." That's why it's in such demand with the
finest perfume companies. It allows the fragrance to linger
many more hours after the perfume is applied to the skin.

Where does it come from? You may find this
shocking: whale poop! That's right, a small percentage of
sperm whales produce it in their gut because they are unable to
digest the beaks (or mouths) of giant squid that they regularly
dive very deep in the ocean to devour. When the chunks of
encased beaks are expelled they then break-up in the ocean
and the pieces float around for decades and after much
exposure to salt water and sun they sometimes wash onto the
beach for some lucky and inquisitive kid to find.

For our U. S. readers, you should know that the U. S.
banned the sale of the substance in 1972 as it comes from an

endangered species. However, there is a ready market in Europe. Claude's father stated that Claude had told him prior to this event that he wants to be a marine biologist. "This will enable him to get a good education and follow his dream."

Sally reads the entire article and says, "You've got to be kidding me. Do you really think that is what we have found?"

"I don't know, but I think it could be."

Sally looks at Gio and asks, "Are you hungry, I'm starved?"

"I could eat." Gio responds.

Sally seats Gio at the kitchen bar and makes two tuna sandwiches and sits next to him and they eat in silence until Sally jumps up to give the begging dogs a treat. Seated again, Sally moves her knee a little and it touches Gio and she pulls it away and then slowly touches his knee again and leaves it there. When they finish eating Gio takes her by the hand and tells her that she is a beautiful woman and bends a little and kisses her. Sally puts her arms around Gio and holds him tightly and they embrace and kiss and Gio brushes his tongue across Sally's left ear and she moans so loudly it almost startles Gio and he asks, "Can we go to your bed?" Sally takes him by the hand and walks him through the house to the master bedroom. As they are walking she says softly, "I think I'm going to hate myself in the morning."

The next hour was very pleasurable and especially so as it had been a long time since either of them had experienced such passion. They did many of the things that new lovers do. And, then they did things that only the animals in the woods do when they are sure no one is watching them.

Finally, when their lust had succeeded in satisfying their pent-up needs she lay on his shoulder.

"I've never, ever, had anything like this happen to me. I must be losing my mind," Sally says softly into Gio's ear. Gio pulls her more tightly to him and he whispers to her, "I think it is the best thing that's ever happened to me."

7

The Tall Mexican

Among the population of Mexicans living on the Baja California Peninsula there were very few with the surname of McCallister. When Fred's great, great grandfather, Frederick, had left Ireland aboard a freighter ship he suffered the misfortune of serving under the notorious Captain O'Reilly. Frederick's suffering was made worse as it was his first time at sea so that both the crew and the Captain made his life more miserable than the life he had fled from in Ireland. Once his feet touched the dock at Tijuana he vowed not to return to the ship and he blended into the Mexican population. At least as well as any six-foot red-haired Irishman with a bit of Norseman's blood could assimilate. Fortunately for Frederick, Captain O'Reilly and the entire crew were glad to be rid of an inept Irishman who towered over them all.

Both of Fred's parents were a little taller than average and their skin and hair a little lighter in comparison to other Mexicans but in conceiving him they had somehow reached back to his great, great grandfather Frederick to produce a fair skinned red-haired nine pound baby boy. Fred had a brash personality that matched his brash looks and he had always been a leader of Mexican boys and now men and he used his skills to gather wealth and in a situation where money and power were at stake he could be quite violent. However, unlike some of the dispensers of narcotics he had given thought to the future and decided he wanted to live to be an old and rich man. He had somehow extricated himself from the life of a drug dealing pimp before his name turned up on someone's hit list, or at least he thought he had, and then he found another less dangerous albeit still illegal profession of dealing in the smuggling of exotic animals, stolen works of art and recently he has taken an interest in something called ambergris. Any activity in Norte Americano that breaks the law is a natural magnet for the unscrupulous and exploitive men of Mexico. Fred is well known to the border guards and travels to Southern California and back again with as much ease as going through a toll booth.

8

On The Beach!

In the three weeks since Gio and Sally first met they have been inseparable. They also own two very happy canines. Just imagine two high school students falling in love for the first time and not having any parents to ground them! And, there you have it! Gio loves jazz and big band and so does Sally. They both enjoy being outdoors and exploring the beaches and the little out-of-the-way places that tourists could never find. Gio has abandoned his beloved condo and has been living fulltime with Sally since the day they met. In Gio's retirement he had "come alive," and had been reborn again when he met the woman he had always been dreaming of.

In the almost non-stop chatter since they had met Sally has told Gio her story. Gio was a good listener and he especially wanted to hear all about this magnificent "catch." Just imagine; Gio having avoided being "caught" his whole life and now he has become the catcher and catch-ee and never once has he thought of this new journey in those terms. Sally and her husband had met in high school and became sweethearts and then drifted away from each other having attended universities separated by the forty-eight states. After graduation and both of them experiencing break-ups with their college sweethearts and back home they started dating again and got married two years later. It was a childless marriage and although both sets of parents kept waiting for grandchildren to be born it just never happened and after a brief period of Sally wanting to be a mother they both forgot all about it never knowing if one or both were infertile. After twenty years of marriage Sally began to suspect that Howard was chasing other women but Howard had finally convinced her that he was above suspicion. At least he thought he had. For many years Sally just put it out of her mind and enjoyed the bounty that Howard's real estate and development company provided.

She traveled throughout the world with women friends and sometimes nieces, who took the place of her remedial need to have children of her own. Then, three years ago, the cruise ship on which she was vacationing, made an unscheduled stop in Cabo San Lucas for a medical emergency. She went ashore and to dinner with her new cruise friends, there in the restaurant was Howard, having the time of his life with his twenty-eight year old administrative assistant. Sally was stung into silence and told her cruise friends she had a migraine as she decided to not face the humiliation of the situation. After she returned home to Howard telling her how busy he'd been while she was gone she waited still. Sally did her own surveillance the next week and it paid off as on Thursday of that week she saw him leaving in their town car with his assistant and she followed them to a condo development that Howard had control of and watched them enter into one of the display condos. Howard had driven the Lincoln Town Car that day and she was driving the Cadillac. She pulled into the parking space next to the Lincoln, entered it and drove away leaving the Cadillac for Howard to puzzle over until he saw their marriage license lying on the passenger's seat. Sally returned home and waited.

"Long story short," Sally had told Gio, "that's how I got this beach house." Not long after that Howard began having heart problems which Sally thought odd considering he had broken her heart! She was once again devoted to him in his illness but silently in her heart was glad when a heart attack took him and then she grieved; the most serious grieving a human being can ever do: the grief for what a relationship could have been and should have been.

After all the legal issues were settled and the outrageous attorney's fees were paid Sally discovered she had enough money to clear the bridge loan if her in-town home sold for at least $2.9 million.

9

Honor Among Thieves

The business matters Jordan and the twins were to discuss at 8 p.m. "before they got fucked up" never happened as the twins were "fucked up" when they arrived and so was Jordan. Jordan is the first to arise Sunday morning and is aghast as he sees Soliloquy lying at the bottom of his cage perhaps dead from spiked water and/or inhalation of second-hand cannabis smoke. Jordan fills a glass with ice water and pours a little onto Soliloquy's head. The reaction is immediate as Soliloquy rights himself and screeches "what the fuck do you want, huh? What the fuck do you want?" Jordan is greatly relieved to see that his old friend is alive and as sassy as ever. Jordan looks around to see if his human friends are similarly alive but maybe not too sassy.

Fred McCallister removes a sofa cushion covering his head and asks Jordan, "can't you shut that fucking parrot up? I thought the fucker was dead."

The noon-day sun, though unobserved, creates inertia among all-night partiers and it now works its magic as one-by-one the revelers crawl out of their reverie and move to the great room, a combination of living room and kitchen. As Ryan or perhaps it is Bryan wanders into the room Fred points to him and says to Jordan, "I'm sure glad I knew that fucker has a twin. I saw him humping so many women last night; it was unbelievable, even for two guys. Does everyone like mushrooms, hamburger and black olives? Fred then calls and orders four large pizzas and agrees to a $12.00 surcharge for the distance of the delivery.

Jordan mixes Bloody Marys in a large pitcher and pours everyone a glass full. A few people pass through the room and depart with explanations of having to go to work or some other imagined necessity and Jordan is glad that only the twins and Fred are left with Tekeysia still sound asleep in the bedroom. Now the business meeting could begin. "Does anyone want a bagel?" Jordan asks, "I can assure you that the pizzas won't be here for an hour and a half.

Jordan opens the meeting by asking Fred, "any luck in finding a grisrock dealer in Mexico?"

"I did find one," Fred answers, "but the fucker is in Mexico City and I don't like going there, it is not a safe place for me."

"Guess we're stuck with the bitch of Copenhagen," Jordan replies, "but as discussed before I think she is making a ton off of us and we never know when our package will be confiscated by the good ol' U. S. of A."

Fred continues, "I want to find a dealer that I can go talk face-to-face with, so I can, oh, what is the word that means to be rough with?" Jordan helps, "intimidate." "Yeah, that's it," Fred says, "so I can intimidate them. I can be very aggressive when I want to be."

Bryan speculates, "I still can't believe that we can't go direct to the perfume companies."

Ryan replies, "those fuckers won't even admit that they use grisrock in their products and still the news reporters keep saying how many thousands a grisrock is worth," it drives me crazy!"

"We've got to get organized on this," Bryan reflects, "I don't know what has happened but grisrock is starting to show up here pretty regular. Jordan, do you think we should try training another beagle to help us find the stuff?"

Fred asks, "What's this?"

Jordan gives Bryan a hateful glance and tells Fred, "oh, I forgot to tell you I was training a hound dog to sniff out the grisrock and I got fucked-up when I met Tekeysia down on Monk's Beach and I lost the dog.

"Have you tried to find him?" Fred asks.

"Not really," Jordan replies, "well, I did run an ad in the weekly sales flyer that my beagle was lost, and that his collar said 'Amber' on it.

Fred gives Jordan a stare and asks, "oh, I get it, you didn't want to give away what the dog was being trained for, huh?"

"Actually, ambergris wouldn't fit on the tag, too long." Jordan replies and feels quite foolish as Fred shakes his head from side-to-side.

Fred excuses himself and heads for the bathroom. He doesn't actually have to go but wants to be alone for a while to do some serious thinking. He recalls seeing that dog: a crazy old guy with a dog doing funny tricks and he had a good looking old lady with him. One of the kids on the boardwalk had asked the dog's name and Fred couldn't catch what he said. Fred had thought he said "amber" but he knew that wasn't a name for a male hound. Fred looks in the mirror and admires his handsome face and smiles widely and quietly says, "I am going to find that fucking dog, but I'm not going to tell those fucking idiots I'm doing it."

10

A Watchful Eye

Perhaps the tsunami in Japan has changed the ocean currents or perhaps the prevailing winds have changed or maybe there is no logical explanation; logic being of human creation and nonexistent in Nature. However, there are many pieces of ambergris washing up on the shores of Southern California and the ambergris pickers are all patrolling the beaches and doing such a good job that the average person does not know of its existence.

Fred McCallister goes to Monk's Beach every day and does not see Gio and Amber for almost two weeks. Gio patrols the beach twice a day, early morning and late evening. Gio now pushes a jogging stroller with a cover so no one can see inside. He first searches the beach and then moves above the high tide line as apparently some beach walkers have done as the government has asked them and moved tsunami debris above the high tide line.

On the eleventh day Fred has been out all night and goes to the beach much earlier than usual and realizes he hasn't seen the old man and his dog because they patrol the beach very early in the morning. Fred backs-off and retrieves the binoculars from his Lexus and pursues his surveillance at a comfortable distance, just as he once did at the border to find and steal dope and drugs from the low ranking "mule" smugglers. That era of his career had almost cost him his life and if he could figure this ambergris thing out he knew he could make lots of money.

Fred tracks Gio back to the beach house and watches him enter the three car garage and on the third day equipped with better binoculars he is able to read the code Gio is dialing to get into the garage. When Gio and Sally leave to get lunch he looks in through the small windows and sees some plastic containers filled with water and bubbling from air being pumped into the water. Fred begins to wonder if maybe Gio is a marine biologist or some bullshit and not picking up grisrock at all. But no, he thinks, I've seen the dog sniff it out and seen him putting it into the jogging stroller. Fred enters the code on the security pad and nothing happens. He tries it again and then realizes he must not have seen the numbers properly and then he fades back into the beach before he is noticed.

At lunch Gio and Sally discuss the recent developments of her financial situation. "I thought the banker told you that the beach house wasn't connected to the sale of your other house." Gio states.

"Well, I don't really understand it, but I do remember him telling me I had to sell the place in town for at least 2.9 million or I risk a foreclosure on both."

Gio responds to Sally, "Damn bankers, they tie up everything down to your socks and underwear. And, worse of all is that we are sitting on a fortune in ambergris and I can't figure out a way to get it sold. I did send a small sample to some gal in Copenhagen to prove that it really is ambergris and I haven't heard back from her yet.

A couple of days later Fred again watches Gio at the garage door security pad and this time he is sure he has the right numbers. However, when he tries it a few days later it does not open. One day Fred notices the couple sitting on the deck overlooking the beach and he approaches from the front of the house and secrets himself under the deck and he can hear part of their conversation through the barking of the dogs. Fred is relieved that there is a gate to prevent the dogs from coming around to discover him and more relieved when Gio opens the patio door and the dogs go inside. Now Fred can hear the couple quite well and discovers that they are soon to shower and dress for an evening out including dinner and an old fashioned big band dance. He hides behind a sand dune near the garage and when Gio backs the town car out and starts up the street, before the garage door closes Fred drops down and rolls underneath it and is safely inside, except that he has broken the beam of light that prevents small children from being crushed, which stops the garage doors descent but Fred quickly pushes the button on the wall and the door descends. Fred's heart is racing but he calms down when he sees the town car turn at the corner. There are now more plastic containers and Fred counts eight of them and each container has exactly five pieces of grisrock except for one that has six. The grisrock is all sizes and shapes and is suspended in the salt water by a bubbler system. "This fucking guy is smart." Fred theorizes out loud, which he immediately regrets as the dogs are at the kitchen door barking their heads off. "Fuck!" Fred wonders how he is going to get out of here without getting his ass bitten but soon is oblivious to that reality and the barking of the dogs as he examines the ambergris and is pretty sure it is the real thing. Fred finds an envelope that's been dropped on the garage floor. It is a statement for condo fees, addressed to a Gio Valducci, that's right, he had heard that bitch call the guy "Gio," and wasn't quite sure what she had said. Fred sits down in an old lawn chair and tries to decide if he should just steal all of it, shoot the dogs, and then burglarize the entire house for valuables. Fred is in sort of a trance as he thinks of all the possibilities. The dogs have stopped barking and he makes his decision: he will take one piece of grisrock from the container that has six and try to exit the garage by pushing the garage door button on the wall and then running and jumping over the beam that had nearly foiled his entry. Fred is sure the old guy will not remember that one container had six pieces and he can use the one piece as bait to find a good broker to sell the grisrock to. Fred smiles widely; why steal the grisrock now? He is thinking. Let the old guy collect a lot more and just sit back and wait until I find a good broker and then do the big heist. He fishes the grisrock out of the container, wraps it in an old tee shirt hanging on the wall and makes his escape just as he planned it and he is sure that no one sees him doing it.

Ryan and Bryan make their way down the beach highway every morning at sunrise. Sunrise is something the men usually try to avoid but they are getting short on funds and they have discovered from some information on the internet that some grisrock hunter in New Zealand can spot it from his car, as the sunrise produces just the right light to pick up that special glistening that grisrock often has. They are driving an old delivery van they bought from Jordan that has "Carl's Meat Market" painted on the side and is only partially concealed by the white paint the twins sprayed on it. After a few days of patrolling the beach they have a few small pieces of ambergris and then one morning Bryan spots Fred looking through a pair of binoculars and they turn the van around and drive back by to make sure it is him. At first they think he has just found a better way to spot the grisrock but then they realize he is watching some old guy with a baby carriage and a beagle.

"I'll bet that's the fucking dog that fuckhead Jordan lost!" Ryan says.

"Yeah, I think you are right. I fucking told you that Fred was up to something. After we started talking about that dog and he went to the restroom his whole demeanor changed. I told you, he just wasn't interested in talking about us working together after he came back, I fucking told you!"

"All right, you were right." Bryan replies, "Let's keep an eye on this fucker and see what he's up to."

Indeed! Fred's only thought since starting his surveillance of Gio is that Gio himself doesn't catch-on that he is being watched. He has given very little thought as to someone watching him. That has made tracking Fred easy for the twins. They watch his every move and they always know where to find him. All they have to do is find Gio, who can be spotted from about a mile away; an old guy pushing a baby carriage with a beagle by his side!

The twins know that Fred has been inside the garage and they too have clandestinely observed the chunks floating in the bubbling water. They have also guessed that Fred's plan is to let the old guy find more grisrock and then steal it all. What has the twins and Fred perplexed is; when will the old guy ship the grisrock? Does he have a broker? Has he had it confirmed that it is really grisrock? There are so many questions standing between them and a small fortune. It is much easier for Fred. He has no qualms about stealing the grisrock and even murdering Gio, Sally and the bulldog if it should come to that.

11

Fred's Big Score

Gio wakes early as usual. He has set no alarm clock but he fills the coffee maker each night and sets the timer to make the coffee early and it is the aroma of fresh brewed coffee that lures him through getting dressed and his morning bathroom routine. Sally is sleeping soundly and will not wake until Gio is well down the beach. He lets Amber out of the laundry room and he joins him on the deck to enjoy the breeze and beautiful sunrise. Sally's bulldog, Wilma, has been gone for ten days. The dog was a nuisance as far as Gio was concerned but he had nothing to do with her death. He knew that Sally and Amber missed her but she was a bad influence on Amber's discipline and Gio hated that Sally was sad but they both had Amber now and a dog like Amber is enough to fill anyone's heart with adoration. Gio downs another cup of coffee and a breakfast tart and gets his baby carriage from the garage, hooks Amber to the leash, and down the beach they go. Amber has only found one small piece of ambergris in the last two weeks. This makes Gio very optimistic as he has learned in life that success comes in bunches and the longer the dry spell the closer he is to reaching his goal. Today his theory rings true when something floating in the surf catches his eye. Gio rolls his shorts up and kicks off his sandals and wades into the ocean to get a closer look. There is a huge boulder floating there and after several tries he is able to push it toward the shore. It is of a lighter color with darker gray lines running through it which resemble the growth rings of a tree. Gio has read of such pieces but soon realizes that Amber doesn't have that frenzied excitement he usually has on sniffing out the smaller pieces they have been finding. Gio speculates that perhaps by finding it first he has truncated the dog's enthusiasm. The piece is too large and waxy to be put into the baby carriage and Gio scoops out a depression in the sand and rolls the boulder into it. He looks all around and sees no one and rushes away to exchange the stroller for a wheel barrel.

Fred has gotten sloppy with his surveillance since noticing that Gio and the dog have found nothing for days. But on this morning he decides to shadow the old man and his dog once again. Fred has even grown fond of watching the sunrise and feeling the freshness of the morning sea breeze. He has purchased an expensive digital camera with a powerful close-up lens and uses it to follow Gio's beach strolls as he thinks it attracts less attention than the binoculars. Fred wonders why he is still watching Gio, as he plans to steal all the grisrock before Gio can find a broker and ship it out of the country. The timing of which has caused Fred to lose sleep. The minute he gets the results from "that bitch in Copenhagen" he will move forward with the plan. Fred has watched the dog grow in his expertise of finding ambergris and on several occasions has seen him digging it out of the sand. It is a lucky morning for Fred as when he pulls into the parking lot he can see a husky man and his little dog through a gap in the sand dunes. He grabs the camera and zooms in just in time to see Gio rolling the boulder into a dip in the sand. He watches Gio look up and down the beach and walk away.

Once Gio is out-of-site Fred snaps a few pictures of the small boulder and wonders if he has time to run down to the beach, grab the object and return to his car. He looks up and down the deserted beach and jumps in his car and drives around the guardrail and through the gap in the dunes and right down the beach to within a few feet of the boulder. He opens his trunk and picks the waxy greasy ball up and when he reaches the car puts the chunk down on the sand, dumps the contents of a plastic tub in the trunk and places his new treasure inside it, enters the car and drives back the way he came, then onto the highway and once he is about a mile away he pulls off the road, gets out, and does a little celebration dance. He makes a quick phone call and heads to his favorite coffee shop where he will meet Tekeysia for breakfast.

12

That Bitch in Copenhagen

Agnes has been away on holiday and as usual it takes her a day or two to settle down into serious work again. She has samples backed up for days and finally just makes a big pot of coffee and starts opening the envelopes. She opens all of the packets and lines the lumps up with their envelopes along a long table. She quickly ferrets out the impostors and puts them back in their envelopes and places them on a pile in the corner of the room. She no longer takes the time to write the wealth seekers to tell them their sample is probably an old rubber toy or dog shit. Those that have successfully done business with her before do receive a stock rejection letter and a brief encouragement to keep looking! She takes the aspiring pieces of ambergris into another room and continues to sniff, feel their weight, rub them between her thumb and fingers and eliminates a couple of them and then she begins to grade the quality of the samples that will determine their proper market, weight, and approximate value.

If the grading of ambergris with great precision were music, Agnes would have been a world renowned child prodigy. Indeed she would have had the talent to rival Mozart. However, the world of ambergris, until recent internet years, was a secret and little heard of by the average person. As an ambergris broker for over thirty years she knows the parts of the world where the ocean is most likely to "cough up" quality ambergris and sometimes it does "pop up" in unlikely places. Most recently the "pop up" is the coast of Southern California. One sample is of particular interest. It is grainy in texture, has strata running through it and is filled with the delicate frothy bubbles formed from tiny squid beaks of great age. The quality is as high as any she has ever seen. Her expertise has made her a very wealthy woman but being able to match the proper grade of ambergris to its final use has made her a legend in the industry. This piece will never go before the buyers from the perfume companies. This piece, sent to her by Gio Valducci, will fetch a small fortune from the

Dutch chocolate makers. Just imagine: a chocolate so rich that it continues to massage the taste buds for hours after being eaten. The list of those who can afford it is quite small and the chocolate maker has been calling, nearly begging for more of the precious substance. So specialized are her capabilities that she can create a shortage simply by temporarily hording her inventory, thus keeping the price high.

Something about its aroma casts her into a reverie and she sits spellbound thinking of her childhood friend, Rene, a boy who was a precious friend until raging hormones overtook them and changed their friendship. She is thinking of the time a flower farmer near the French town of Grasse hauled her into the bank and told her father how she and her friend had trampled some of his crop of jasmine. Her father showered harsh words upon her but the minute her accuser was gone he turned to Agnes and confessed that he too had scarred the fields as a boy and he loved being immersed in the sanctity of the wonderful aromas the fields provided.

Now sixty years old, she was born Agnes Antoinette TuBakken to a French father and Danish mother and spent most of her childhood in the south of France in Grasse, where they grow beautiful aromatic flowers and manufacture the World's most expensive perfumes. Her father was a banker and was heavily involved in the storage and sale of ambergris. Her mother never really wanted a child and there was no closeness there so she spent most of her time with her father and her friend Rene. Agnes started learning the art of the ambergris trade at the age of three that she recalls. She learned to recognize the texture, even able to distinguish the quality. Her parents divorced when she was twelve years old and her mother moved back to Denmark, gladly leaving the child in her father's care. Agnes visited her mother in the short Danish summers, which she hated, because she had to give up the beautiful French hillsides and the adoration of her father.

A funny thing happened when she reached her late teens; as her mother began to see her as a young friend she enjoyed spending time with her, without the pressures of being a mother. Over the years her father remained president of the Napoleon National Bank but most of his banker duties were handled by his first vice president and really he had become a broker for the sale of ambergris with the prestige and integrity that was then afforded bankers in that time.

In Agnes' second year at university her father died of a heart attack while in the middle of an ambergris sale in the conference room adjoining the lock box vault. The purchaser absconded with all but a token amount of ambergris in his brief case and tells the bank staff that he thinks Mr.TuBakken has had a heart attack and quickly exits the bank. With her father gone Agnes was the only one that knew anything about her father's brokerage and she made an attempt to step in and run it but eventually the bank's board of directors cast her out as they had not realized the extent to which her father was involved in what they regarded as a "shady" business.

In spite of the old resentments of her mother's near abandonment, after her father's death, her mother became her best friend and after being cast out by the bank's board, Agnes retreated to her mother's villa in Copenhagen, but soon began traveling to France and used the leverage of having been by her father's side for so many years to connect with most of the perfume companies' ambergris procurers and by the time she was thirty she was regarded as a major player in the mostly unknown ambergris trade.

A seagull lands on the corner post of the terrasse and makes a loud squawk and wakes Agnes from her pensive probing of her life. Now she must send out some emails. This is so much easier than sending letters, she thinks, and as much as she sometimes hates the new technology she gets on her laptop and finishes up the morning's work.

From: agtubakken@Dannet.com

To: giovalducci@cablestat.net

Subject: Your ambergris sample

Mr. Valducci,

I have examined your sample and find it to be ambergris of a high quality. It looks as if you may have broken it off from a larger piece. How much of this do you have? Please reply by email at your earliest convenience.

Agnes Tubakken

From: agtubakken@Dannet.com

To: fredmccallister@freeshare.com

Subject: Your ambergris sample

Mr. McCallister

I have examined your sample and find it to be ambergris of a high quality. It looks as if you may have broken it off from a larger piece. How much of this do you have? Please reply by email at your earliest convenience.

Agnes Tubakken

From: agtubakken@Dannet.com

To: bryanryan@cablestat.net

Subject: Your ambergris sample

Mr. Bryanryan,

I have examined your sample and find it to be ambergris of an average quality. It looks as if you may have broken this sample off of a larger piece, how much of it do you have? Please reply by email at your earliest convenience.

Agnes Tubakken

Agnes sends out several more emails to sample providers in Southern California, her new hotspot. She is thinking ahead and depending on the amount of ambergris available will determine if she will make a trip to Tijuana, Mexico. It is so much easier to do business in person and she never knows if she is competing with other brokers. The internet has changed the business dramatically and for the time being it seems that everyone that is new to hunting ambergris finds her quickly. She knows from all her years of experience to always be truthful with her clients as to the quality and value of their ambergris. This fact has been well established in the online blog pages where ambergris hunters compare notes on finding reputable brokers and avenues to get the ambergris out of the country without any hassles. Although the blog postings attest to her knowledge and honesty, a couple of them refer to her "as that bitch in Copenhagen." Agnes doesn't mind that, in fact, she relishes it. She knows she is definitely not a "people person."

She looks at her watch and sees that it is 11:30 a.m. and just as she is thinking that Angelica will be here soon, the doorbell rings and she opens the door to greet her new lover. They embrace and Angelica asks, "How was the holiday?"

"Splendid," Agnes responds, "what a pity you couldn't go with me, perhaps next time if we are still together."

"I wish you wouldn't say things like that."

"I seriously doubt that a twenty-two year old will stay interested in an old bird like me. What do you choose, lunch or bedroom?"

Angelica throws her head back in laughter and glides the tip of her tongue across her perfect teeth, "perhaps we'll find something to eat in the bedroom." Both women laugh and scamper off to the boudoir.

13

Let's Play "Dress-up"

Gio is sitting at the kitchen table next to Sally. He is holding her hand and sipping coffee. "I didn't tell you this because I didn't want you to worry. Plus, in my older years I don't trust my memory so much. Since that big ball of ambergris was taken I've been thinking. I was quite sure that I had six pieces of ambergris in that plastic storage bin closest to the garage door. The next time I looked there was only five. I racked my brain to try and think if I had done something with it. Also, when I check the oil level in our cars I always use an old T-shirt to wipe the dip stick with. That is also missing." Gio reaches down and pats Amber on the head. Amber gives up on getting any coffee cake and trots into the laundry room to his bowl of food.

Sally reaches for another piece of the coffee cake in the middle of the table. As she reaches her right breast pops out of her robe. She quickly covers it and asks Gio, "are you sure that's not the piece you sent to that broker in Denmark?

"Absolutely, I broke that off of a bigger piece in the first bin. Also, how does it happen that I look up and down the beach and not a soul is in site and when I return a few minutes later there are tire tracks down the beach right to the grisball and it is gone?"

"Sounds like someone was watching you and also knew what you were looking for."

"Exactly! You are such a smart little girl!" Gio reaches out and pushes her robe aside to expose her breast again. He runs his finger around her areola and watches her nipple become erect. "umm, I've forgotten what we were talking about."

"Only about how the successful sale of our ambergris could save the beach house for us."

"Just kidding," Gio takes another sip of coffee and pulls Sally closer to him. "Can we go back to bed?"

"That's what I'm thinking."

As they walk to the bedroom Gio says softly, "I have a plan to catch that thief, I'll tell you later."

After love making and showering together Sally and Gio get dressed and carry their coffee onto the deck. Amber explores the deck with his nose and then lies down on the mat next to the shower. It is a splendid day. Gio stares out to sea. Yesterday evening there was a storm. Now the wind is stacking the waves up as it presses to the shore. One of the waves contains a pod of dolphins swiftly swimming along. As the bright sun clarifies the wave the dolphins appear to be nearly flying through the air. "Look at that!" Gio shouts. Gio is still reveling in living in a beach house with a beautiful woman. He still can barely believe his luck and yet, as wonderful as it is he still has this internal struggle as to how to sell the ambergris, his need to catch the prick that took his big grisball, how to bring up to Sally that he wants his name on the deed when they pay the lien off on the beach house. It just seems every time he gains something he has always wanted it comes with complications. How simple and calm his life was the last few years he worked at the bakery. He has no desire to go back to that life; he just didn't realize what responsibility real love would bring.

Gio clears his throat and says, "Here is what we do: We are about the same height, give or take an inch or two. I'm going to beef your shoulders up with padding and have you wear my clothes, boots and hat. You will then go out and walk the beach with Amber just as I have been doing. I will stay back on the beach road and see if I can spot our thief and confront him."

"Isn't that a dangerous thing to do? I don't think law enforcement would consider the grisball a theft. Wouldn't it be just like if you had left a conch shell on the beach and someone picked it up? I mean really, they might think they found it."

"If the authorities saw someone driving their car on the beach wouldn't they give them a ticket?"

"Sure, there is a $500.00 fine. When they passed that law it quickly stopped people from doing it. But we have no way of proving that this person did this and you might get beat up or worse."

"I suppose you are right. Maybe I'll just get their license number and -- I know what I'll do: If they show-up, I'll just approach them casually and chat-it-up with them about how beautiful the beach is and see what I can find out and of course, get their license number."

"You promise?"

"Yes, we have to do something."

Gio goes into the house and boots up the computer and checks his email. He pulls the email up from the broker in Copenhagen. He prints it out and walks back onto the patio where Sally is sweeping sand into the space between the boards. "Take a look at this."

Sally reads the email and says, "We've got a whole fucking garage full of this stuff. Soon, God willing, we will be able to pay off our beach house and I've been meaning to tell you; I want your name to be on the deed as well. In fact, if you are ready, and I am, let's get married."

"Jeez, I never thought this would happen to me. Better late than never I suppose. I am crazy about you, you little snatch cake. But first, let's find out what our cache is worth. Also, if someone stole a piece of it, then they must have a key to the house and they must also plan to steal all of it. In fact, I believe the reason they stole that small piece was to have it analyzed. I'm going to have the locks changed. Just think how much that grisball must be worth. I found it and I want it back. I have a couple of things I need to pick up from my condo. Also if we are getting married I will need to sell the condo. In fact that will be a big chunk of change to put toward the beach house. I'll be back in a little while."

Gio drives to his condo and inside finally finds the box with the treasure he seeks: a stun gun and the Colt .45 that his father had acquired in WW II. Gio wonders, will these bullets still work after all these years? He looks around and finds the box the cartridges came in. They are only a few years old and then he remembers having bought them on a vacation trip, just in case he ever needed them. He says aloud, "What a smart little boy you are." He loads the clip with seven bullets and pumps one into the firing chamber, ejects the clip and adds one more. He knows he doesn't dare tell Sally about this.

14

Size Does Matter

"Hello, is this Bryan or Ryan?" Jordan asks.

"Yes," replies Ryan, "is this Jordan?"

"Yeah man and I need you guys' help. That fucker Fredirico stole Tekeysia away from me." Jordan was barely able to get that out as he fought back the tears.

"You mean he fucking kidnapped her?" Ryan asks.

"Well, not exactly." Jordan replies. She's been gone a lot lately and I knew something was up and then that fucking Fred shows up here and takes her stuff."

"How the fuck did he get in there?" Ryan asks.

"I don't know, followed someone in I guess. He tried to provoke me into a fight, like I could fight that big motherfucker." Jordan breaks out in tears again. "She's the best fuck I've ever had man, you gotta help me get her back."

There is a long silence on the other end of the phone.

"You there man?" Jordan asks.

"Yeah, I'm here, just thinking." Ryan replies. "We've been following that dick early mornings. He's been spying on some old guy that has been finding some grisrock using a dog. We think he's going to steal this guy's cache of grisrock and we fear he might even kill them. You know, you can't force Tekeysia to come back to you."

"She called me man, she says he's too rough with her and that she's made a big mistake, but she's afraid to leave, he might really fuck her up."

"Just a minute." Ryan finds Bryan and tells him what is going on. "O.K., Jordan, here's the deal. Meet us at Frank's; it's about half way, so we can figure this thing out. We need to get this fucker."

"Sounds good, when?"

"How about noon? And don't be late."

"I'll see you there!"

15

Revenge

Sally "dressed up" like Gio for two days and decided to tell Gio that she didn't want to do it anymore. Soon after having this thought Amber went crazy and started digging in the sand. She helped dig as well and soon pulled out a piece of grisrock about the size of the very first one she found with Wilma. Sally was transformed and suddenly was looking forward to the next day. The third day; was the day that Gio saw a man in the parking lot following Sally through the lens of a rather large camera.

Gio is talking to himself, just be friendly and make a little small talk.

"Nice day," Gio says. "Are you a professional photographer?"

Fred turns to Gio and gets a huge menacing smile on his face. "Nah Gio, just watching your fucking girlfriend trying to look like you."

Without any hesitation Gio charges the big man and knocks him off the asphalt and into the sand. Gio has caught the big man off guard and for a moment Gio is in control. Fred soon recovers and pushes Gio off of him and jumps up and starts kicking Gio. In his desperation and anger Gio has forgotten about the stun gun and pistol he has in his jacket. As he pulls out the gun, a white van goes by on the beach road, stops suddenly, and three guys jump out and tackle Fred. The cavalry has arrived just in time. One of the twins tells Gio to get some bungee cords in the back of the van. By the time Gio retrieves the cords Fred has been pummeled and punched into submission. The three young men bind Fred up like a mummy and throw him in the back of the van and slam the door.

Amber has heard the ruckus and starts pulling Sally up the beach toward the commotion. She arrives as Fred is being tossed into the back of the van where he promptly starts yelling insults and then starts calling for help. Ryan goes to the front of the van, retrieves a roll of duct tape and wraps it around Fred's head covering his mouth.

Gio realizes he still has the gun in his hand and quickly puts it away and says, "That fucker has been spying on me and he stole my largest piece of ambergris."

Jordan puts in, "he stole my girl."

Ryan, Bryan, and Jordan look at Sally and then Gio. One of them says, "What are you guys doing?"

Gio and Sally answer simultaneously, "catching a thief."

Jordan looks at the collar on Amber's neck, "hey, that's my dog."

Without hesitation Gio starts giving Amber commands and runs through several of Amber's crazy tricks. Gio asks Jordan, "Did you teach him all those tricks? I ran an ad in the local paper. How much do you want for him? I'll give you a thousand dollars."

Jordan thinks it over for a few seconds and says, "I might make more using him to find grisrock."

"Possibly, "Gio replies, "but will you walk the beach twice every day? It's hard work."

Jordan thinks that over and quickly answers, "I'll take the thousand."

"What are we going to do with this guy?" Gio asks.

Ryan replies, "We've been watching him watch you. We saw him go into your garage and believe me this guy would kill you both to get what's in there."

Gio says, "Maybe you would too, you should have called the police when you saw him go in there. Does he have a key?"

There is a moment of silence and then Ryan says, "Didn't we just rescue you from a horrible beating or maybe worse?"

More silence and Gio replies, "you're right, I'm sorry I said that. What are you guys going to do with him? We can't just leave his car here."

Bryan tells Jordan, "I think you should take his car to his house and we'll follow you. You can get Tekeysia and her things and we'll take Fred to your place.

Gio asks, "Can we follow you guys? I'd like to know what's going on."

Jordan offers, "jump in Fred's car, oh good, the keys are in it."

Gio says, "this baby buggy folds down, can you please open the trunk?"

Gio puts the stroller in the trunk, retrieves Fred's camera from the sand and he, Sally and Amber get into the back seat and Ryan gets in the front with Jordan. As they drive to their beach house Gio gets his checkbook from Sally's purse and writes a check for $1,000.00. On the back he writes, 'This signature acknowledges that I have conveyed complete ownership of a male beagle dog named Amber to Gio Valducci.' He hands the check over the seat to Jordan, half hoping that he has decided not to take it. Jordan glances at the check and says, "Oh, thanks."

When they reach the beach house the twins tell Gio and Sally about how Fred rolled under the garage door to get in.

As Gio puts Amber inside the house Sally asks him, "are you sure you are ok?"

Gio responds, "a couple of my ribs are hurting, but I'll be alright in a day or two. Sally, I think you should stay here at the beach house."

Sally turns to Gio, "not on your life buckaroo, I'm going where you go." Gio exchanges cell phone numbers with Ryan and off they go. Ryan and Jordan lead in the Lexus, then the van with Bryan and Fred, then Sally and Gio in the town car.

16

Looks Like We've Got Ourselves a Caravan

When they arrive at Fred's seaside villa, Jordan and Ryan go in and start gathering Tekeysia's things. Gio starts looking through the cabinets, closets, any place large enough to hide the grisball.

Jordan asks, "what the hell are you doing man, we already kidnapped this dick, we can't steal his fucking stuff too."

Tekeysia looks at Gio. "You look for de big ball, yes?"

"Yes."

"Fred, he gived it to de Mexicanos. He show dem de email from de Copenhagen women. He gived dem some money and de email and de big ball for de money he owes dem. Dey punch him just one time and leave and dey tell him he better not bullsheet dem or dey cut his throat. Tekeysia pulls her index finger across her neck.

Gio stands astounded with the new information and says, "I'm going to beat that fucker about the head repeatedly. He stole a fortune from me."

Tekeysia replies, "he say you leave de big ball and dat he found it de same as you."

Jordan and Ryan are looking at each other in amazement and Ryan asks, "what the fuck are you guys talking about?

Gio tells them the whole story and Jordan speaks to Gio, "listen man I know how you fuckin' feel but he's probably right. He could tell the law that he just found it on the beach, the same as you!"

"Not to mention that it's illegal to posses it," Ryan adds.

Gio asks, "What do we do now? We can't let him go. He'll fuck us all up one-by-one."

"Let's take him to Jordan's dad," Ryan suggests, "he can probably figure it out. Let's get out of here."

The caravan snakes its way to Jordan's. Each motored vehicle holding its own tailored conversation:

The Lexus: "Jesus, Jordan, we got ourselves in a big ol' fucking mess. Bry and I never been in shit this deep. Well, not since we were fucking the same girl in high school and she got pregnant."

Jordan asks, "what happened?"

"Well, we lucked out, she had a miscarriage."

"Shit man, that was a close one."

The White Van: Fred has wiggled the tape from his mouth, "you fuckers are going to jail. You assault me, steel my fucking car. This is kidnapping you fucking dick head."

"Shut the fuck up, Fred, or I'm gonna pull over and really fuck you up."

The Town Car: "All I wanted to do was get that beach house paid off! I knew dealing in ambergris was a little shady. But I've been straight as an arrow my whole life. I worked hard and saved my money. Jesus, we're hanging out with a bunch of hoodlums."

"We can turn around, go back home and throw the ambergris back in the ocean or put it in the trash. We don't have to go on with this."

"Yeah we do, I've worked too hard to give up now. I want to see this through. But it just scares the shit out of me."

"Me too."

The Lexus: "Fred must have really pissed those Mexicans off. Do you know what he did?"

"Yeah, he was in cahoose with some border guards. They were rippin' off one of the cartels. Fred was working as a dealer and informing the guards when and where the shipments were coming through. But I don't get it because he did that months ago. It just seems to me they would have got to him sooner. They'll be back. Their big boss is not just going to accept an email and a ball of something he's never heard of as payment.

"Maybe we can hand him over to them. You know who they are, right?"

"Fuck no, man. He'll tell them about Gio's cache. He'll do anything to save his ass.

Jeez Jordan, can't you guys wait until we get to your apartment?"

The White Van: "Shut the fuck up man, I don't want to hear your shit!"

The Town Car: "I'll have to say, this is really exciting. I've never felt like this before. I guess we're on an adventure."

"I love you."

"Me too, with all my heart."

"I feel like we are in a fucking movie."

17

Jesus Freak

Jesus Garciá is following the little caravan, but staying back a half-mile or so. This is only possible because he attached a GPS transmitter to the undercarriage of Fred's Lexus a few days ago. El Capitán has told Jesus to follow Fred a few days and see if he can get any leads on any wealth that Fred might have. Jesus knows this is his last chance. When he took the big valuable ball to El Capitán it only took him a week to find out it was a worthless ball of grease.

Jesus was deep in thought when the little caravan stopped at Fred's place:

If when I took the ball to him with the email, and it had turned out to be real ambergris, I would have been a hero. Well, not a hero. But El Capitán would have thought I was doing my job. But now, El Capitán has blamed me for the lies Fred told. I'm going to get that motherfucker. But, right now, someone else has got him. This Fred man has many enemies. I wonder what he did to piss these people off? If they kill him, what will I do? I'll be ok if I can find his body and cut off one of his hands. If I go back to El Capitán without-well, I can't go back with nothing. I know the penalty for failure. These guys are really fucking me up. What a fucking shit. This Fred guy, Jesus chuckles a little, if you want to kill him, you have to get in line. What a fuckhead!

When the caravan turns into the lane to Jordan's place, Jesus starts to curse. "This is the fucking road to the fucking stolen car place. I'm sure of it." Jesus stays back and watches as all three vehicles go through the gate."I am so fucked." He turns around and heads back to the main road. What can I do, he thinks, what can I fucking do? Then he remembers there is a small motel, not far up the main road. He pulls into the parking lot and is glad to see the GPS signal is still strong. The motel has a small restaurant. Jesus is thinking it through: I can go in here and get something to eat and maybe get some tequila at the little store. If they don't come out for a few hours, then I will get a room and wait. What else can I do? I'm sure this is what El Capitán would want me to do.

18

Fred Rises Up

When Jordan's father, Theo, sees a Lexus and Town Car coming in the gate with Jordan's old white van sandwiched in the middle, it raises his curiosity to the highest level. He starts to head back to Jordan's apartment but is stopped short by a phone call. He soon reaches Jordan's apartment and is quite puzzled at the scene. He sees Jordan and his twin friends, the unsavory character that is known to him as Fred McCallister, tied to a chair, and an elderly couple that does not belong in this picture.

He looks at Jordan and says, "just what in the hell is going on? I've just about had it with your shenanigans Jordan." Soliloquy shouts out, "What the fuck do you want? Hmm…what the fuck do you want?" Theo grimaces, looks at Soliloquy and shakes his head in disgust.

Jordan answers, "it's a long story dad, let me explain."

"Stop Jordan! Theo looks at Gio and asks, "do you know what's going on here?

"Yes, I can tell you the whole story."

Theo gives a command, "Jordan, you and one of the twins take your old van and go to Fred's place and get his passport, the registration on his car and pack some clothes in whatever luggage he has."

Tekeysia jumps in, "I know wey heez passport is. Can I guh wid dem?

"What if we can't find all those things Dad?"

"Jordan, I did not ask you to give me excuses before you even try. Go! And go now! Take the girl with you. One of the twins will stay here and keep a loaded gun aimed at Fred, and if he tries anything at all, blow his head off. Here's a pistol, it's a .44. Theo looks at the elderly couple and asks, "Can you folks join me for some lunch up at my house? I can listen to this "long story" there."

Gio and Sally follow Theo out to his car. Gio asks, "Can we just follow you in our car?" Theo answers, "Why of course you can."

Gio is desperate to discuss the situation with Sally.

Sally asks, "do you think he's taking us somewhere to kill us?"

"I doubt it very much. As you can see, he's a successful business man. And, it sounds like he is air mailing Fred out of here. If he's not shooting that bum, I really doubt that he will harm us. I mean, it's obvious he's pretty disgusted with his son."

"I guess you're right. I'm so glad we are following him and could talk about this. I've been scared-to-death all morning."

They are following Theo around a hill and as they turn to go up the hill a beautiful home sits atop the incline. Sally says, "Holy shit." Gio agrees, "It's palatial."

Theo's maid serves some sandwiches and beverages. Gio does most of the talking, with Sally adding a little here and there. Theo listens attentively and asks a few questions. "Tell me," Theo asks, are you aware that dealing in ambergris is against the law in the U. S.?"

"Yes, Gio replies, "but it seems to be an ambiguity. I've contacted one of the world's top brokers and she has told me what I have is quite valuable and wants to know how much I have of it. I'm hoping to send it to her via FedEx."

"Well, Gio, it won't be ambiguous if you are caught with a quantity of it in your possession."

"I've read that they usually don't imprison people, they usually just confiscate it."

"Gio, Fred is in a lot of trouble and I'll show you why." Theo reaches over to a nearby table and hands a newspaper to Gio.

It is a San Diego newspaper and the lead story tells how the clogging of the sewer lines has been so severe that the city has been forced to flush a large quantity of the grease and oil into the ocean. There is a picture showing a grease ball someone found on the beach. The object looks very much like the piece that Fred "confiscated" from Gio.

"Gio, once Fred's henchmen over-the-border discovers it is worthless they will find Fred and carve him up; slowly. I suggest that you and the missus ship your ambergris out of the country soon and we'll keep our fingers crossed that Fred hasn't told anyone else about it."

"My broker in Copenhagen has verified that what I have in my possession is genuine ambergris and of high quality. So, what's going to happen next?"

"Do you have a weapon?"

"Yes, a Colt .45."

"I don't wish to unduly frighten you Sally, but if I were you guys, I'd stay close to home for a while and keep your .45 nearby. I'm putting Fred on a plane to Madrid. I think he knows the danger he's in. I don't expect him to return."

"Thank you Theo, for the lunch and the advice. If it's O.K. with you I think we'll head for home. We really appreciate your hospitality." And then Gio holds his breath.

"Sounds good, but you do know that you must not tell anyone about all of this. For the protection of all, we don't need the gendarmes jumping into this."

"Oh, no, of course not."

Gio and Sally shake Theo's hand and he walks them out to their car. Gio asks, "Should we exchange cell numbers, just in case we need to talk more on this."

"Good idea, but I hope like hell that never happens."

Gio and Sally exit through the security gate, drive up the narrow lane and turn onto the main road. As they pass the little motel, Sally says, "You know I've never been a religious person, but sometimes I think Jesus is watching over us."

19

Betrayal

Gio and Sally decided to heed Theo's advice and they have stayed home for a few days now. Gio has moved the ambergris to his condo, just in case Theo's clan can't be trusted. They are both more at ease now, however, Amber has not figured out that he hunts at his master's pleasure and daily brings his leash to Gio and drops it in front of him and then Sally.

The sun is setting and tonight the misty spectrum is more special than any other evening they have shared on this seaside perch. It causes Gio to get a lump in his throat like he did as a child. He feels loneliness at such times. It is a reaction to the knowledge that the day is ending and as a child it meant no more play and the loss of his friends as bath-time had arrived, followed by bed time. It does seem odd that sixty years later a beautiful sunset brings that on. They each have had a couple of glasses of wine and Amber has decided it's a good time for a little snooze. The sound of the surf is so soothing.

When Gio gets up and goes inside, Sally thinks he is going for another bottle of wine. He returns with something in his hand and a book of matches. He holds the object out in the palm of his hand and Sally says, "Jeez, I haven't smoked one of those since college, where did you get that?"

"I found three of them when I ripped through Fred's things looking for my big ball of grease." They both laugh. Sally teases Gio, "you were sure charged up! You wanted your big ball of grease back!" They laugh again and Gio lights the chubby joint and hands it to Sally.

Sally says to Gio, "Mr. President did you smoke pot when you were in college?"

Gio replies, "Well, I did, but I didn't exhale." Sally giggles and hands the joint to Gio, who takes a puff and holds it down a long time, passes it back and says to her, "do you know Sally, how much I love you?"

"Yes, I think I do, and best of all, I love you just as much. Which reminds me, when do you want to get married? You haven't said anything about it since you agreed we should."

"Sally, when I was a young man I had something happen that has scared me single ever since."

"Gio," Sally takes his hand, "tell me about it, I'd like to hear it. What happened?"

"I was deeply hurt by someone. It was a total betrayal and I was so in love I didn't even suspect her. Are you sure you want to hear this bullshit? I am so high."

"Have you ever told anyone this before?"

"No."

"Then it's time you did, I'm all ears."

"I had only worked for the Mid-States Bakery three or four years and I knew I was the best baker they had. Any special orders that came in were handed over to me. I must say, I was very creative with a trough of sweet dough. Most people don't realize that all the fancy stollens and rolls are all made from a huge trough of sweet bread. It is just slightly sweet and depends on filler and toppings to please the masses. You can fill it with fruit and make a turnover; you can braid it, use scissors to create an affect and many other things. In my fifth year the brass called me into their offices. I really thought they might be firing me because I was pretty outspoken in regard to conditions in the bakery. They asked me to be the bakery manager for that facility. I was totally shocked and asked if I could have a few days to think it over. Apparently they hadn't overheard any of my condemnations of the cleanliness and dangerous conditions we worked in. I decided I didn't want to do it. I was a strong supporter of the Baker's Union and just didn't want to be "one of them."

"Management was just as shocked that I didn't accept the promotion as I was that they offered it. All the union guys loved me! Turning management down was such a slap-in-the-face that the next term I was elected the Union Shop Steward."

Gio stops talking and Sally sees he is lost in his memories. "Go on."

"Where was I?"

"You were elected the shop steward."

"Oh yeah; well, as shop steward I really gave the bosses hell about the bakery conditions and they got some bad press from it. About the time our union contract was up, I met this girl. She was a beauty and really stacked and we fell head-over-heels in love, or so I thought. I certainly did. She catered to me; she laughed at my jokes and did things in bed that I had never experienced before."

"Like what?"

"Doesn't matter, I was pretty inexperienced. She was such a great listener and of course I told her every single plan we had for the upcoming negotiations with the bakery. I fought those guys hard but it just seemed that they were always a step ahead of me. Our plan was that we would talk only of striking the plant where I worked. Back at that time, we knew that they would bring in thugs and scabs to keep the plant going. Anyway, so our plan was we would get signs printed and all the other bullshit that it takes to plan a walkout at the plant where I worked but when the day arrived we were really going to have a walkout in the Indianapolis plant. That would have given us a great advantage at the startup of the negotiations."

71

"Go on."

"So the day arrives and Indianapolis walks out. The company was ready with their thugs and scabs and somehow they knew we were walking out in Indie. The negotiations were very tough. A couple of weeks later we voted in a new contract and I couldn't get hold of Sondra. She wouldn't return my calls and when I went by her apartment she was gone. Then it hit me like a ton of bricks. She had been playing me that whole time. My fucking ego was so huge that I thought it was about time a good looking, really smart, girl fell for me. I didn't let on to any of the union guys at the bakery. Every one said they knew who had sold us out. They blamed George Bacon and he was a strange guy. I was a coward. I never said a word."

Sally rubs Gio's shoulders and kisses him on the cheek. "Let's go inside."

Once in bed, Sally gives Gio the most active and jubilant fellatio of her lifetime. Then she swirls the pasty liquid around in her mouth, first she holds up one finger in front of Gio's face, then two and finally three; at which time she swallows the entire mouthful.

Lying back on her pillow Sally tells Gio, "I think we should have the wedding next month, here on the beach. Can I start planning it? "

"Absolutely, that sounds like a great idea."

20

What Goes Around, Comes Around

Fred is desperate. Theo has showed him the newspaper article and he knows that El Capitán will be angrier than ever. Damn it! He thought he had covered his tracks when he was in on stealing those dope shipments at the border.

Now that he has cashed his ticket in and rented a car he begins to wonder if going to Madrid would have been the smart thing to do. But stealing cars? Fred thinks that would be a big step down for him. Theo has told him that Seve Alverez will be waiting for him in Madrid. A business contact Theo had established years ago. He was to be a car thief! As he is driving out of the airport his hands are shaking. The danger he is in has just descended on him. He pulls the car over after exiting the airport. "Why didn't I just go to Madrid? Fuck me!"

Most people that have achieved a treasured success in their life have done so because the conditions were perfect when they made their effort to succeed. The human ego being what it is means that each individual thinks they have achieved this success in spite of the conditions. The great danger is: they think that they can do it again following the same path they used before. This is especially true of criminals. Life is full of falls and tumbles, but this is dramatically true in the underworld of crime. Thus, Fred has a plan to repay El Capitán by stealing Gio's cache of ambergris. It was the plan all along. Except that now it won't just lead to money. It is to save his life and he now really understands that and it is all he can think about. Fred also assumes that Theo has his Lexus dismantled by now and the parts available for sale. He also knows he can't return to his house.

Fred stops at a fast food chain and grabs something to eat. He drives to Gio's beach house and pulls his rented car right up to Gio's garage. He jumps out and looks in the garage door windows. The ambergris is gone! Such frustration! Fred feels like he's on a conveyor belt slowly propelling him into a giant buzz saw. He checks into a cheap motel not far from the beach house. He shaves his moustache. He buys some cheap sunglasses, a touristy hat and shorts and sandals. Back at the motel he puts his new purchases on and looks in the mirror. He thinks it is enough to pretend to be a tourist, maybe enough to keep an eye on Gio and that dog of his. But is it enough to throw El Capitán's henchmen off his trail? He doesn't know, but he must try. He looks in the mirror again, admiring the handsome man there and says, "Well, one good thing, Gio thinks I'm in Madrid."

Theo told Ryan to make sure Fred got on that plane for Madrid. However, without a ticket he was unable to get past security at the gate where the plane was departing. He hung around the gate for a while until the departure time had passed and then got back in Fred's Lexus and headed for Fred's house. He was going to meet Bryan there and then leave Fred's car in the driveway. He was still unaware of the GPS device attached to the underside of Fred's car and did not notice Jesus Garciá following him. Sitting in Fred's driveway Ryan sends a text message to Bryan and asks him where he is. Bryan texts back; be there in ten. Ryan places his phone on the arm rest and waits. At that same time headlights blind him as a big black S.U.V. pulls in next to him. Jesus approaches Bryan as if he is lost: "Hey buddy, can you tell me how to get to the freeway?" Ryan is about to tell him when Jesus brings his .45 automatic out quickly and hits Ryan on the temple with the sturdy pistol grip. Ryan slumps onto the steering wheel completely unconscious. Jesus looks in the trunk to see if Fred is in there. "Fuck!" Jesus closes the trunk lid and leans on the trunk and wonders; what the fuck am I going to do now? Jesus pulls Ryan out of the driver's seat and shoves him into the back seat where Ryan remains unconscious and face down. Jesus gets in the Lexus and starts it up. He is filled with dread and thinks; I have to take this to El Capitán. As he backs out his right elbow slides onto the armrest and pushes Ryan's cell phone into the back floorboard.

Just as Jesus pulls onto the coastal roadway and his tail lights are out of site, Bryan pulls in with the white van. He doesn't see a silhouette in the black S.U.V. and he approaches the driver's side cautiously. The window is down and he pears inside. He sees a device on the center console with a red light blinking. He picks it up and gives it a closer look. There is a small display screen and typed into it is, "Fred's car." Bryan exclaims, "Fuck, fuck! Something has happened to Ryan." He carries the device to the van and an arrow is pointing south on the coastal roadway.

21

Ignorance is Bliss

It's the next morning, after Gio and Sally's big adventure.

"I feel much safer now, with Fred on his way to Madrid." Gio tells Sally.

"Do you think those other guys will try to get our ambergris?" Sally questions.

"No, I think Theo has put the damper on that. I don't think they would have anyway. Those twins weren't thugs. They had good manners, appeared to be educated and they seemed alright to me. Don't you think?"

"I suppose you are right, but they still seemed a little shady, being involved in ambergris and all."

"You mean like us?"

"Good point."

Gio asks, "Can you hold off a week or two on setting a date for our wedding? I'd like to get our ambergris shipped out and see how much it is worth. What do you think?"

"As long as you don't have cold feet about it. That worries me sometimes."

"Not to worry! I'm just as thrilled as you are."

"OK, then, I can still start looking at dresses and planning it out and then we'll set the date. Can you make me a list of your relatives you want to invite?"

"That I can do, do you think we should invite Theo?"

"Please, all I want to do is forget that all this has happened."

"Yeah, you're probably right, but I kind of liked him though. I'm going over to the condo, I need to check on the ambergris and, and a few other things." The few other things are to put the pistol and stun gun back in their hidden cardboard box. Gio is so relieved that Fred is headed for Madrid. He thinks that Theo is one cool character. As Gio drives over, he has to chuckle and thinks, I'm a guy that has never stolen anything, but I've got Fred's camera and he doesn't have my ambergris. Gio received an email this very morning from Agnes TuBakken in Copenhagen. She is flying over in two days to meet with Gio face-to-face. Gio hasn't told Sally yet. He wants to find out what it is worth and how long it will take to get paid before he says anything. He plans to bring Agnes to the condo. He is also worried that to show his ambergris to only one broker is a mistake. But, based on what he has read on the internet, this is an honest woman, and he knows it is impossible for him to market his cache direct to the users. It just isn't done.

Fred keeps his rental car at a safe distance. Just a few blocks away, Gio pulls into the condominium parking lot and enters his condo. He leaves the patio door open to let some fresh air in and goes into the kitchen, where the ambergris is still floating in the bubbling containers. As he places the items he brought on the table, his phone rings.

"Hello."

"Is this Gio?"

"Who is asking?"

"Gio, this is Theo."

"Oh, yeah, hey man, how are you doing?"

"I've got some bad news Gio, Fred didn't get on that plane and I have no idea where he is."

Gio is struck dumb.

"Are you there?"

"Yes," Gio answers. "I just left Sally and the dog at the beach house. I'd better get back over there quick. When did you find out?"

"Just now, thought I should give you a heads up."

"OK, thanks, I've got to go."

"Good luck."

There is a problem that the pursuit of wealth creates, especially when the pursuit involves dealing in illegal goods and products. When things go awry one can't go to the police. One can go, but that must be done before the illegal activities have commenced and every official properly paid. There is no doubt that Fred is guilty of trespassing, and theft. However, Gio is more worried about what Fred will do in the future. He puts the .45 pistol in his waist band and the stun gun in his pocket. He lays the digital camera on the table and thinks, awe fuck, I stole this, this is a valuable thing and I did, I stole it.

As he heads down the hallway to rush back home, there is a man standing at the end of the hallway. Gio is stunned. The man's body is backlit and all he can see is his silhouette. "Hello Gio. I don't see any of your friends around now. Going somewhere?" Gio is thinking that he knows that voice and then it hits him: It's Fred.

22

Like a Canary

Armed with the GPS receiver Bryan has easily followed Fred's Lexus across the border, telling the border guard that he's following the guy in the Lexus. "Yes, the one with the drunk passed out in the backseat."

When Jesus turns into a darkened street Bryan goes on past and down to the next street and pulls up to the back of the giant abandoned warehouse. Bryan gets out of the van and makes his way across the end of the warehouse and peeks around the corner. Jesus is on his cell phone, pacing back and forth and there is no sign of his brother. Ryan has gained consciousness and is able to recall what happened and so he is pretending to still be out. He finds his cell phone and slides it into his front pocket, unwilling to take a chance on, whomever this thug is, hearing him. A big black S.U.V. pulls in and three men get out and Jesus points to his phone and then to the Lexus, he covers the phone's transmitter and says, "he's in the back, sleeping like a baby." The men pull Ryan out of the car and carry him into the warehouse where they place him in an old straight-back chair and bind him with duct tape. So tightly that he can't move his arms at all and his ankles are taped to the chair legs. He is still pretending to be unconscious, when one of the men walks up behind him and cuts part of his right ear lobe off. "Oh, Gringo, so now you are awake from your little nap. Good, we need to get some information from you." The man punches Ryan in the nose.

Through tears Ryan says, "What do you want to know? Just tell me and I will tell you all I know. Please don't hit me again."

Jesus' boss smiles a wide grin, "So, the canary sings. We want to know all you know about Fredirico McCallister."

After the interrogation the men decide to get some dinner and talk about what to do with Fred's car and what they should tell El Capitán. They wrap duct tape around Ryan's head covering his mouth. Bryan makes sure all the men are leaving and after a few minutes he decides to go into the warehouse. He is surprised to find the door locked and it is a heavy duty metal door with no window. He fears Ryan is dead but then he hears his brother making sounds through the tape on his mouth and rocking the chair to make more noise. Bryan shouts, "I'm going to get you out bro. I just have to figure out how to get in before they come back."

Bryan makes his way back along the nearly pitch-black end of the warehouse. He feels for his cell phone, wanting to know if there is a signal here. Bryan had been lucky on his first trip across the back of the warehouse or perhaps he was more careful for fear of making noise. But this time he trips over a large piece of metal and falls flat on his face. His nose is bleeding and his face is scraped up. He carefully makes his way to the van and does not find his cell phone there. He must do something. He decides to find a place with a phone and make a call to the local police and he is thinking that his fingers are crossed that the police are not part of the gang doing this. What did his brother do? It has to have something to do with Fred. Fucking Jordan, he caused all this with his "underworld" contacts and the man does not realize the havoc he is perpetrating. Bryan can't keep his nose from bleeding. The first business he sees is a small restaurant and he finds a rag in the van and puts it under his nose. He walks in and asks, "teléfono?" As he is walking to the phone some Mexican men look astounded and jump up from their table. He knows it is the men that beat his brother. Bryan sees that the back door in the kitchen is propped open and he runs out the door and down the alleyway with the men in hot pursuit. He hides around the corner and though the men are nearby they do not find him. One of the men says in Spanish, "how the fuck did he get out of that fucking chair?" Jesus says, "What do we care? We know everything we need to know. Let's go to El Capitán. Then tomorrow we can go get Fred and also steal that ambergris shit, unless it is like the big ball and is worthless."

Once the men are gone back into the restaurant Bryan makes his way back to the van and waits until the men get in their S.U.V. and he is relieved to see them heading away from the warehouse. Only then does it hit him that they thought he was his brother. Only then does he realize it is safe to try to free Ryan. He goes back to where he was parked before at the back of the warehouse. He finds a long two-by-four and sticks it through a gap in one of the overhead doors, bends it wide enough that eventually he squeezes through. Bryan is in bad shape but very glad to see his brother. They unlock the metal door to exit and as they are about to turn the corner of the building to make their way back to the van they see headlights and wait and listen. The men have returned for Fred's car. They don't bother going inside the warehouse. Ryan and Bryan carefully make their way along the back of the warehouse. As they turn the corner, somewhere in the van Bryan's cell phone is ringing.

23

Gender Confusion

When Agnes was twelve or thirteen years old her life-long friend Rene started trying to kiss her. And then one day they were having lunch on a blanket under a giant sycamore tree and she let him kiss her on the mouth. But then he touched her budding breasts and she pushed him away. He did it again and she shoved him away. Rene was quite angry and kicked over the picnic basket and ran away into a nearby field of flowers. They didn't see each other again for a few weeks and when Agnes saw Rene at the spring carnival he had just won a stuffed animal and given it to a girl standing next to him. A girl she knew to be a couple of years ahead of them in school. Agnes missed her childhood friend. She missed the one she had known, not the one he had become. Rene ignored her as they passed and he quickly put his arm around the older girl.

Agnes had felt nothing when Rene had kissed her and was repelled when he touched her breasts. She and Rene in later years would chat a bit when they ran into each other and sometimes talked and laughed about the times when they had gotten into trouble. She dated a few boys when she was in prep school but quickly dropped them when they became sexually aggressive. In her last year of prep school she met Thomas Chevalier. He was incredibly handsome and talented. His great uncle was the famous entertainer Maurice Chevalier. She was very fond of Thomas and he never offered more than a kiss on the cheek and a good hug from time-to-time. Like many women she enjoyed the company of a flamboyant homosexual. After all, why wouldn't she? He liked to shop and would spend hours with her picking out their clothes for the next dance. He helped her with her hair and makeup. Sometimes they would lie in bed for hours talking about fashion, art, the cinema, and Thomas' favorite subject: the ballet. Agnes' father never cared much for Thomas. It was clear to him that Thomas was a homosexual but one must understand that during that time, around the late 1960's, and even in France, homosexuality was not openly discussed and unless it was exposed in a criminal way, most people ignored it. The plus element for her father was that he knew he didn't have to worry about his daughter getting pregnant. Her father just let it go as his daughter would be going away to university the next year and Thomas was going to be attending a school of dance.

At university, in her freshman year, Agnes received her first kiss on the mouth since Rene. There was also much touching of her breasts, long interludes of the licking of her nipples and nearly endless kisses and caresses all over her body. She had her first orgasm with another person in the room. That person was Alouette de Gaulle, a girl that lived just down the hall from Agnes' dorm room. She was a quite distant relative of the President of France; Charles de Gaulle and Alouette played it for all it was worth. They were nearly inseparable for almost a year and so in love. There were no limitations or restrictions on what they could do together. They were just two school girls paling around with each other. Often on Saturday mornings they would lie in bed together and paint their nails and drink coffee, smoke perfumed cigarettes and speculate on which of their classmates might be of their persuasion. Agnes would often sing to her special girl a French folksong, her namesake:

"Alouette, gentille Alouette,

Alouette, je te plumerai.

Je te plumerai le bec,

Je te plumerai le bec,

Et le bec, et le bec

Alouette......."

It is an old French children's song, something about plucking the feathers from a lark. Sometimes, filled with wine, they would sing the song together loudly and stumble around arm in arm. The next year Alouette broke Agnes' heart when Agnes saw her on the commons, nearly hidden by a tree trunk, kissing an older girl that Agnes detested. When she confronted Alouette she claimed she was only trying to bring another girl into their love making. Agnes was clear: "Then go find another girl and then you will have your little mánage á trois, but I won't be there, I'll be out looking for someone better than you." From that time on Agnes had one long affair after another, each lasting about two years and then a few months of abstinence until she discovered someone that liked the same things as she. Then about every third affair she chose someone that was just the opposite of her. So it seems that opposites do attract, they just don't stay together long. Mind you, Agnes was clueless that her life had been following this pattern. People can never understand themselves as others do and it took years of therapy before Agnes understood what she was doing. It made no difference to her behavior, but now she could savor the moments of her dissatisfaction without guilt or depression. Once her father passed away and she came to grips with life without him, she also discovered that what she had considered great fun in assisting her father all those years was a marvelous way to make a lot of money. Her expertise was astounding and most of the ambergris buyers had witnessed her by her father's side just taking it all in. He had at times asked her opinion in front of certain buyers and her reply was proof of her business savvy. Her knowledge gave her power, prestige and money, all very nice things to have when looking for a new lover.

Her latest love, Angelica, twice has told Agnes that she doesn't want to go to San Diego with her. It is the morning before Agnes is scheduled to fly out the next day. Angelica is propped up on pillows against the headboard. Agnes is watching her masturbate. She loves watching her. Angelica is pawing at her breasts and her right hand is just a blur. Agnes loves how loud she gets and then at orgasm a shrill sort of scream that she never emits when Agnes gives her head and she reaches orgasm. Angelica slides over to Agnes and pulls her into a full body hug. Angelica is trembling and she has told Agnes before that when she has a masturbation orgasm her lips feel nearly numb and tingling.

In a few minutes Agnes asks Angelica; "are you sure you won't go with me to America? I checked last night and they still have first class tickets." Angelica pulls away, irritated that Agnes is asking about something that she thought they had settled days ago.

"I don't want to go, you will be doing all that business stuff and it is such a long way, I just don't want to go. Why can't you accept that?"

"I will tell you why. I think you are seeing someone else and if you think you are bringing them here to live-it-up while I'm gone; drinking my liquor, smoking my dope – well you're not doing that and I want your key - now!"

"Guess you wanted to see one last "show" before leaving." Angelica is getting dressed and gathering her things. Some things that Agnes doesn't think she would take except that she is not planning to come back.

"Here is your fucking key." Angelica tosses it onto the bed. I'm taking that bottle of absinthe, I stole it from a friend and it is mine."

"Fine, my lovely. We can talk when I return if you like. I'm not ready to let you go."

"You already have!" Angelica grabs the bottle of absinthe from the kitchen, stuffs it in her bag and slams the door. She decides to take the steps instead of the elevator. On the landing between the 3rd and 4th floor she sits down on the bottom step and takes a drink from the bottle of absinthe. She cries softly and takes another drink; "fucking bitch!"

24

Gio's New Friends

Gio is still standing in the hallway of the condo, looking at Fred's silhouette. The seconds have clicked by like hours. As his eyes adjust a bit to the hallway lighting he can see that Fred does not have a weapon aimed at him. Gio is also hoping that Fred has not seen the gun in his waistband. Feeling he has no choice, Gio pulls the gun from his waistband, clicks off the safety and puts one foot forward for balance and brings the pistol up and holds it in both hands.

"Fred, you need to sit down on the floor, with your hands on your head; now!"

Fred can barely believe his eyes and it takes him a few seconds to realize what is happening. Fred barely utters, "Fuck me." He is shocked by Gio's forceful voice and the rather large handgun that is pointed at him and he does as he is told. He had planned to pick Gio up by the collar and toss him across the room. Then having subdued him, make him tell where he is hiding the ambergris. His thinking was that a knife retrieved from the kitchen would be adequate to keep Gio under control and could also be used to cut his throat if necessary.

"O.K. Fred, scoot using your feet into the room to your left." As Fred is making progress scooting into the bedroom Gio is walking down the hall with his gun trained on Fred and as he reaches the end of the hallway and turns toward the bedroom Jesus Garciá brings his pistol butt down on the back of Gio's head and he falls against the wall and slides down on to the floor.

Fred says almost imperceptibly, "motherfucker, why didn't I go to Madrid?"

Jesus' two henchmen drag Gio into the kitchen. They return and duct-tape Fred's hands behind him and his ankles together. Jesus makes a call on his cell phone and after waiting a few moments he hears El Capitán's voice.

"This is Jesus. I have Fred tied up and the old man with the ambergris is just coming around from being knocked in the head. What should I do?"

"Let me think about it. Just sit tight, I'll call you back in a few minutes."

As Gio regains consciousness he very quickly understands what has happened. He is relieved that Fred is no longer his problem. But he realizes that now he will lose his ambergris. All his work and now nothing and if he goes to the police, even then, they will confiscate his cache. As he is thinking this through it occurs to him that those issues are the least of his problems and he knows, really knows, that this might be his last day on planet earth.

About ten minutes later Jesus' phone rings and it is El Capitán. Jesus listens intently. Then he turns to Gio and says, "If we let you live will you forget all this has happened?"

"Yes, absolutely."

"Also, you also understand that if you don't keep quiet we will also kill your family."

"Yes."

Jesus goes to the door and looks up and down the street. He comes back and tells his men. "Take Fred to the car and get him down out of sight." He looks at Gio, "Grandpa, do you know how lucky a man you are?"

"Yes."

"Hasta luego."

Gio feels like it is a really dumb question but he knows he has to ask it:

"Are you coming back for the ambergris?"

"No, Senor, the boss says we have no business fooling around with something we know nothing about. It is yours. Hasta luego grandpa, sorry for the little bump on your head."

Just as suddenly as they had arrived now they are gone and Gio is sitting against the wall knowing that he can't get up for a while and he is so glad that he didn't bring Amber with him. Gio doesn't remember ever having a worse headache, but this one was delivered by Jesus himself. Gio chuckles a little but it hurts his head so much he stops. As he sits against the wall, a breeze makes its way through the condo and he manages to get up by going onto his knees and then he pushes on his hands and gets to his feet and feeling dizzy, he leans against the wall while still standing and waits for the dizziness to clear. Next, he makes his way into the bathroom and looks into the mirror. He grabs a hand mirror from a vanity drawer and turns so that he can see the back of his head in the hand mirror. It doesn't look as bad as it feels. He takes a washcloth and wets it with cold water and dabs at the wound and then presses it there for a while. He then goes into the kitchen, looks in the fridge and is relieved to see there is a bottle of Gatorade there and he drinks half the bottle. Since Gio discovered ambergris and its promise of riches his use of foul language has grown exponentially and as he sits down at the kitchen table he says out loud, "Holy fuck, more shit has happened to me in the last few weeks than the whole rest of my life. Motherfucker!" Motherfucker indeed, as always, greed takes many and sundry paths. The advantage in life that Gio has is that his greed developed to achieve one specific goal and once that goal is achieved, he believes he will be able to return to his old self and maybe he will.

25

A New Identity

It has been two weeks since Ryan was kidnapped and his ear lobe, now disfigured, has nearly healed and his nose, though just slightly crooked is looking pretty good. The twins are nearly out of money and they have been trying to come up with some new way to make money. They have a small cache of ambergris and have an appointment to meet with Agnes Tubakken for the second time. She has told them that their cache is of average quality and her offer is based on that fact, but the twins have told her they want to think it over. They have been cautioned that the day after their next meeting Agnes will be traveling to Mexico City where she will board a flight to Copenhagen with all her ambergris acquisitions, well packaged and in the plane's cargo hold.

"Look, I think twelve grand is probably a good price, but we have to get every cent we can." Bryan says to Ryan, and stares at his brother and can barely believe that they are no longer indistinguishable. The ear lobe is obvious, but the nose is a subtle difference, but side-by-side it is still quite noticeable.

"I agree bro, but we've got rent coming due and all the rest. Plus if we change our lifestyles a little that money should last us a couple of months. That still doesn't give us much time to come up with a new money-making idea."

Ryan laughs.

"What's so fucking funny?"

"It just seems funny. With all our talk about some new scam, never once has either of us suggested getting a job."

"What's that? They both laugh.

"When we quit college, didn't dad say that if we ever wanted to go back that he would pay our tuition?"

"Yeah, Yeah, I think he did. But it's been four years now, do you think he would still do it?"

"I'm not sure about that, but don't you feel that we can't go on living like this forever?"

"I haven't really thought about it."

"I have. I look in the mirror now and I see me. I see a different earlobe and a new nose and I see me. Don't you get it? Now I'm me and you are you."

"But we're still twin brothers."

"We are still twin brothers, but we are no longer identical. Remember when we went on that binge after we quit school? After a few days, one-by-one our friends had to get back to their lives, for one reason or another. We never had that feeling. For Christ's sake we stayed down there another week. For the first time in my life I know what I want to do. I'm going to go talk to Dad and see if his offer is still good. You can come with me if you want."

"What do you mean? Are you just assuming I want to go back to school?

"I'm not assuming anything. I'm just saying, give it some thought. I started thinking about changing my life the day after those Mexicans fucked me up. Don't you see? I could have easily been killed."

"Yeah, but I rescued you."

"No shit Sherlock and I'd do the same for you. I'm not sure if it has anything to do with the ambergris thing or not but I want to be a marine biologist."

"What the fuck?"

"Yeah man, I do. And I realize how hard I'm going to have to study and I'm sure there will be some hardships along the way. But that's what I want."

"Wow, I'm shocked, I'm truly shocked."

"Don't you see, Bryan? We've been fucking around as far back as I can remember. Our whole lives have consisted of fucking people over with our little switch-er-roos. Just all fun and games. We've lived in our own little world and looking back I can see that we must have drove mom and dad nearly fucking crazy."

"Not so much mom." Bryan adds. "I think she kind of liked some of it and thought it was funny."

"We'll have to ask her."

Bryan looks at Ryan and puts his head back. "Wow, I never gave this any thought. Can you give me a few days to think about it?"

"Sure, we've got to get squared away with Tubakken no matter what. I've got a window of about a month before registration begins."

"Where will you go?"

"Good old San Diego State University offers a B.A. in ecology and marine biology. That will give me everything I need to get into the U of Cal in Santa Barbara and they offer a masters in marine biology. Why are you looking at me like I just grew another head?"

"I can't believe how quickly you came up with all this bull shit. It has seemed like you've been kind of quiet, even subdued, the last couple of weeks. It must be…..what is it those guys get? You know those military guys that have been in Afghanistan."

"You mean post-traumatic stress disorder?"

91

"Yeah, that's it."

"Look Bryan, if you have to think I've got some psychotic disorder going on to accept this, fine by me. But I'm serious about this. And I hope somewhere along the way I'll meet a good looking chick that also digs marine biology and we can marry and maybe even have some kids. I don't want to be the type of marine biologist that spends all his time in the lab. I want to be working out in the ocean, finding ways to preserve the world's barrier reefs, before it is too late. Maybe we'll even do a few shows for National Geographic as a husband and wife team."

"You know what, Ryan? You have grown another head and mine is spinning. I have to catch up. So really, pretty much what you are saying is soon, we both go our separate ways."

"We'll still be brothers; we just won't be together 24/7."

"Yeah, but remember, we've always discussed everything we planned to do. And you haven't said a word about this until you had it all planned out, with no consideration for me!"

"Not true. I've asked you if you want to go see mom and dad together. You can go with me and you can still decide on your own what you want to do in the future. Then, at least you'll know if dad will still pay for school."

"What if I just ask him for the money it would cost to get a master's degree?"

"Funny, oh real funny."

"That's kind of the way I'm feeling right now. I just need to think it through."

"Sure, absolutely, but I won't be asking him to support me. If I can convince my professors of my great interest in saving the barrier reefs I'm pretty sure there will be summer jobs I can get related to marine biology. Also, a major part of earning a master's degree is working in the field and conducting experiments or making discoveries to put together a thesis. I'm really excited about it!"

"Wow, my brother, my now un-identical twin, is going to marry a fucking mermaid and live happily ever after."

"Fuck you!"

"No, fuck you!"

"I said it first you dick!"

26

Give Me a Hand

When Fred's body washed up on the beach about a mile down the coast from Sally and Gio's beach house it caused quite a sensation. Not that it was that unusual for a body to wash ashore on this stretch of the Pacific Ocean. It usually happened about once or twice a year. However, generally the bodies do not have one hand missing and certainly not such a clean cut. The coroner said it was as if someone gave it a huge whack with a machete, and this coroner was known for his accuracy.

When Gio read that the police department was asking for anyone with any information on the incident to call Detective Watson in the homicide department Gio did feel a little sense of abandoning his citizen's duties. But how could he feel any sense of regret or responsibility? Fred was his own worst enemy. He had a chance to leave the country and he didn't take it. For Fred McCallister, it was just a matter of time before someone whacked him. The truth is: Gio is so glad he doesn't have to fear this man anymore and he also doubts if there is a single person on earth that would morn Fred's departure.

Just to think that he had come so close to shooting, maybe killing Fred, in his condo. Just that act alone would have tumbled Gio's world up-side-down. It would also have made him a much poorer man, in more ways than one. But, Gio thinks, who would expect to become the owner of a fine beach house in Southern California without having to go through a lot of shit to get it? Gio had gained so much in such a short time: The woman of his dreams, Amber and his skill, the luckiness of ambergris showing up in a place that rarely produces it.

It is a beautiful evening and Gio is sitting on the deck enjoying the cool evening breeze, starry sky, sipping a little brandy; just a man and his dog. Sally is out with a lady friend looking at wedding dresses. Gio feels like he has been on a long journey and now he has arrived. Now, he feels, everything will fall into place and he should have knocked wood. And the entire deck was made of wood.

27

The Lobby of Opportunity

The big day has arrived and Gio is sitting in the lobby of the Crown Royale Hotel. His plan of having Agnes Tubakken come to his condo was cast aside the moment he suggested it in a phone call with her a few days ago. Something like; "Mr. Valducci, I'm going to be meeting with over twenty potential clients, tell me how I would have the time to visit your home."

Gio has thought this "cattle call" scenario through several times. He wonders about the wisdom of going out with a suitcase full of ambergris, which may be more valuable than gold, without being surrounded by armed guards. After all, he was nearly ripped off when he thought he was keeping his cache a secret. When he brought this up to Agnes she told him that anyone can ascertain the value of gold based on the carat signature and the weight. "What you have, Mr. Valducci, is of no value until I evaluate it further." Maybe she's right, Gio is thinking, after all, a Mexican crime kingpin had a chance to take it all and chose not to.

Just to be on the safe side, Gio is wearing a suit to help conceal the .45 automatic he is carrying in a shoulder holster. Although for many years the weapon was stored in a box, now Gio has developed a feeling that it is a direct link to his long absent and undoubtedly dead father. Gio struggles to suppress the great feeling of power he felt when he had this keepsake trained on the torso of Fred McCallister.

Sally has asked to accompany him to the appointment to see Tubakken but Gio insists that it is better for him to make the negotiation alone. He has promised her to consult with her before he accepts an offer. He points out that it is a negotiating ploy that he learned as a shop steward in the baker's union: "I'll have to get back to you after I've consulted the other decision makers." All of this was true but he also still felt there was a hint of danger involved and he wanted to protect Sally from that.

As Gio enters the lobby of the exclusive hotel it very much has the appearance of a doctor's clinic. There are people killing time with their laptops and other electronic paraphernalia. Gio stays busy doing something that he and Sally love to do; people watching. He is surprised that he doesn't see the twins and tries to recall their names. There is a man with a briefcase that looks familiar and Gio falls into a reverie of thought trying to place that face. Finally he recalls where he has seen him before: he is one of the fishermen that he used to see on the beach. Damn, Gio wonders, did I give him the idea to hunt for grisrock? He recalls an old comedic line of the showman Jimmy Durante, "everybody wants to get into the act." Time is passing slowly and Gio chuckles a little to think that he had never considered any other outcome other than the lady broker coming to his condo, evaluating his grisrock, weighing it and making the arrangements to have it shipped. Oh well, he thinks, maybe there is safety in numbers.

A large, tall, very dignified looking gentleman comes into the lobby followed by Ryan and Bryan; the twins. The gentleman has a touch of indistinguishable European accent and calls out to the lobby: "Is Mr. Sandusky here?" The gentleman Gio knows as the fisherman jumps up and lamely offers his hand as Mr. Dignified turns and heads for the elevator.

Gio stands and greets the twins and asks, "O.K. which one is which?" Ryan and Bryan stare at him a moment before they recognize Gio. It was Gio's only way to get their names as he is having a senior moment.

"Hey," Ryan shakes his hand and says proudly, "I'm Ryan; I'm the one with the disfigured earlobe and broken nose and this is Bryan."

Bryan shakes his hand and they all stand there a moment looking around, each realizing that the conversation that is about to ensue is not one to have publicly. Bryan waves his hand and all three walk around the corner where there is a small area with seating where a bank of land-line phones were once located. Gio looks at Ryan and asks, "What happened?"

Ryan looks at Bryan and asks, "Should I tell him?"

"Sure, are we not, partners in crime?"

Gio sits down with his suitcase in front of him and he asks, "What time was your appointment?"

"Nine O'clock, when's yours?"

"Ten-forty five."

"Then don't worry, we've got plenty of time. Are you sure you want to hear this?" Ryan asks.

"Absolutely!"

Ryan starts out softly and Gio bends over to make sure he can hear.

"Did you know Fred was found on the beach with one hand missing?"

"Yes, I saw it in the paper."

"We heard it from Jordan."

Gio responds, "That guy scares me and I think he scares his father as well."

Ryan continues, "Yeah, we feel the same way, we are trying to stay away from him as much as possible. Our lives have changed drastically and we are trying to steer clear of him. Here goes; when I drove Fred to the airport I could almost tell that he wasn't going to get on that plane for Madrid. I couldn't go through security without a ticket and so I waited until after the departure time and I saw him exit the gate and

98

head for the rental car companies. I didn't know what else to do except to go back to Fred's place where Bryan was going to pick me up. Unknown to me, the whole fucking time I was driving Fred's car some Mexican cartel punk was following me. Fred's car had a GPS tracking device attached underneath. Some Mexican fucker pulled in next to me at Fred's in a big black S.U.V. and I didn't know who he was. I thought he was lost and the next thing I knew I was regaining consciousness in the backseat of Fred's car."

Gio's hair is nearly standing on end. At first he's pissed that they didn't let him know about what had happened and then he realizes they kept quiet for the same reason he's not sharing his story of Fred and Jesus' visit to his condo. "Unbelievable."

Ryan and Bryan tell him the whole story and Gio wants so much to share his experience as well, but he knows it exposes him to some liability in Fred's murder and he doesn't say a word.

"So," Ryan finishes his story, "I talked to our parents and they've agreed to pay my tuition so I'm going back to school this fall, in fact, in a couple of weeks, to complete my education and forget about all these crazy schemes to make money."

"What about you Bryan?"

"I'm still thinking it over."

"So, Ryan, do you have a major yet?"

"I do," Ryan says proudly, "I'm going to be a marine biologist."

"You guys are lucky," Gio tells them, "there are a lot of young people out there that have lost their way and then when they want to get on the right track they are clueless. I could tell you guys had a good background. It just showed through."

"Yeah, we've got great parents. Hey Bry, we had better get going we're supposed to have lunch with mom and dad."

Gio is blunt, "did you guys make a deal with her?"

"Nah, we're coming back tomorrow to see if we can get a little more."

"That's my plan too! Do you think we can really trust her to pay off?"

Bryan looks at Ryan and says, "That's kind of what we've been talking about for days now. We've decided that there are just too many happy customers online to ignore. There is no way she could have posted all that on her own. Like some of them say, she's a tough old bitch, but apparently she knows what she's doing and we've decided to stick with her and Jordan says that he knows people that have used her and thought they did well. Whatever that's worth." Bryan shrugs his shoulders and they all stand up.

Gio reaches in his jacket pocket and pulls out a wedding invitation. "Hey, if you guys can make it, please come to our wedding."

Ryan and Bryan look at each other and Ryan says, "hmm, we thought you guys were old married folks."

Bryan jumps in, "I told you they were too lovey-dovey to be married." They all laugh.

Gio says, "We'd love to have you come, it's going to be on the beach and there will be a ton of booze and some great food."

The men shake hands and Gio returns to the lobby, which is unchanged, still a doctor's waiting room.

28

A Surprising Offer

Having learned something from "the fisherman" when Gio's name is called he walks with Agnes' protector to the elevator and then offers his hand and introduces himself, "Gio Valducci, and you are?"

The man shakes Gio's hand and offers; "I'm Alsace L. Wohljung, retired Interpol officer. They enter the elevator and between floors three and four Mr. Wohljung pushes a button and stops the elevator. He looks down at Gio and pulls Gio's coat lapel out exposing the Colt .45 pistol. He says to Gio, "with your permission I'll remove your weapon, that is, if you still want to see Miss Tubakken."

"Yes, I'm a little embarrassed, but I was worried about my safety on the trip here."

"No need to be embarrassed. I knew you were carrying the moment I saw you." Mr. Wohljung unsnaps the safety strap and removes the weapon and puts it in his suit coat pocket. He flips the switch and the elevator continues to the 20th floor, where he leads Gio to room 2001 and nods his head for Gio to enter.

As Gio steps into the room he expects to see an old ugly broad, which is based entirely upon the things he's heard and the sound of her old lady smoker's voice on the phone. Wow, Gio thinks, she's a good looking gal. Agnes is still busy organizing some things behind the folding table she's using as a desk and it gives Gio a little time to look around the room, which is quite elegant and probably very expensive. So far everything he has seen regarding this woman is first class. Agnes sits down in the chair and looks up, "Mr. Valducci?"

"Yes, that's me, please call me Gio." Gio waits to see if she will shake his hand, when Agnes smiles and says, "Have a seat Mr. Valducci."

"A pleasure to meet you, is it Miss or Misses?"

"You may call me Miss Tubakken."

"I have your sample here Mr. Valducci; let's see how it compares to the rest of your product."

Gio places the suitcase on the floor, opens it and begins placing "the product" on the table. Miss Tubakken picks up a piece and runs her fingers over it and sniffs it a bit and looks Gio square in the eyes and says, "Mr. Valducci, this product appears to have just been pulled from the ocean. I thought it had been on hand for a while."

"Well, yes, I've been keeping it in plastic containers with sea water and bubblers."

"In an attempt to increase the weight and thus take advantage of me?"

"Oh, no, I hadn't thought about it in that way. I just thought it was a good idea to keep it fresh."

"Oh, I see, so you were just keeping it fresh."

"Yes."

Miss Tubakken looked at every piece and used a small torch to heat a long needle and plunged it into a couple of pieces. "Mr. Valducci, this is all of the high quality of the sample you sent me. It's really quite extraordinary. However, you must understand that from the moment you removed it from your plastic boxes of sea water it will dry out and I can't weigh it until it has dried out enough to be representative of what I'll be submitting to my clients."

"So, how does that effect our transaction?" Gio asks.

"Damn, I wish you hadn't stored it in sea water." Agnes scolds.

"Tell me what to do."

"Let me think about this for a moment." Miss Tubakken stares at the ambergris as if lasers in her eyes are drying it out. "Damn, this complicates things. If I stay another day there will be extra expense for the hotel and Mr. Wohljung. Quite frankly, I've never had anyone do this before."

Gio sits forward in his chair, thinking that he had kept it in sea water to keep the quality high, not thinking it would be such a problem.

"Mr. Valducci."

"Yes."

"As I said, your ambergris is of very high quality. In fact, I'm fairly certain that I can market it to a Dutch chocolate maker, and that means you will be making top dollar. I can submit the sample you sent me to the chocolate maker. By that time the rest will have dried out enough to weigh and make the sale. However, you must trust me to be fair with you or this just isn't doable."

"Can I think about this for a moment?"

"Yes, I need to use the rest room, so, yes, by all means think about it for a bit."

When Miss Tubakken returns Gio says, "How about this: can we weigh it now in its damp condition?"

"Mr. Valducci, I don't think you understand."

"Miss Tubakken, will you please let me finish." Miss Tubakken nods her head yes.

"Let's weigh it now and then we'll cut a piece off one of the larger pieces about the same size as the sample I sent you which has already dried out. Then you will have some idea how much the dried out weight will be. Does that make sense?"

"Somewhat."

"What do you mean "somewhat?""

"Well, the larger pieces will dry out more slowly than a small piece because of the mass of it."

"True, but at least that will give us some idea of the final weight. Listen, Miss. Tubakken, I'm going to trust you on this. Honestly, I did not intend to create a problem, I was just doing what I thought was best. So you have to trust me as well."

"I will have to say that the relative freshness will probably appeal to the chocolate maker. So, let's weigh it quickly, we are nearly running over our appointment time."

They work together to weigh "the product" and after deducting 15% for the drying out process the total should be approximately 15 pounds and 14 ounces.

Gio asks, "As a ballpark figure, what do you think it will bring with the chocolate manufacturer?"

"What is a "ballpark figure? What does that mean?"

"Oh, I guess you could say it's like using your best judgment without me holding you to the figure."

"Hmm, I like that, a ballpark figure. Yes, well, I would say, depending on how urgent the need of the chocolate maker is; perhaps between seven hundred fifty and eight hundred fifty thousand American dollars."

Gio is so astounded he forgets his good manners: "You have got to be shitting me!"

"Excuse me?"

"Oh, sorry, just another American expression. Should I take this to the bank around the corner and store it in a safe deposit box? I had no idea it would be that much." And, Gio is thinking; what if it was "just" three hundred thousand, a safe deposit box would still be a good idea. All his thoughts up until now were just blue sky, something that might be achieved. But now, one of the foremost experts in the world has evaluated it. Motherfucker, we are rich beyond belief! Gio refrains from rubbing his eyes to make sure this isn't just an illusion.

"Mr. Valducci, do you know a man named Fred McCallister?"

"Why are you asking me that?"

"A man from this area sent me a sample very similar to your product. I've emailed him and tried to call, but I haven't heard from him."

"He is in prison. He stole that sample from me and was planning to steal all of it from me but he got caught and now he is in prison."

"Oh, thank you for the information. I'll add that piece on to your total."

"ChaChing!" Gio shouts.

"Excuse me?"

"Oh, nothing, just a way to celebrate this."

"Fine, Mr. Valducci, if you wish you can leave your product here. Alsace is a retired Interpol officer and has an adjoining room. It will be safe here. I've been working with him for about seven years now and he is quite excellent at security."

Although still a little cautious, Gio places the ambergris back into the suitcase, including the stolen piece and asks Miss. Tubakken where he should put it.

"Just over there in the corner." Miss Tubakken tells him. "Here, put this sticker on there."

Gio looks at the sticker where Miss. Tubakken has printed his name, the date, the weight and some sort of code as to the quality of the product.

Miss Tubakken tells Gio, "Turn it around so the information doesn't show. Are you abandoning the suitcase?"

"Ah, yes, that's fine."

"It's a pleasure doing business with you Mr. Valducci. If you haven't heard from me within three weeks, give me a call or email. Here is a receipt with all the pertinent information on it signed by me and please sign both copies and leave one with me."

Gio signs the copies, gives one to Miss Tubakken and wonders how he got through this without shitting his pants.

As he closes the door behind him Alsace is waiting in the hallway and he quietly says to Gio, "Will you please wait here until I bring the next appointment up, there is something I want to discuss with you?"

"Sure."

Jeez, Gio thinks, I wonder what he could possibly want to talk to me about?"

When Alsace returns and escorts the next appointment inside, he signals Gio to follow him and they enter the adjoining room. Alsace leaves the door open. There is an Uzi submachine gun lying on the bed in its opened case. Alsace lays a pillow from the sofa to hide the Uzi and walks to the bar and asks Gio if he would like a drink.

"What are you having?"

"When in Rome, as they say; I think I'll have a shot of Jack Daniels."

"Me too, so what's up?"

"Let's see, I believe that is a phrase Americans use to greet each other." Alsace chuckles.

"Oh, yeah, in this case it's just to ask what you want to talk about."

Alsace hands Gio a business card: Alsace L. Wohljung, Retired Interpol Officer and Security Expert and the usual contact information.

Gio asks, "What does the L stand for, Lorraine?"

"How the fuck did you know that?"

"I thought maybe you were named for the Alsace Lorraine part of France."

"As you Americans say, bullshit, that region rightfully belongs to Germany."

"Are you a German?"

"Well, my name is German, but I'm part French. There are no pedigrees in that region, I assure you."

"Is your last name pronounced Wohl-young?"

"Correct."

Alsace takes Gio's pistol from his pocket and asks, "May I examine your gun thoroughly?"

"Certainly."

Alsace removes the clip and holds the gun up to the light and looks into the clip area. He points the gun towards the outside and high and pulls the slide to eject the cartridge in the chamber. As it falls on the bed he says, "You were ready for a fire-fight Gio, good man. Gio, this Colt .45 is a weapon made by Colt for the German army before Germany provoked World War II. Only officers Colonel and above were allowed to carry it. How did you acquire this weapon?"

At first, after entering the room, Gio had no idea what this man was going to ask him and now he is wondering if he is going to confiscate his gun.

"My father brought it back from World War II. I found it in the basement when I was a teenager. I was sure it had belonged to my dad and I hid it in my room so my brothers and sister wouldn't come across it. I never told anyone in my family about it and hung onto it because I like guns and it was all I had from my father."

The men click their shot glasses together and down the Jack Daniels. Both men make a sound, "Whew!"

"I love this stuff," Alsace utters, "your father probably took this pistol off a German officer, perhaps killed him, perhaps not, but probably did. How much will you take for it?"

That question totally baffles Gio; it was the last thing he expected to hear. Oh well, he thinks, that's much better than confiscation. "Why do you want this pistol, is it valuable?"

"I'm not sure about the value. I recognized it as soon as I looked at it. My father had one; he was a Colonel in the army. I think guns are in our blood. My older brother has my father's pistol. I'd love to wave this in his face the next time we go target shooting. Does it have a great deal of sentimental value to you?"

"Not exactly, my father left us before I really knew him. It is the only thing of his I have. So I guess the answer is yes."

"Would I insult you with an offer?"

"Go ahead, insult me."

"Allowing for the sentimental value, my offer is two thousand U.S. dollars."

"Not much money for a newly rich man."

"Yes, that was a very big suitcase, crammed full of ambergris?"

"Yes, pretty full."

"I'll trade you my Uzi for it."

"Alsace, how in the fuck did you get that gun into the country?"

Alsace reaches in his breast coat pocket and produces a very fancy leather holder which he flips open. There is an elaborate badge there and some other very official looking information that proclaims him an Interpol Officer."

"I thought you were retired."

"Yes, I am, but as long as we keep our record clean, we keep our badges. It is a way for Interpol to increase their eyes on crime. I'm told it has paid off numerous times. So I can pretty much move about with any weapon. The airline employees usually about shit when they see my I.D. If they question it, there is usually someone on their staff that is aware. So how about it, Gio, do you want to trade?"

"You really want my gun don't you?"

"Indeed I do, is it a deal?"

"So Alsace, you're carrying a pistol, right?"

"Yes."

"What kind?"

Alsace reaches under his coat to the middle of his back and pulls out a Glock 19. It is a combination of synthetic parts and metal parts blended together to make a state-of-the-art pistol. He hands it to Gio. Gio carefully takes the weapon and surveys it. "How many bullets in the clip?"

"Fifteen, 9mm, plenty of firepower."

Gio hands the weapon back to Alsace and says, "O.K., I'll trade my colt for your Glock with three thousand cash."

"Hmmm.."

"Is that a yes?"

Alsace laughs. "Are you an attorney?"

"No, I'm a retired baker, now fortune hunter."

"O.K. tough guy, how about this?"

Alsace goes to his luggage and pulls out a plastic case and opens it up. He pulls another Glock pistol from its case and says, "This is a Glock 21, the clip holds thirteen forty-five caliber rounds and it has an internal laser site." Alsace points the pistol at a painting of Thomas Jefferson hanging on the wall. The laser beam held steadily on Mr. Jefferson's forehead.

"Holy shit," Gio exclaims."

"The Glock 21," Alsace offers, "and two thousand dollars." Alsace hands the pistol to Gio. "Go ahead; assassinate your former president right between the eyes.

Gio takes a shooting stance and points the laser at the historic president's head and watches it wiggle around his whole face.

"That's the strategy of the laser light; as long as you can see the light on the targets body, you can make the shot. The Glock 21 and two thousand."

"The Uzi is worth more, right?" Gio asks.

"Absolutely, but you can't conceal and carry with it. Well, unless you want to carry a large briefcase around."

Gio counters, "The Glock 21 and three grand."

"Meaning three thousand, right?"

"O.K. Gio, it's a deal." Alsace opens a briefcase and takes a stack of money out and peels off 30-one hundred dollar bills, puts the stack on the Glock 21's plastic case and puts his hand out to shake on the deal. Alsace picks the Colt .45 up and says, "I can't wait to show this to my brother. This Colt is in pristine condition, our father's gun shows some wear. It's a great deal for both of us. As you Americans say, a win-win situation!"

There is a tap on the adjoining room door. Alsace crosses the room and opens the door. Miss Tubakken is standing there. "Alsace, please escort Mr. Chandler to the lobby and retrieve the next person on the list."

Alsace quickly grabs a shopping bag from the bed and puts the gun case into it and hands Gio the cash. "Let's go Gio." As they wait for the elevator Alsace tells Gio, "can you come to my room for dinner this evening, I really enjoyed our conversation."

"In your room?"

"Yes, I'm guarding your treasure, I can't leave the area."

As the elevator reaches the lobby and the doors open Mr. Chandler exits and Gio pushes the "close door" button and pushes the fifth floor button.

"What did you see Gio? You're turning pale."

"I just saw Jesus in the lobby."

"Excuse me?"

Gio steps out into the fifth floor hallway and Alsace follows; there is no one else in the hallway.

"Alsace, there is a man in the lobby, a Mexican thug. I don't know his last name, his first name is Jesus. I'll try to make this quick. He killed a guy who tried to steal my cache of ambergris and I then thought he would take it but when he called his boss he said they didn't want to deal in anything they weren't knowledgeable of. Now I see, they were really waiting to steal everyone's ambergris. The guy they tortured and murdered knew Tubakken was coming and when she would be here. He knocked me out with the butt of his gun. They are killers Alsace."

"So am I Gio." Alsace looks at his list and tells Gio, "Look at this."

Gio looks at the list and the next name is Jesus Garciá. "What are we going to do, Alsace?"

"So glad you said "we" Gio, I may need your help. Will you be here for dinner this evening at seven?" "Yes I will."

29

"The Fam"

Ariel Lynn Fishman is a beautiful young woman that recently came home from school just days before final's week telling her mother that college just isn't her thing and that she wants to get a job as a legal secretary, which probably won't happen since she's been home two months now and hasn't been to one job interview. Not long after she returned home her mother, Judith, noticed that some of her jewelry was missing. At first Judy thought perhaps she had misplaced it, but soon realized many things of value in her house were disappearing. This led to a confrontation that also included accusations of, "This is my house and it just isn't fair that I am working everyday and you lounge around here never cleaning up your messes and not even doing basic things like loading the dishwasher or doing the wash and you are stealing valuable jewelry and other items from me and for what I don't even have a clue." As Ariel, or Lynn, as she prefers to be called, looks on with indifference the tirade goes on for a while and then exists only as stares between the two participants. Soon, Lynn bursts into tears and desiring to explain all those accusations with one mighty excuse blurts out, "I'm on cocaine mom, I'm addicted to cocaine." Though not untruthful, the ploy works, and mother and daughter share an embrace and tears flow in great volumes all around. After all the accusations of "I've given you everything" and "how I miss having my dad in my life" and "you must do something" and all the usual family horror that plays out across America every day, Lynn nixes going to rehab in favor of quitting cold turkey and promises to do better around the house and to look for a job. In the two months that Lynn has been home the same scene of confrontation and accusation has been played out four times now with fewer items being stolen and a bit of cleaning and lies of having gone to numerous, yet unfruitful, job interviews. Under such circumstances a parent is plunged into the role of caring for that child as if they were a baby again. They can't be left alone without circumstances, they can't be reasoned with, and unlike a baby they can leave the home and do evil things. Therefore, Judy was delighted when she received her half-brother's wedding invitation.

Lynn rolls her eyes and says, "I don't even know him, isn't he like a hundred years old or something?"

"He's retired and never been married, not even engaged before, as far as I know."

"So, why do you want to go?" Lynn asks.

"The invitation says the wedding and reception will be held on the beach and I looked up his address and Google-earthed it and the house is on the beach. Gio wrote a note saying there is no need for a hotel, that he has plenty of room for us to stay there, that evening beach attire is fine for the wedding and he was adamant that there should be no gifts. This could be almost like a vacation, we can walk the beach, and you can meet some of the family......" Judy looses concentration and is thinking how she will be able to keep an eye on Lynn and this may be the perfect answer and alternative to doing rehab. She doesn't mention it to Lynn but she wonders how-the-fuck her brother, the retired baker, happens to now live on the beach in an upscale community near San Diego? He must be marrying money, she thinks, and realizes that she doesn't know much about Gio. She was five years old when Gio left home and became a baker's apprentice. He was always really good to her, getting her gifts and making her feel very special. They seem ancient memories now and she looks forward to getting reacquainted with her older brother. Gio had been a solid rock when her husband Sol died, helped her financially and gave her the courage and confidence to go out and find a good job.

"Mom, you can go and I'll stay here, what if I'm offered a job, I really need to be here."

"Look at me Lynn, if you think I'm going to leave you here to lounge around and party with some of your friends, you need to know: that is not going to happen. So just put the attitude away. If you get a call about a job, I assure you, we will manage for you to respond to it without losing the opportunity. You are going and you need to make up your mind to enjoy yourself, because that's exactly what I'm planning to do."

Gio's brother, Jonathan, sends his regrets, as he will be in South America working on his employer's latest oil drilling project. However, Jonathan's two grown children, Maya and Jason, plan to attend.

Sally has invited several relatives of her deceased husband, and really, she hopes they don't come, but realizes a few will attend just out of curiosity. Sally is sure her brother John and her sister Sylvia will be there, as for the nieces and nephews, she is not so sure.

So, it's to be a small wedding, with a wooden dance floor, situated in a gleaming white tent, just in case of rain. There will be a five piece jazz band; "Spencer and the Bell Tones," that can play anything from Dixieland to be-bop and all somehow "danceable."

30

Full Disclosure

When Gio arrived home Sally was out on the deck with Amber, sipping some white wine. The sun had passed over and the sea breeze was magnificent. Gio poured himself a glass of wine, grabbed the agreement with Ms. Tubakken and was immediately greeted by Amber, who was petted briefly and then told to "come" - which to Amber means "sit."

"I was beginning to think I'd be tipsy before you got home."

"I really don't need any wine, I'm on a high baby, I'm on a high! But it might help to settle me down."

"How rich are we, did you make a deal?"

"Tubakken tells me that our "product" as she calls it is of a very high grade and she's sure she can market it to a Dutch chocolate maker and in the range between seven-hundred fifty and eight-hundred fifty thousand."

"Is that what we get or what she will be selling it for?"

Gio unfolds the agreement and shows it to Sally, "I believe that it is what we would end up with."

Sally reads the agreement over and points to one line of the document: "It says here that if it is confiscated by any government we may not receive anything."

"I know, but since this is borderline illegal, we just have to put faith in her and Alsace. The twins were there, Ryan and Bryan, and we talked about the risk. They seem to think that there are just too many happy people that have posted good things about her online. I see their point. Apparently she's been doing this for a long time."

"Did you say Alsace?"

"Yes, he is a retired Interpol officer and is guarding our grisrock with an arsenal of weapons."

"You left it there?"

"I know, I know, but believe me, it is much safer at the hotel, Alsace is camped out in the next room and her room is at the end of the hall. You'd have to be there to appreciate the set up."

"I wanted to be there, you didn't want me to go. I thought you were going to tell her you would have to get back to her after consulting with me. What happened to that strategy?"

"That's a fair question. I can tell you are upset and I don't blame you. I have lots of other things I need to tell you. I kept quiet about them because I didn't want you to worry and after I tell you, well, you can decide if I was wrong or not."

"I'm all ears."

"We talked about Fred McCallister when it came out in the news."

"We did, he was a fool, he could have gone to Madrid."

"As you know, Fred didn't get on the plane; he rented a car and left the airport. Ryan saw him go but didn't know what to do but follow their plan and meet Bryan at Fred's place and leave Fred's car there. One of the Mexican thugs had a GPS tracking device on Fred's car and he followed Ryan to Fred's place and then pretended to need directions and knocked Ryan out. So when Bryan arrived, Fred's car was gone and he looked in the SUV Jesus Garciá had left there and saw the tracking device. So he used it to track Jesus across the border and found his brother, Ryan, in a warehouse being tortured for information about Fred. They broke his nose and cut part of his earlobe off. It's kind of confusing!"

"Go on."

"So now it is easy to tell the twins apart and they seem very changed. I think facing death woke Ryan up and he's going back to school to be a marine biologist. I invited them to our wedding."

"You've got to be kidding me."

"I knew they had a good background, I told you that. I think they are good kids; I'm not sure why I invited them. They probably have better things to do anyway. Remember that day when I went over to my condo to check on the ambergris and stow away my pistol?"

"When you fell off the ladder and hit your head?"

"Yes, exactly, only I didn't hit my head. I left the patio door open to get some air in the place and when I started back down the hallway Fred McCallister was standing there. It took me a minute to see if he had a gun and when I saw he didn't I pulled mine out of my waistband and told him to get down on the floor and I told him to scoot into the bedroom, which he did. Then when I turned to go into the bedroom that Jesus character slugged me with his pistol's butt. I was out for a little while and when I woke up they were carrying Fred out the door and Jesus called someone named El Capitán and asked what he should do about stealing our ambergris. Then he told me his boss said they had no business dealing in something they knew nothing about. He actually apologized for slugging me and out-the-door he went. It was all a huge relief to me, Fred was no longer my problem and they didn't steal our cache."

"What a fucking mess."

"There's more: After I talked to Ms. Tubakken, Alsace asked me to wait in the hall until he brought the next person on the list up. When he came back he took me into his room and wanted to buy my father's pistol. It's a special one made just for high ranking German officers just before World War II. Alsace's brother has their father's pistol and he asked to buy mine. Alsace asked me to join him for dinner in his room tonight at seven. Then when we escorted the gentleman back downstairs, I saw Jesus walking into the lobby. I pushed the up button and I was pretty sure he didn't see me, but I realized that they had passed up stealing our stash so they could steal from everyone. Fred sent Tubakken that piece of ambergris he stole from us and he apparently told Jesus about her coming to town to buy from a number of people. So, we made a plan and Alsace goes down to the lobby and tells everyone that Ms. Tubakken has a migraine headache and she forgot to bring her medication with her and that she is arranging for the medication as we speak and she will be fine in the morning. He has a clip board and tells them they need to sign up for a time tomorrow. He hands the clipboard to Jesus so that his fingerprints will show up on the back of the clip board and then he flips up a card he had carefully taped to the back of the board and it prevents the others from spoiling Jesus' finger prints. He called a friend of his at The National Central Bureau in Washington D. C., the agency Interpol works through in the U.S., and Garciá is wanted on drug smuggling charges and kidnapping and torture. Alsace used a field fingerprinting kit to process the prints and he was sending them to N.C.B. on a special encoded internet link to make sure it is the same guy. So, when Garciá shows up tomorrow, he and his henchmen will be taken into custody by a Federal Marshall. Alsace told his friend that he was in San Diego running security for a Copenhagen diamond dealer in town buying and selling diamonds. I guess that is everything, well, and I traded my pistol for a brand new Glock 21 with built-in laser and this:" Gio pulls the 30 one hundred dollar bills out of his pocket and shows Sally.

"I think we are in over our heads on this one."

119

"I feel that way too, but what can we do, we have to follow through so we can get our money."

"So, if you hadn't seen this Garciá character, he would have stolen all the ambergris she had."

"I doubt it, I think Alsace would have killed them all, but anything is possible when you are outnumbered."

"You should have gone to the police the day they knocked you out."

"We would have lost our whole cache!"

"Well, I suppose when one gets involved in something shady, you run with shady people."

"Actually, I'd say much more than shady. This Alsace is unbelievable. I think he will get us through this and I think we will, in a little time, get our money."

"How much time?"

"She told me that if I didn't hear from her in three months to call or email her. I can tell she's a real pro, I'm confident this will all work out."

"Three months?"

"Oh, sorry, three weeks, she said three weeks."

"Won't you have to be a witness in this Garciá's trial?"

"No, no, no; Alsace seems to think they may discover blood in their SUV that can be linked to Fred, he said he would keep me out of it and I believe him."

"Well, he certainly has made an impression on you!"

"So, are you mad?"

"Life's too short for that Gio. Will you promise me that after this is all over and we get married; we will be able to have just a simple life? I've had enough excitement for a lifetime. We can still cash in my annuities to pay the house off. If we do, I'll probably need to work a little to pay real estate taxes and living expenses. Marge said I could work at her studio, selling her paintings and things.

"Sally look at me. I promise you. This is a once-in-a-lifetime opportunity, we can't pass it up."

"Do you think we are in danger until this guy is arrested?"

"I don't think so, they have their plan and I think they will stick to it."

"I'll find out more when I have dinner with Alsace at seven this evening."

"Did you say, in his room?"

"Yes, he can't leave our valuable "product," even for dinner."

"And you think I'm waiting here?"

"Call Marge, you guys can have dinner in the hotel restaurant while I'm upstairs." Gio hands Sally three one hundred dollar bills. "It's on me."

"Briber!"

"Guilty as charged!"

31

Dinner For Six

The Way There

Amber has been walked and fed and has continued to be a very confused little dog for a while now. It's as if all the rabbits in his territory have been caught. The walks are short now and ambergris seems to have gone from being an endangered species to extinct. Amber was even more excited than Gio about the hunting of his namesake and at least Gio, in his quietude, has the satisfaction of having achieved great wealth. Gio plans to start taking longer walks, maybe along the boardwalk. Gio doesn't want Amber to forget his goofy tricks and love of performance.

Gio and Sally take the Town Car and pick up Marge. It is a continuation of an adventure near it's end.

"Marge, I have three one-hundred dollar bills. Do you think we can manage to spend them on dinner?"

"Well, including drinks and dessert, I don't see a problem." The two women giggle like school girls.

Gio asks, "Is it OK with you if I ask Alsace to be my best man?"

"Aren't the chances pretty slim that he'll fly back here to be best man for someone he's only known for a couple of days?"

"Well, when you say it like that it does sound a bit silly. So, I ask you again, is it OK with you if I play the long-shot?"

"Go for it Gio, he can be best man and provide security for the wedding."

Everyone laughs.

Marge asks, "do we get to meet this guy?"

"Sure," Gio speaks up, "I'll take you up and introduce you and then you can head for the hotel restaurant."

When they arrive, Sally, being on the passenger side, pulls the vanity mirror down to check her makeup and Marge in the middle pulls the rear view mirror down and does the same.

The Trip Home

Strangely, Gio thinks, the girls sit in the back seat. As Gio drives along he looks in the rear view mirror and sees that it has been moved. Just as he starts to move it back into place he stops short, as he can see in the mirror that Sally and Marge are holding hands. This really piques his curiosity and also gives him an erection. Oh my, what can be done with a naughty old man?

The girl's hands dapple in and out of the random light that casts itself through the Town Car's skylight window. Gio keeps watching as best he can while driving somewhat intoxicated, both from the whiskey he shared with Alsace and the femme fatale hand holding. Where does that manly gene come from? Clearly, the enjoyment of two women caressing in any way haunts the mind of most men. Perhaps Mother Nature has programmed the male mind to relish such behavior to keep his harem together and happy. Such a pity that modern society has no place for such antics.

Gio pulls up and stops at a red-light and Marge says, "I can understand why you were so taken with Alsace, there really aren't any men around here like that."

"So," Gio asks, "you really like him?"

"Well, yeah, but so what?"

"Good, then you won't mind – he asked for your phone number and I gave it to him."

123

"Gio!"

"So, is it OK?"

"Sure, fine, I mean what's he going to do, call me from the airport? How much longer will he be here? Is he single?"

"He didn't mention a wife. I think he'll be here a few more days."

Gio asks, "how was dinner?"

"Very interesting," Says Marge, "your Copenhagen money-maker is a dyke."

"She was there, in the restaurant?"

Sally puts in, "she had dinner with that Jamaican girl we saw at Jordan's dad's place."

"Tekeysia?"

"Yes, and sparks were flying. They drank their dinner and soon left."

"So while I was talking to Alsace they were in the next room getting it on?"

"Did you hear any strange noises?"

"I could tell someone was in there with her, I thought maybe it was a customer. Tekeysia is one wild woman, remember, she spent time with Fred before going back to Jordan."

"Yep, she must have come with Jordan when he brought his ambergris in."

"What ambergris? I didn't think Jordan even had any."

"He must have had some, why else would they have met?"

"When I see Alsace tomorrow, I'm going to ask him about that."

In a moment, Sally asks, "why are you going to be seeing Alsace tomorrow?"

"He needs my help, in case those Mexican thugs come back to steal the ambergris."

Sally and Marge look at each other and stop holding hands. Sally asks, "Gio, why would you risk your life doing something you know next to nothing about?"

"It's to protect our future." The tension in the car stops all conversation.

Gio adjusts the rear-view mirror and soon they drop Marge off and Sally gets in the front seat. This is the first confrontation Sally and Gio have had and it silences them completely as they each try to find a way to get through it. As they arrive home Sally says, "Gio, I don't want to be a widow before I'm a bride."

As Gio ponders Sally's thought the excitement and camaraderie of the event leave him drained and he knows that Sally is right, but how will he withdraw? Gio thinks Sally's statement requires no answer and he attaches Amber's leash to his collar and takes him for a walk.

Sally somberly goes to the bedroom and takes off her dress and wonders, why do men have to be so, well, so boyish? Why does the thought of a battle so excite them? She had seen it in her now deceased husband. The excitement he exuded when trying to put a big deal together. How high he was when he beat out the competition. And she knows that now, for Gio, it is all about losing face. Thank goodness the Japanese gave it a name, too bad they didn't find any resolution. At first Sally thinks the best thing is to pretend to be asleep when Gio returns, but she knows she has to find a way to keep him safe.

Gio is gone for over a half-hour and then seeing Sally sleeping he laments how he had planned to fuck her and whisper to her that he saw them holding hands and that he knows that Sally wants to lick Marge's clit and how excited Sally would become as they both had earth jarring orgasms. Gio slips quietly into the bed. After a few minutes Sally asks, "can we talk about this?"

"There is nothing to talk about."

"Oh, but I think there is."

"Alsace called me while I was walking Amber. He told me he had just spoken to the local law enforcement and they don't want me around tomorrow. He said he thinks they are right, there is no reason for me to risk taking a bullet when they can handle it."

Sally turns to Gio, looks him in the eyes and says, "I'm so glad he called you."

"I'm glad too, I just got carried away with all that macho shit and I didn't know how to back out. Hold me tight my love, you are the rock of my life and I love you oh so much."

32

Tekeysia's Story

Tekeysia arrived in the United States of America as a stowaway on a low flying "mule" airplane used to smuggle cocaine and heroin into the country. The pilot loved fucking her in Jamaica and although he initially scolds her, he is soon mounted and he is glad she came.

Tekeysia was born in a village high in the mountains of Jamaica. Although most of the villagers have proper English names; Edward, Joseph, Daniel, Elizabeth, Mary, Mildred, that is the only such acumen in this village of abject poverty.

Tekeysia, whose mother broke with tradition in naming her, is twelve years old and is headed for the village's "gathering area," a kind of village park. She has heard the acoustic bass guitar of Big Brenda and Tekeysia knows that soon a crowd will gather as Big Brenda begins to sing her bawdy songs. Tekeysia is hoping to get her first hit of the day to help pass the time away. Incest is so rampant in this village that when a baby girl is born there is a competition between male relatives as to who will stoop the lowest to be the first. Age is not important, opportunity is.

As Big Brenda begins to sing, a crowd gathers. Arthur, though in a wheel chair and stinking to high heaven, is there with his drum. Another brings an African thumb harp and still others sit down at the primitive picnic tables and join the rhythm of the song, a Big Brenda original, "I'm Going Home." Klatches of chickens are roaming the grounds, digging out earth worms, rustling insects and covering the ground with their feces.

Big Brenda is smoking a big joint and sitting atop the table her upper body swaying back and forth to the rhythm she is laying down on the big acoustic bass guitar. One of her huge breasts seems in danger of popping out as she moves to her music. Tekeysia looks at Arthur in his wheel chair and yes, he does have a huge hard-on, although they say he can't even feel it.

Tekeysia has been sexually abused since she can remember. Mostly by men and boys in her family and sometimes by her older sisters and aunts. She slowly navigates her way through the chickens and chicken shit and manages to grab Joseph's cigar sized joint to get the first hit of the day. Someone points to her and Joseph catches her. Damn, she thinks, now I'll have to go into the bushes and blow him.

The rhythm of the music is hypnotic as Big Brenda sways to and fro on her huge ass that's spread across the table. The wood carvers are here today, sending chips of exotic wood flying through the air. They are smoking big cigar sized joints, sending up clouds of smoke punctuated by the crisp wood chips. Some of the villagers walk by with chickens, their tied-up feet slung across a stick and carried along for the journey to the city market in Montego Bay. Other villagers traipse by carrying all manor of agricultural products, on their shoulders and on their heads. Some of them move a little to the music but give the joyous music makers a hateful scowl that they do not earn an honest living like them. After the next song and Tekeysia's fourth hit, Joseph takes her by the hand and guides her into the bushes, which she hates because he is so big. But she manages it in spite of the size and then spits her mouth's contents out on to the ground as the chickens run to see if it is edible.

Tekeysia returns to the musical gathering and takes several long tokes on Joseph's ganja. One of her older aunts leaves the entrepreneurial pathway and grabs Tekeysia by the hand and tells her, "you are going to the market with me today." Tekeysia doesn't mind, she's flying quite high now. As they walk to the bus stop she continues to spit to get the bad taste from her mouth. She knows that Aunt Consuela will buy her a meal after she helps her sell the handmade jewelry pieces. Then back at her aunt's hut she will lay back while her aunt pleasures her. She is so happy. Aunt Consuela gives her a little money that she will use for small food purchases at the village store or maybe some ganja of her own.

33

Jesus in His Homeland

Jesus is headed for a face-to-face meeting with El Capitán. Jesus always feels a great sense of dread as he drives into El Capitán's complex. The security guard opens the gate when he sees that the driver is Jesus. Jesus lowers the driver's side window and says, "Hey, Paco, que Paso?

"Ola Jesus ."

"I haven't seen you for a while. I've been mostly on the other side, trying to make my big score." Both men smile wide grins. "Paco, what kind of mood is El Capitán in?"

"Ahhh, so-so. Hector was here this morning, he left without stopping to talk, he didn't look too happy, but maybe his wife is giving him some trouble." Both men laugh, knowingly.

"O.K. Paco, thanks for the warning."

Jesus drives his black Escalade into the compound, the flowers and shrubs on each side of the drive are impeccably groomed. He drives up the circle drive to the palatial home, striking enough to please a Spanish Nobleman. Jesus recognizes another black Escalade by the license number and knows Roberto will be in attendance. This could be good – could be bad, Jesus thinks, I'm not sure which. Jesus can see just a corner of bright light amongst the shade. El Capitán's children are playing on the playground of his private school.

Jesus takes one last sip of his morning coffee and hopes that El Capitán doesn't start doing tequila shots. Jesus says aloud, "he thinks it is truth serum – like I would lie to El Capitán, well maybe just a little."

He stows his weapon in the glove box, though he will be surrounded by armed men, and walks into the King's castle. Jesus hopes that El Capitán doesn't bring up the whale shit thing. It could and should have been a big score, but Jesus is quite sure if he had gone to the hotel to keep his appointment he would be arrested or shot. Jesus smelled a rat when the big man came down and changed their appointment. Jesus purposely didn't say anything to José and after they reached the Escalade José said, "something is not right there, what do you think, Jesus?

"I think you are right, I didn't want to say anything about it to see if you noticed also."

"That guy reeked of cop man. I think he got your finger prints. Did you notice he flipped a paper up on the back of the clipboard when you signed-up for the new appointment?"

"No, I didn't. He did that?"

"Yes, I could see from the side. I've been meaning to tell you this whole whale shit thing freaks me out man!"

So, that settled it.

If El Capitán brings it up Jesus will tell him it was a mistake. But, he will also remind El Capitán that "Fred the Red" is dead now and a score was settled there. El Capitán can be very unforgiving when time is wasted. But the good news is: Jesus tapped into a smuggling ring that allowed him to meet his monthly obligation to El Capitán, plus, he stashed some aside for his own use with no trail showing.

Snake Eyes meets Jesus at the door and escorts him to the veranda where El Capitán is having breakfast and watching his children playing on the playground. Snake Eyes pats him down, as if anyone would be foolish enough to attend a meeting with the boss armed with any weapon.

"Jesus, how nice to see you on such a beautiful day!" Jesus is glad to see that his boss is in a good mood. But, it is a cruelty that he can change as quickly as the sun goes behind a storm cloud.

"Good to see you El Capitán, I trust you are in good health?"

"As you can see Jesus; watching my little tribe of los hijos."

"They are all growing so fast!"

"Yes, and all very healthy as well!"

"I can't remember Jesus, do you have children?"

"Yes, I have many, but I don't know where they are." Both men laugh. Even Snake Eyes smiles a little.

"I looked at the numbers this morning Jesus, you are doing well."

"Thank you, El Capitán. I've been working hard."

"Just one question: how is the whale shit; ambergris heist going?"

Jesus hesitates a moment and then says, "I think I wasted precious time on it and I, and José, think that in the end we were being set up. With your permission, I won't spend any more time on it. I'll dig up some new opportunities."

Just as the sun is shaded by a dark cloud El Capitán's face changes. "Jesus, are you holding out on me?"

"No sir, El Capitán, I am sorry I wasted time, but as you said we are doing well and please consider that Fred McCallister is dead and a score settled."

"That is true, I have his hand in my body parts collection. So are you saying that the ambergris opportunity is being abandoned?"

"Yes sir, it has already been abandoned."

"So, Jesus, then you took the decision upon yourself and are confident that your decision was in the best interest of El Capitan?"

Jesus hates when his boss speaks of himself in the third person, but he quickly says, "that is correct El Capitan. I detected a plot to draw us into taking the ambergris for the purpose of arresting us. José separately assessed the situation in the same light."

"O.K. Jesus then you are learning to make decisions without having to check with me at every step of the way?"

"Yes, El Capitan."

"Good! That is why I chose you to work across the border. And Jesus, I have a surprise for you."

"A surprise El Capitan?"

"Yes, I am going fishing in Cabo the first two weeks of September. Would you like to go with me?"

"Yes, of course, what will I do?" Thinking again of El Capitan's cruelties Jesus sees himself being thrown from the boat to circling sharks.

"We will fish and drink tequila and fuck whores and there is a fishing contest we will try to win."

"Sorry, El Capitan, do you mean I would be fishing and the other things too?"

"Well, you will also be protecting me of course, but you have served me well and I want you to have some fun with me."

"I am honored that you have chosen me El Capitan. I will make sure that José keeps our men in line and there will be no interruption in income while I am away."

"Excellent! You are doing well Jesus - now get out of here and make me, uh, us some money!"

Without thinking Jesus comes to attention and salutes El Capitan, does an "about face" and marches off the veranda and down the hall. As he reaches his car he says out loud, "that was really stupid, some how I thought I was back in the army." In fact, he thinks maybe he heard El Capitan laughing a bit as he marched away.

Jesus looks around at the great wealth of El Capitan and thinks maybe some day he will be this successful and he feels on top of the world. The boss is happy and he is taking me fishing!

34

Ring, Ring

"Gio."

"Hey Alsace, how you doing?"

"Oh, you recognize my accent."

"Just your voice, what's up?"

"Well, your Mexican cartel guy didn't show."

"He smelled a rat!"

"I guess so. Listen Gio, I've been trying to figure this thing out."

"Thing?"

"Yeah, I can be your best man. I'd be honored to."

"Really Alsace, I know it's asking a lot."

"Here's the deal. I used to go to Baja, Cabo San Lucas every year fishing for sail fish. I talked to a friend of mine and he's going this year. It's the week after your wedding. So it works out."

"Cabo?   That's   where   we're   going   for   our honeymoon."

"That's what Margaret told me."

"Margaret?"

"Yes, Sally's friend. I called her the other night and she's been staying with me since then."

135

"Man, you move fast."

"Yeah, I know, she's quite a lady and she seems to be crazy about me too. In fact, I think she's going back to Stockholm with me."

"Are you kidding?"

"No, I guess I have her talked into it. I pulled some strings, she's out getting her new passport right now. And you know that Jamaican chick?"

"You mean Tekeysia?"

"Yeah, Agnes wants to take her home with her. She's got no I.D. - I'm going to have to put handcuffs on her and take her in as a prisoner."

"Jesus, Alsace, is there anything you can't arrange?"

"No big deal. So Gio your best man and brides maid will be international guests. Don't worry, you don't have to go fishing with us.

"Unbelievable, I'll tell Sally as soon as she gets back from shopping. When are you guys flying out of here?"

"The day after tomorrow. Agnes is out with whatever-the-fuck her name is buying clothes. I put my ear on the adjoining door last night and got an ear full. I've never seen Agnes like this. So, anyway, I'll keep in touch."

"Just get my fucking ambergris to Stockholm safely for me, please!"

"Don't worry. It's all packaged and going in via FedEx. Anyway, just wanted to let you know the good news."

"Sally's going to shit a brick when she hears this, I'm surprised Marge didn't call her already. Hey, if I don't talk to you before then, have a safe trip!"

"Will do, and thanks for introducing me to Marge – well, I call her Margaret, but thanks!"

"Good deal, I'll talk to you later, bye bye."

"So long."

It seems like hours before Sally returns forty-five minutes later. As she steps through the door Gio says, "you're not going to believe this!"

"I bet I will, I just got off the phone with Marge, I think she's flipped her lid!

"She told you what's going on?"

"Yes, and it worries me."

"Why?"

"We really don't know this guy. He seems to be a miracle man, it kind of scares me. What if she gets over there and things don't work out?"

"She'll fly back early. I don't think her safety is an issue."

"I suppose. I've never seen her like this, she's totally "head-over-heels" with this guy."

"Did she tell you about Agnes and Tekeysia?"

"Oh brother, what's going on there?"

"Agnes is taking her back to Stockholm with her."

"You've got to be shitting me!"

"No, Alsace is putting handcuffs on her. She has no I.D. of any kind. He's taking her as a prisoner to get through customs."

"See, that's what I mean, this guy scares me."

"You didn't know me and it worked out. All I know is we can tell people that our best man and bride's maid will be flying in from Stockholm."

"I think they will be in France by then, at, get this, "Alsace's family estate."

"Who knew that Ambergris could be such a life changer?"

"I know, I think there could be a movie about all this."

"It would be a good one."

"I'll say! What about our ambergris?"

"It's going FedEx."

"I guess that's one good thing, we'll have a friend to keep us informed."

"Alsace is my friend, albeit a new one."

"I hope you're right."

"It's going to be fine."

Three weeks later, to the day, Agnes wires Gio $873,469.58. The chocolatier came through. As Gio and Sally were nearing getting her mortgages worked out her old house sold. It brought less than she needed to clear the loan, but

138

using their ambergris money, everything was quickly settled to clear the loan by using their new found money and they were left with over a half-million dollars.

35

A September Wedding

Somewhere off he western coast of Africa, near the Canary Islands, not far from the Sahara Desert, a cyclone is being born that will become Hurricane Ormando. Other than some introverted forecaster, surrounded by the best weather prediction equipment money can buy, there is little interest in this weather disturbance.

Actually, a hurricane is the last thing on the mind of Gio's sister, Judith. She has stood her ground, insisting that her daughter, Ariel Lynn Fishman, will accompany her to Gio's wedding. Judith has great hope that getting Lynn away from her so-called friends for a while will help her change direction in her troubled life. In fact Judith has stealthily arranged for them to occupy Gio's unused condo for two weeks. They will arrive a few days before the wedding to "help out" and stay on after Gio and Sally depart for Cabo San Lucas. Judith figures it is worth a try and certainly a lot cheaper than a detox clinic. Lately, Lynn has spent most of her time on her phone with friends, trashing her mother for such a horrendous intrusion on her life. "She's like" – "I'm like" – "and like I don't" - - you get the idea. Lynn finally acquiescing to accompany her mother is quite important as it shows that she still has some control over her daughter. A lesser mother-daughter attachment could have coalesced into the daughter disappearing onto the streets. How much parental hope has been squandered on hopeless children? Judith, not a religious woman, has prayed for a miracle. The prayer goes unheard, but the miracle, through a series of uncontrollable events does occur.

36

Lust at First Glimpse

Lynn and her mother are quite impressed with Gio's good fortune. The beach house is magnificent because it is large and on the beach. Lynn has met one of Sally's nieces and she has joined them in Gio's condo. Madison is three years older than Lynn and just graduated from USC with a bachelor's degree in pre-law. She plans to specialize in environmental law. Immediately, a side of Lynn that Judith has not seen for years begins to emerge.

Things that Lynn has said to Madison:

"Like I just decided to take a year off from college and work a while, but I like plan to go back soon."

"I'm not like sure what I want to major in, so I'm just like going to take general studies classes for a while."

"I like really admire that you knew when you were twelve years old what you like wanted to do with your life, like I still really don't know."

"I like, don't get, like how can someone just study so much and just let their social life go into ruins?"

Things that Madison said to Lynn:

"If you don't know where you are going, any road will take you there."

"It takes the human condition about three weeks to adapt to change. If you change your ways for 21 days you will be that new person you want to be."

"Lynn, that was wonderful at the coffee shop today. I didn't know you played piano, and you have a great voice, you need to do something with that."

"This is the dress for you Lynn, so much better than what you were planning to wear to the wedding. I think you should buy it."

The wedding went as planned. The side curtains on the large white tent were opened to allow the gentle ocean breeze to pass through. Speeches and toasts were made. Spencer and the Bell Tones played beautifully, at least that was true in the ears of the bride and groom. To the ears of Lynn and Madison it was at best "historical" music. Margaritas flowed freely to all that cared to participate and when the band took a half-hour break Madison talked a rather tipsy Ariel Lynn Fishman into playing the piano and singing a pop song. It went very well until….. there is an old rock and roll song that goes something like this: "we both knew what would happen the moment you walked into the room." And that is an accurate description of what happened when Lynn glimpsed Ryan for the first time. She stumbled slightly in her vocalization and quickly recovered and sped up the tempo and was drawn like the proverbial moth to the flame and that flame was Ryan who gazed at her with abandon. It was so obvious to everyone that it would have been embarrassing had Lynn and Ryan been aware of anything else in the world besides themselves. This may be sickening sweet to some but if you have ever been lucky enough to have it happen to you I'm sure your heart is pounding now.

Gio quickly stepped in to free the unacknowledged embarrassment and handled the introduction.

"Ryan, this is my niece, Lynn Fishman."

"Lynn, this is a friend of mine, Ryan Osborne."

"Shall we have a drink?" Ryan asks.

"That sounds like a wonderful idea, did I sound horrible?"

"Like an angel singing in heaven."

"I really doubt that, I probably wouldn't have done it if I hadn't been slightly drunk."

"Well, I probably wouldn't have enjoyed it so much if I hadn't been slightly intoxicated."

Both laugh.

The couple has nearly identical piercing blue eyes. The only eyes like his that Ryan has ever stared into are those of his brother, Bryan. And right now Ryan has no thought of telling Lynn that he has an identical twin except for the missing earlobe and slightly twisted nose. The band is playing again and it's a slow one. Lynn and Ryan are not dancing as new acquaintances but as a young couple very much in love and this magical moment is noticed by some of the guests and particularly by Judith, who is both excited and cautions about what she is witnessing.

"Want to take a walk on the beach?"

"Oh my God, like yes!"

"OK, go say something to your friend and I'll get another drink and slip out the other side. You start up the beach with your friend and I'll join you."

The threesome is walking the beach just out of the high water line.

"I'm freezing," chirps Madison, "I'm going back."

"OK, we'll see you later." Ryan places his sports coat around Lynn's shoulders and holds her as close as walking will allow.

"How do you know my Uncle Gio?"

"Well, we've had some adventures together."

"Like what?"

"Well, without going into any great detail, we are in the same business."

"I thought he was like retired."

"Sort of, but let's talk about you."

Ryan turns to face Lynn and gives her a full body hug and kisses her full on the mouth. Through Lynn's soft dress she can feel his hardness and shifts her weight to her toes. He is touching her in just the right place and she feels lightheaded as Ryan lifts her off her feet.

"I have somewhere we can go."

"You do?"

"Yes, my uncle's condo, it's not far from here."

"What about the key, you left your purse."

"We hid a key."

As they enter the master bedroom Lynn turns on the stereo and as they undress each other in a nearly ritualistic way Joy Winter is singing, "You're My Only One."

"You're my only one," the tops are off.

144

"That's fair to say," only underwear left.

"I'll be true to you, every day," naked and moving to the bed.

"You mean more to me than life its self," passion has overwhelmed them.

Back at the wedding things are winding down. Judith only knows that her daughter has disappeared down the beach. Gio tells Judith that Ryan's a good guy and that she doesn't need to worry, and Sally only hopes that it is true.

37

Ormando

When babies are born, regardless of their "pedigree" we have no way of knowing what they will grow up to be; saint or serial killer? Is that inside them? Are they born with a kernel of greatness or devastation deep inside? Such was the birth of Ormando on August 30th. A dust storm kicked-up in the Sahara Desert and as a big wind pushed these particles out to sea they became a nucleation point for water vapor; causing rain. How a great ocean and a vast desert convene and interplay is not fully understood. There is little reason for any great concern. It is just rain, a lot of it, thousands of miles out to sea.

September 8th is the day after Sally and Gio's wedding and they spend the day saying goodbyes to the relatives that they have lodged and fed and as planned they now have one day to recover before departing for their honeymoon. Alsace and Marge are flying down the day before and are staying at a different hotel. Gio's sister Judith has agreed to stay ten days to keep an eye on the beach house and walk and care for Amber. Judith has seen some very positive things out of Lynn since she met Ryan and he seems like a wonderful young man.

Gio and Sally fly out of San Diego's International Airport on September 10th just as Ormando, disguised as a mild tropical depression, is crossing the Caribbean Sea, dumping rain all along the way. There is much speculation as to where it will go next but probably no one in route to the tip of the Mexican State of Baja California Sur is concerned about it or perhaps even aware of it. Ormando crosses Central America dumping more heavy rain and kicking up the surf and stalls out a bit over land but manages to find his way to the Gulf of Tehuantepac, off the coast of Southern Mexico in the Pacific Ocean.

When Sally and Gio arrive in Los Cabos the short flight has caused no fatigue and they are ready to get settled in their resort and go exploring. Sally has booked a room with an ocean view and as they follow the bellboy carrying their luggage up a very steep hill, it is obvious that their "ocean view" will be far from the ocean. Sally is the first to open the closet doors and she watches wide-eyed as mosquitoes billow out the closet doorway and fill the room. There are hundreds of them.

"How do you say mosquito in Spanish?" Sally asks.

Gio starts smacking mosquitoes as fast as he can and then gathers several together onto a Kleenex and folds it over. "Close your suitcase Sally, we're going to the main desk." They slog down the hill carrying their bags with more difficulty than the trip up and Gio walks into the main lobby on a mission. He has traveled extensively in Mexico and knows that a legitimate complaint is often met with great generosity. There doesn't seem to be anyone on duty that speaks much English so he makes a gesture of opening double doors and makes a sour face and then he opens the Kleenex on the counter and displays the dozen or so mosquitoes and says, "hay muchos!" The clerk holds up one of his index fingers and says, "un momento." He goes in the back and returns with an older gentleman who speaks a little English and he fully understands what has happened. He calls the bellboy, hands him a key, and speaks to him in Spanish and smiles at Gio and Sally and says, "please follow."

As they leave the lobby Gio looks up the hill at all the villas and is already tired of their new accommodations. However, the bellboy strides across a sort of plaza with a water fountain in the middle and enters a three-story building which clearly contains the finest rooms the resort has to offer. The building of perhaps one hundred villas is built directly on top of a cliff, overlooking the ocean. In their villa the floors are made of marble and there is a large living area, a separate bedroom and a large bath with an ocean view window over the large tub.

The bellboy asks, "is ok?"

147

Gio smiles and says, "you bet your sweet ass!" The bellboy smiles a wide grin and Gio tips him again.

"Geez, this is better than home!" Gio says, "it's making me horny, how about you?"

Sally tugs at his belt and says, "come on outa there big boy, mama needs you!"

It is of no surprise to them that their cell phones are useless in Cabo San Lucas and they are able to reach Alsace and Marge and make plans for dinner using their room phone. There is a small balcony just outside their bedroom and the patio door is left open during their love making. There is a strong ocean breeze and the surf can be heard pounding the rocks sixty feet or so below their room.

The couple showers together and nearly go back to bed but give in to their hunger and desire to explore the area, they get dressed. Briefly Gio walks onto the balcony while waiting for Sally to get ready. He looks over the wrought iron railing straight down to the rocks below and it makes him a little dizzy. He is surprised at how rocky the coast is and peaking out a bit he does see a small stretch of sandy beach that must have been pictured in the brochure and wonders how many hundreds of steps there must be to access it from the hotel. Gio looks out to sea and sees not a hint of what is to come.

They take one of the taxis waiting in the plaza area of the hotel and are dropped at the waterfront, where hundreds of boats of every size and description are moored in the huge marina. Although it is mid-afternoon they have not yet had lunch and they quickly find an outdoor restaurant overlooking the magnificent harbor.

They both order Corona beers and today's special, red snapper.

"This is absolutely delicious."

Gio looks at Sally and smiles, "yes it is."

"What are you smiling about?"

"I think you are absolutely delicious, as well."

"I'll bet you tell that to all the girls."

"The girls, yes, but not usually the women. I wonder what Amber thinks about all this?"

"He was a lost dog when you found him, previously owned by that moron Jordan, I'm sure he's adjusting quite well. I'm surprised that Judith decided to stay so long."

"Well, I told her she could have the condo for a couple of weeks a while back. I was talking to her about it yesterday when we were walking on the beach. She has tons of vacation and they told her that if she doesn't take it this year she will lose it and she won't get paid for it either."

"Seems like companies are really cutting back now."

"Also, I think she's glad they are staying a while to give Lynn more time with Ryan. They've only known each other a couple of days and already seem inseparable."

"And who does that remind you of?"

"Yeah, but they are just kids and these kids are not like we were, they don't have a shred of shame. She told me that she's had lots of problems with Lynn in the last year. She's involved with a group of kids that totally think they are entitled and only want to party and she's been hooked on drugs as well."

"You said that in past tense, has she given them up?"

"I think so, for the time being. I talked to Ryan briefly at the wedding. Apparently he is determined to get a graduate degree in marine biology. I just hope he rubs off on her rather than the other way around."

"Oh, I'm sure they are rubbing each other off right now," quips Sally."

"You always make me laugh."

38

"A Chance Meeting"

After they've finished eating and study the harbor a bit, Gio tries to get the waiter's attention. Gio has been in Mexico enough to know that the service is good until time for the check. He thinks it is because the waiters do not want to make patrons feel they are being pushed out or perhaps the theory is that it might lead to another round of drinks; but how did the whole country decide to do this? Gio visits the restroom and finds the waiter on the way back and he and Sally are now walking on the maze of gangways that access the boats in the harbor. Some of the watercraft are easily accessible but there are also many gates with security keypad access to protect the property and privacy of the marina's patrons. As they peer over a security gate in the middle of the harbor they hear a familiar sound. It is Alsace's powerful voice, followed by Marge's silly girl giggle. Such a combination leaves no doubt that their friends are somewhere nearby in the secured area.

"Alsace!" Gio shouts.

"Is that you Marge?" Sally adds.

Soon they see Alsace striding up the gangway with a big smile. He's wearing a Hawaiian style shirt, dungaree pants and has a kerchief tied around his neck, topped off by a Greek fisherman's cap. He opens the security gate, gives Gio a hardy handshake and gives Sally a hug and a kiss on the cheek.

"So glad you're here, how did you find us?"

Gio answers, "I planted a bug in your shoe after the wedding and we tracked you here." Alsace looks a little puzzled. Gio goes on, "gotcha, quite by accident actually."

"Follow me."

Sally and Gio follow Alsace a few boats down and there is Marge sipping a martini, engaged in conversation with a very rotund man with a hat that leaves little doubt that he is the captain of the "Mañana." It is a good name for a Mexican boat. Most gringos think that it means tomorrow but to the Mexican people it means simply, "not today."

"How did you know we were here?" Marge asks.

"We just had lunch and were walking around and heard you guys talking." Sally replies.

Alsace introduces them, "Captain Rodriguez, this is Gio and Sally, our friends that just got married, we were telling you about."

The Captain is leaning against the ships wheel and simply nods in their direction and asks them, "would you like a nice cold beer?"

"That sounds great." Gio replies.

The Captain shouts, "Pablo, dos cervezas para nuestros huéspedes." A teenager emerges from the shadows and retrieves a couple of beers from an ice chest, wipes the droplets of water from the cans with a towel and hands them to Gio and Sally.

"As I was saying," the Captain suggests, "we need to go make some arrangements regarding the bait and tackle."

"Let's go," Alsace gestures with his hand toward the gangway.

The three men mount the gangway.

"Do you mind if we wait here? Will you be long?" Asks Marge.

"No, not long," replies the Captain, "Pablo is at your service, let him know whatever you need."

39

The Women

Sally asks, "can I get one of those?"

Marge gets Pablo's attention and points to her martini, "dos, por favor."

Pablo brings the drinks out and asks, "is OK?" And as Marge nods he retires back into the shadows and is absorbed in reading a comic book.

"I didn't really get a chance to talk to you much at the wedding Marge, bring me up to date, how is the romance going."

"Oh, Sally, I was so glad to get home and now we're here to fish and maybe ruin your honeymoon. I had a blast in Europe and wouldn't trade it for anything, but now I can't wait to get home and settle back into my own life."

"Alsace is a bit too much at times, "larger than life" as they say."

"That's true, but a lot of fun and he knows somebody everywhere he goes to arrange things. I think he may ask me to go back to France with him, but I'm not going. I don't want to ruin this big fishing trip of his but I'm not going."

"I've known you a long time Marge, if you really loved him you would go."

"Guess you do know me pretty well. He's a great guy, but for me he's a little overwhelming. He's like they say about Paris, it's a great place to visit, but you wouldn't want to live there."

"Well, I'm glad you are not going, I sure would hate to loose my best friend. But if you were "head-over-hills" I would certainly wish you well. And don't worry about ruining our honeymoon, Gio and I have talked about it and he may go out fishing with them one day but we're going to do a lot of exploring and shopping here and if you want to join us, you are welcome to."

"I may just do that."

"I mean, it's not like we haven't been together 24/7 before. Getting married at this age has its advantages but it's not the same as being twenty-something."

"You are so right. Seeing you and Gio together these past months is one thing that helped me to realize that Alsace was just an affair, a really great one, but still. Right now I'm living in dread of him asking me to go back to France with him and when I say no I'm not sure how he'll take it."

"OK, so, start back in Copenhagen and tell me all about your trip................

40

The Men

Alsace and Gio walk along with the captain and find themselves in a seedy bar.

Gio asks, "what about the bait and tackle?"

The captain shrugs, "just a way to get away from the women and do some serious drinking. Alsace, tell him about the fishing contest."

"Sure. This is the first contest of the season. Which means the fish may not be as big as later on, but the competition is not so tough right now."

The captain adds, "not so many rich gringos as later on."

"Right," Alsace agrees, "the entry fee is only $6,000. This covers a six man team. Now let's suppose you decide to go out one day with us. We can substitute you for another team member, it just costs an extra $100 to get you in. The entry fee has already been paid for and we've got all the equipment you'll need. All the boats are restricted to a forty mile limit. Anyone reported outside of that forty mile limit that gets caught forfeits the entry fee and can no longer compete in the event. We document catch and release billfish with a video camera, but anything over three hundred pounds can be brought in and weighed for the big prize. We also signed-up for competition on yellow fin and big eye tuna, wahoo and dorado. The daily prize goes to the boat with the heaviest fish in each category."

Gio says, "wow, sounds like Vegas might be involved?"

Captain Rodriguez asks, "who is Vegas?"

"He means Las Vegas, you know, gambling."

"Oh, I see. Yeah, I can see that, we are gambling our money." Acknowledges the Captain.

"You are on your honeymoon, so you let me know if or when you want to go fishing Gio, no pressure." Alsace assures Gio.

"Well, it would be nice to get out on the water while we are here. I'm thinking of buying a sailboat. I see some of the boats here are for sale. Captain, if I find one can you check it out for me?" Gio asks.

"Sailboats are not my forte as you can see, but I can tell you if the boat itself is sound and I have a compadre who knows sailing, we can bring him along as well. You can sail it all the way to San Diego?"

"I wouldn't risk it. I would probably have to hire someone and learn along the way."

Some young tourist women are walking by and the breeze lifts up one's dress, exposing her buttocks, unclothed except for the T-strap of thong panties.

"Look at the ass on that bitch!" Alsace exclaims.

"Hmmm…. I think I'm in love." The captain puts in.

"Very nice," Gio agrees, "look at her, she knows she's showing it off."

"Gio, you are a married man. Not suppose to notice such things." Alsace kiddingly scolds Gio.

"True, and just married, but not dead." The men all laugh.

"What about you Alsace, aren't you a one-woman man now?" Gio asks.

"Best blow-jobs I've ever had and a really nice lady. I think she thinks I'm going to ask her to go back to France with me. But things are still very good, a perfect time to end a love affair. What do you think Gio? Will things get ugly when I tell her I'm going back home alone?"

"Oh, I couldn't say, I haven't known her that long. I'll see what Sally says. They have been close friends for a long time. Sally was a little shocked when Marge left the country with you. I'll see what I can find out."

"Great, I have an insider, a spy." Alsace quips.

"If Sally asks, should I tell her you plan to go home alone?"

"Not just yet, I'd like to fly back to San Diego and spend a little time there. I don't want her to be hostile."

"OK, I'll see what I can find out, but if Sally tells me not to repeat what she says, I'll honor her request."

"Some fucking spy, huh captain?"

"Once aboard, we'll keelhaul him, then he'll talk!" The men all laugh.

"I keep thinking there is something I want to ask you, Alsace.......oh, yeah, what did your brother say when he saw the pistol?"

"Oh, it was very delicious. First I asked to see our father's gun. I examined it closely and told him, too bad it isn't in better condition. And then perfect: he tells me I will not find another in any better shape." Alsace is smiling widely. Then I showed him my new acquisition. He nearly turned green and asked if it was a replica. Thank you so much Gio, it was great – I really got him – so well, I almost felt a little sorry for him. But only for a minute."

Alsace looks at the Captain and realizes he has no clue what they are talking about. "Gio had a pistol his father brought back from the war, like my father did, so I traded him a Glock and some cash so I could shut my brother up. In my country the oldest son gets the family treasure. So now I don't have to watch him gloat."

A few more shots of tequila and the men return to the boat.

"How's the bait and tackle?" Marge asks.

"What?" Asks Alsace.

"Didn't you go to check on it?"

"Oh, yes, everything is fine."

Drunken people have no ability to spot another drunken one, although they are quite good at noticing a sober one. All on board, except Pablo, are well inebriated. And what better way to be when on a honeymoon or on the eve of a fishing contest? A large fishing vessel is coming down the marina's main channel and as it turns into Captain Rodriguez's lane it is plain to see that it is not a chartered boat, but a very expensive private boat rigged for billfish and also luxury. There are several young women sunning themselves on the top deck. As the boat passes Captain Rodriguez tips his hat.

Alsace walks a little toward the passing boat and stares. "I never forget a face, I know that guy, but I can't think from where."

Gio is having the same thought and as the name "El Capitan" on the back of the boat comes into view he realizes who it is and says, "that's the guy that was going to steal our ambergris, remember? He is the guy that knocked me out and was on the phone with his boss that he called El Capitan. That's the fucking guy that tortured Ryan trying to get information. His name is Jesus."

41

"Lust Finds Love"

There are lots of young people from all walks of life that go astray and find themselves swept away by crime, drugs, lack of respect, and deep feelings of entitlement. For many, there is a day when something happens that fills their minds with feelings of regret and an urge tugs at them to do better. Lots of these young people have never been taught the values of the mainstream of society nor had a mentor to pattern themselves after. When they decide to do the right thing and plan a future, without a sincere helper to assist and guide them, they often are clueless and quickly fall back into old habits. This is not the case for Ryan and Lynn. They've both had many role models in their life and they also have backing from those same role models who will offer financial and intellectual support once they decide to be "somebody."

Ryan is on fire with regret of the time he has wasted in his life. He is driven to seize his goal of participating in the fight to save the World's oceans and all the flora and fauna that once thrived there. It is a goal that he cannot achieve with anything less than a master's degree in marine biology. He also realizes that he will have to stand out scholastically in order to be chosen to work on summer projects in that field.

Led by their lust and genuine affection for each other, Lynn has seized the opportunity for a new life. All the crazy sex wrapped in bodies that struggle to be one has led to many long hours of discovery in laying their souls bare through the most candid conversation they have ever had. Here is my soul and you may crush it if you want, but I trust that you will not nor will I yours. Ryan's enthusiasm has harkened Lynn back to when she was a child again, interested in turning rocks over to see what was there, collecting all manner of shells on the beach and a desire to be with nature that she has long since abandoned.

Lynn is lying on her back across the bed with her buttocks at the edge with legs spread wide. Ryan is on his knees on the floor and has his mouth locked by suction around Lynn's clitoris and vulva. Inside his mouth his tongue is very pointed and going in a circular pattern around Lynn's clitoris and she is moaning deeply. Ryan knows that she will soon orgasm and he also knows he has her close to the point when Lynn's nerve endings will max out and she will push him away, overwhelmed by too much stimulation. Ryan now begins lightly touching her clitoris in an up and down motion and Lynn shouts "ah fuck, fuck!" Ryan reaches up and pinches her left nipple between his thumb and index finger and Lynn shouts, "yes, yes, you fucker, yes." Ryan climbs onto her and kisses her deeply, "taste your cunt you little cocksucker. You like it don't you, if you could reach it you would spend all day sucking yourself."

"Not true, I have you."

"If I fuck you, can you come again?"

"Yes, fuck me hard, I want you to come once more."

Ryan enters her as hard as a rock and her vagina is so tight and yet so wet that he plunges to the hilt and hammers her hard and soon they orgasm together. It is the first time they have attained orgasm at exactly the same time and no matter what anyone says it is the very best sexual experience you will ever have and couples that can achieve that usually stay together and are the happiest of all people in a relationship.

42

Hmmm…. That Was Good!

It is the afternoon of Gio and Sally's second day of their honeymoon. Gio has discovered that the sofa in the living room makes into a bed and he has commandeered the mattress and placed it right next to the open patio doors and the breeze feels wonderful on their skin and wicks away the perspiration of their sexual exploits.

Now sated, Sally lies on Gio's shoulder and he is holding her tightly and kissing her eyes and nose and licks her lips.

"So, you are OK with Marge going with us while Alsace is out fishing?"

"Sure, I told you it is fine, she's fun to be around. I cracked-up today when I heard her bargaining for that crazy hat she bought. That's a side of her I've never seen. I would have just given the guy what he asked or maybe a little less. We were at least a half-block away when the guy came charging down the sidewalk and gave her the hat for what she offered."

"Yeah, that surprised me also. She would shit-a-brick if someone made a low offer on one of her paintings."

"Really. Well I suppose that hat wasn't a work of art. I'm finding out all sorts of things about Marge."

"Like what?"

"Oh, I can't divulge things that were told me in confidence."

"Did Alsace say something? He did didn't he."

"Well, I really can't say."

161

Sally grabs Gio by his left earlobe and pulls on it. "Stop teasing me you little prick or I'll pull your ears off."

"That's funny, just moments ago you were telling me how big it was." Gio is laughing loudly, which only makes Sally more determined. She grabs his testicles and says, "spill it or lose these." And now she is laughing as well.

"Ok, Ok, Ok, leave those guys alone. Alsace said that she gives the best blow jobs he's ever had."

"That's not big news, I could have told you that."

"She told you about sucking Alsace?"

"No, but my departed husband knew a couple of guys that dated her and they said the same thing."

"And why didn't you tell me?"

"You think I'm crazy? Why would I put something like that in your head? Just like I haven't told Marge what a great fuck you are. She doesn't need to know that."

"Well, I'm not about to tell Alsace or anyone what a great cocksucker you are!"

"Better than Marge?"

"You'll not catch me on that one. You're my favorite at everything, in and out of bed."

"Well, thank you, and I feel the same about you."

Less playful now, Gio asks, "did she say anything about going back to France with him?"

"Yes, she did, but I'm not suppose to tell."

"Touché, come on now, spill it."

"She didn't actually tell me not to say anything. She really enjoyed their sojourn to Europe and she said she had a blast, but, she's ready to get back to painting and running her gallery. But she doesn't want to cause a blow-up until we get back home. Did Alsace say anything about that?"

"Yes, he did, and don't grab my nuts, I'll tell you. He essentially said the same thing. He had a great time, he thinks she's a great lady, and - gives great blow jobs, but he is fearful of the same thing: of it ending badly when he tells her he is going back alone."

"Should we tell them?"

"I think we can, but I'm not sure how."

"I'll just tell Marge not to worry, that Alsace is on the same page and you can do the same with him. What's wrong with that?"

"I guess that's fine, but I wonder if they will both be let down that the other isn't going to be heartbroken."

"I hadn't thought of that, but I think Marge will be greatly relieved."

"Yeah, I'm sure Alsace will be too. So, fire at will and I'll do the same."

"Are you going fishing tomorrow?"

"Are you absolutely sure it is Ok?"

"Of course, I want you to. I know you want to get out on the water. Marge and I will shop 'til we drop."

"I guess you've noticed I've been checking out the sailboats in the harbor."

"I know you want one. After all the work you did to get the ambergris and what it put you through, you deserve it. But I think you need to keep one thing in mind."

"What's that?"

"We made a lot of money in a short period of time, the tax man is going to stick it to us. I've gone through this with Howard too many times. You have a great year and then you get gouged by the IRS. So just please keep that in mind."

"I had Agnes put that money in an account at Royal Bank, in the Bahamas. The wire we received to close on the beach house was wired from Royal Bank. We will indeed have to pay taxes, but my accountant researched it and he thinks we're on solid ground for a substantial reduction of the tax. I don't exactly understand it but he can explain it to you, if you like."

"Oh brother, here we go, ambergris was wonderful, but it sure has stuck us on uncomfortable ground."

"Patience is a Virtue"

As Ormando sits off the Western coast of Mexico, West of Oaxaca and hundreds of miles out to sea he has sensed that any movement further West feels less warm and diminishes his strength. He is taking his time and the eighty-five degree ocean is making him large and strong and the sensation is a blessing from Mother Nature and Ormando wants to please Her in the constant struggle She is having with an Earth overpopulated with Homo sapiens. He is possessed by wind speeds of sixty miles an hour and gusting to seventy-five miles an hour.

It is the general opinion of the meteorologists that Ormando bears watching but there is a good chance he will move further Northwest and loose strength and fizzle as colder waters deny Ormando the fuel he needs to make an aggressive land fall. One computer model predicts possible landfall at the tip of Baja California Sur. However, that is just one of many path predictions that weather prognosticators may choose. Most dangerous entities by their very nature are unpredictable and Ormando is no exception. And for now, at least, he is happy to feel strong and growing stronger and will wait until his Mother calls upon him.

"Something Fishy"

Gio is having breakfast with Alsace, the captain and the four other team members. Alsace introduces the men and they all shake hands. Gio arrived excited about going to sea and had a feeling of being "on a Lark." However, it has become apparent that this fishing contest is serious business. There are stories from two years ago when two fishing crews got into a fight back on the docks over who arrived first in a hot fishing spot. Gio had hoped for a jovial breakfast as he met Alsace's European friends, but man-by-man they are instructing him on the "dos" and "don'ts" of the fishing competition. Gio is thinking that he doesn't need this rigid regimen while on his honeymoon. But he also knows it is too late to back out and vows to rely upon the rest of the team to get him through the day.

Gio takes the camera from around his neck and places it under his chair. Gio had grown tired of the challenge of using the expensive camera he "inherited" from Fred and recently purchased a "point and shoot" camera described as bridging the gap between the digital single lens reflex cameras like Fred's and something easier to use and it has a 50X telephoto lens, which would cost many thousands of dollars to add to Fred's camera.

Gio is letting most of the comments from the experienced fisherman filter through his brain without any effort to comprehend the advice. He has already decided not to make a move on the boat without assistance and knows he will never do this again.

As the men leave the restaurant Gio rushes back as he has forgotten his camera. The captain asks Alsace, "do you think any of that information was soaked up by your friend."

"I'm not so sure, I thought he would be excited about it, but it's only for today, he has already told me just one day. Cut him some slack Cap, he's on his fucking honeymoon."

The men go aboard and do the routine chores to make the boat ready for the 7:30 am start. As they are about ready to enter the lane leading to the main exit from the harbor the El Capitan boat passes by.

"So apparently that fucker is in the competition." Alsace states.

"He's flying all the right flags." The captain observes.

"What do you think Gio?" Alsace ponders.

"I think we should just pretend that we don't know who they are and what they are capable of."

"You're probably right. Let's just enjoy this beautiful day."

The captain says, "tequila for everyone Pablo, " as they head out to sea.

There is a forty mile limit and many of the contestants think that all the best fish are somewhere near that marker and proceed to that goal in all directions from the harbor.

As the harbor disappears from the horizon Gio's malaise lifts instantly as the beauty of the ocean and the clear blue sky work their magic. Soon the captain slows the Mañana to trolling speed, believing that it is possible to find a "hot spot" for fishing on the way to the forty mile limit, he instructs Pablo in Spanish to troll two baits on each side of the boat and a downrigger in the middle. All the men are excited that they will soon be fishing as the captain passes a large bottle of tequila around. Each man rubs the palm of his hand on the bottle neck before drinking, as if the tequila isn't strong enough to kill any germ in its path. Pablo baits the hooks with large dead fish baits and soon the men watch the baits skipping across the water, where they look very much alive. Gio figures out that there is a pecking order to be followed as fish are hooked and released as too small or the wrong species and he is last on the list, which is only fair for a "day tripper." As Gio has this thought, the Beatles song starts playing in his head and will loop there for the rest of the day.

Gio is slightly drunk and high from being on the water as Alsace says, "you're up next."

Just minutes after Gio is "up" something grabs the bait and Alsace yells over the engine noise, "take him Gio, take him."

Gio steps up and grabs the rod and reel and quickly his fishing skills come to him as he takes up the slack in the line and then sets the drag. All the men can tell it is a large fish as the line is peeling off the reel. All the men are prepared to step forward and offer Gio advice but no one makes a move as it is obvious he does know fishing with a rod and reel. The captain looks at Alsace and puckers his lips slightly and moves his head up and down as if to say, "not bad."

Every time Gio gains a length of line the fish goes deep and the reel is singing once again and droplets of water are being propelled onto Gio's shirt and face.

"It's a big fucking tuna, yellow fin." Shouts the captain as he watches the fish jumping out of the water desperately trying to throw the hook . "He'll start to tire soon and then just bring him in, he's a big one, I'm sure."

Gio's arms and back are aching from the forty-five minute battle but he barely notices it as he is about to land the biggest fish he has ever caught in his life. As he pulls the fish to the stern of the boat Pablo uses a gaff hook and sinks it in deep to bare the weight of the great fish and pulls it aboard.

"Motherfucker," Alsace exclaims, "what a fish!"

All the men are congratulating Gio, shaking his hand and slapping him on the back.

"I'm sure this will win the tuna category for largest fish today and maybe for the week is possible too. Plus we can sell the loin to a local restaurant for a good price. Ice him down Pablo, good job Gio, you are one hell of a fisherman." The captain hands Gio the half empty tequila bottle and Gio takes a good tug and hands it to Alsace who is relieved that not only did his friend not embarrass him, he is wondering if he can talk one of the other men into giving up a day so Gio can fish again. That's the thing about fisherman; once the fish is hooked and landed all the credit goes to the man with the rod in his hands. The pure luck of the random catch is forgotten and the man with the rod, who persevered over nature is a great fisherman. If the fish throws the hook it will cast doubt on that man and all will think how lucky he was to have hooked that fish and how his lack of skill let it get away.

It is mid-afternoon and each time a man lands a fish comments are made, "nice fish, but nothing compared to Gio's." They have brought several black marlin to the boat and made a time and dated video of the catch with there official boat number included and released them. This will count in the "catch and release" portion of the contest. A marlin has to be three hundred pounds or more to be brought to the dock for weigh-in and there are stiff penalties for underweight fish.

It seldom happens, but Gio's age is starting to show and the tequila hasn't helped. He eats a sandwich and a few potato chips and drinks two bottles of water. As he starts to feel a little better a black marlin is spotted following one of the dead baits.

Captain Rodriguez shouts, "he's a big one, Pablo, give him a live fish."

Pablo carefully eases a live bait back to the marlin and hands the rod to Gio. Gio knows there is no way he can bring this fish in, he is too spent. He hands the rod to Alsace and says, "Take him, Alsace, I'm wore out."

"Thanks." Alsace sits down in the fighting chair and secures the reel and waits to see if the big black will take the live fish. Gio goes below to use the head and as he is returning he sees his camera wedged between two seat cushions. Then it hits him, why in the hell didn't he have someone video his catch? Or, did the captain get him on the boats video that is used to track black marlin catches? He has no idea, but he picks up his camera and will record Alsace's big fish if he can hook him.

Out on deck he sees that the marlin has taken the bait and from what he has heard Alsace may be in for a grueling fight. Gio zooms the camera lens all the way out to see if he can see the bill of the giant fish, but he has gone deep for the time being. He videos the curved rod and the surf that's coming in over the stern of the boat. Alsace is sopping wet from the waist down. Gio looks to the horizon and sees another boat, a speck on the horizon. He zooms the lens in on the boat and loses it because of the movement of the Mañana. He steadies the camera against a bulkhead and pulls the lens in and locates the boat again and puts the viewfinder on his eye and zooms in. This time he can clearly see the boat, he can even read the boats name. It's the El Capitan. Another boat approaches the El Capitan and lines are hauled in and the two boats are as near as they dare in the restless waves. The deck hands of the other boat throw another rope onto the stern of the El Capitan. El Capitan's crew drag a huge marlin across the gunwales of the two boats. El Capitan himself takes something into his hand and then tosses it in the other boat. A man in the other boat picks it up and opens some sort of container and takes something out. Gio can't actually see the money, but he can tell the man is counting it. The man waves to El Capitan and the boat dashes off over the horizon.

Although excited about the video he has just captured Gio doesn't say anything and continues to video Alsace's battle with the big sail fish. After a while the excitement of hooking a giant fish wears off and it is so much like work except that the fisherman has paid big money to do this. Alsace says, "he's coming up!" Gio has his camera in-hand and is able to get a shot of the black marlin breaking the surface and he also fires off several still pictures that the camera is capable of while in video mode. The black marlin goes deep again and the line spills out as the reel's gears sing along.

The big fish would easily be pulling Alsace out of the fighting chair if he wasn't strapped in. Alsace gains back some line and again there is a surge. And suddenly nothing.

"You lost him." The captain shouts.

"I feel something." Alsace replies. "He's still fighting, I can feel it."

"Your fish has been eaten by sharks, you may still have his head."

Alsace reels the dead weight in and it appears at the surface. Pablo reaches over the stern and grabs the long bill and lifts the partial fish head aboard. One eye is missing and the rest of the head looks crushed.

"The bill will make a nice trophy." Explains the captain. "Too bad Alsace, we might have won the contest with that fish. Pablo, get the camera, I think this will at least count in the catch and release. Alsace, you would have been fighting him for at least two more hours. We might as well leave these waters, the sharks are still hungry. We will not feed them our prize fish."

A great sense of loss overcomes the fisherman. There is still a bottle being passed around, but with little enthusiasm. Gio is so glad he handed the rod and reel off to Alsace; first of all to give his friend a chance to land a big fish and now because his catch of the tuna isn't sallied by this loss.

171

Gio turns to Alsace, "you and the captain need to see some video I took of our "friend" Jesus and his El Capitan." The men all look puzzled.

"Here take a look at this." The men gather round, but with the bright clear blue sky it is hard to see on the small camera screen.

"Let's go below, just us three." The captain motions for Alsace and Gio to follow him below. "Give me the memory card."

Gio removes the electronic storage card from the camera and gives it to the captain. He boots-up a laptop computer and inserts the card into the slot and the video starts to play. The men all watch wide-eyed.

"Son-of-a-bitch! We've got that fucker." Alsace exclaims. "But, unless they stole it from a huge aquarium, there was no guaranty they could produce a fish like that. How did they do that?"

"They probably got it from a drag-net boat. There are huge boats from Japan, Sweden, from all over that put out nets that catch everything. I can't imagine a marlin would get caught though, they are so fast."

Alsace adds, "you know what, it doesn't matter how he got the fish, we have proof he didn't catch it and he will be disqualified and barred from ever competing again."

"It's worse than that my friend," the captain informs, "he will be claiming prize money, it is against the law. They will want to make an example of him so others are not tempted to do the same. Let's head back to the harbor, we need to get this to the contest promoters and get law enforcement involved."

Gio and Alsace look at each other and burst out laughing. Alsace says, "we've got that fucker."

45

"Girl Stuff"

On Gio's big fishing day Sally and Marge have met for a late breakfast and spent the next few hours shopping and exploring. They take a taxi back to Sally's hotel soon after lunch. The hotel is typical of construction throughout most of Mexico. It has been built very close to the edge of the rocky cliff on which it rests. The three-story building's foundation consists of concrete blocks being cut to fit the cliff's rocky contour instead of concrete being poured deep into bedrock. Throughout the building construction methods were used that were deemed unsafe in the United States many decades ago. Concrete floors held up by large concrete columns that can be seen in some of the rooms. If an earthquake of serious magnitude occurred the building would sway back and forth breaking the upper floors from their supporting columns causing the concrete floors to yield to gravity and fall, pancaking onto the first floor, crushing all in between.

Sally and Marge are sitting in the large bathtub overlooking the ocean having a good soak. Marge takes another drink of the wine they are enjoying and turns around facing away from Sally and scoots back to her. Sally has a sip of wine and puts her arms around Marge, holding her tightly and kisses her on the neck.

"It feels great to be able to just sit here holding you without the need for sex." Sally observes.

"Funny you should say that, I was just about to turn around and give you my tongue."

"Don't ruin it Marge, I've told you I'm being faithful to Gio."

"I know, really I'm not even horny, Alsace makes sure of that. It's just that it's different with you and I miss it.

"Me too, but I'm sure it would interfere with my relationship with Gio. I won't take a chance on that."

"Really Sally, I'll bet if he caught us in the tub he'd want to watch and probably participate."

"But then it would be a three-way relationship, and I don't want that."

"Do you mind if I masturbate"

"If you must, but I won't do more than hold you."

The movement of Marge's hand makes little wave splashes on the sides of the tub and she says, "let me know if you change your mind."

Sally stares out to sea and knows this thing with Marge would never have happened if she hadn't been so lonely after Howard died. She feels guilt for just doing this and makes a vow to never let it happen again. She knows the trick will be to keep Marge's friendship. That's why she was glad to see Marge go off to Europe with Alsace. She missed her, but mostly in a platonic way. Still, there is something very comforting about holding another woman.

Marge stops masturbating and stands up. "It's not much fun by yourself." She steps out of the tub and grabs a towel. "I don't want to lose my best friend, can we go back to the way we were before Howard passed away?"

"That's what I've been hoping for, and I hope you can find someone to be happy with. I never thought I would and then one day there he was on the beach."

"You were lucky Sally, very lucky."

"I know and I'm ever so grateful."

They get dressed and continue drinking a little wine out on the deck. Somewhere in the background a television is broadcasting the weather, telling of the possibility that hurricane Ormando will make landfall in the vicinity of Los Cabos. The warning is in Spanish and goes unheeded by English speaking tourists and is ignored by the locals, who have the attitude that, "they always say that and then it never amounts to much except a lot of rain." Ormando is still hundreds of miles out to sea. He is building his strength and is now over three hundred miles wide. Soon his time will come.

46

"Retribution"

The old cliché; "throw enough money at the problem and the problem will go away," couldn't be more true than in Mexico. This is true from top to bottom. Police officers have traditionally been underpaid and the average citizen expects to bribe a little along the way. There is even a word for it; mordida, literally "the bite." Even with his vast experience with Interpol Alsace is unaware of how prevalent it is in Mexico and in Gio's many vacations in Mexico he has not needed to use "mordida." El Capitan could not avoid being banned from future competition in the fishing contest, although he believes intimidation will get him back in by the next year. However, he never saw the inside of a prison cell and is now back in his vacation villa. He has bribed an official of the fishing contest to get the name of the person that took the video that has now cost him a lot of money.

He has summonsed Jesus from his room in another part of the resort to come to him.

"I hope you are feeling better by now El Capitan."

"I never feel better when I am throwing money away."

"Of course."

"Jesus, I have a job for you."

"I'm not sure I can get back to Tijuana, I think they are closing the airport because of the hurricane threat."

"The job is here. I have the name of the man that took the video of us and I want him dead. His name is Giovanni Valducci."

"Gio, fuck, he never goes away."

"You know this man?"

Jesus quickly realizes his mistake, but it is too late.

"Jesus, do you know this man?"

"Yes El Capitan, he is the man who had the Ambergris. The one who we suspected was setting us up if we had tried to steal it. I thought I saw him on another boat when we were leaving the harbor, but I figured I was mistaken."

"Jesus, you were mistaken when you didn't kill him when you had the chance."

"Yes, El Capitan, but if you recall, you told me we didn't want to bother with something we knew nothing about, and then I got the idea for stealing all the ambergris. I was so glad we got Fred that day that it didn't seem......"

"Enough! Jesus you find this man and kill him and bring me his balls, they will look good sitting in a jar next to Fred's hand. I've talked it over with the man that takes care of my boat. He thinks this hurricane won't amount to much, but could still do major damage to my boat if I leave it in the harbor. So we are leaving at 5 p.m. today, to take her up into the Sea of Cortez and ride it out. On second thought, you don't need to bring me his nuts, just bring the body by the harbor before we leave, we'll feed him to the sharks.

As Jesus is walking back to his room he is thinking, so this is a vacation? Tip-toeing around El Capitan, worried that I might displease him and be fed to the sharks. And now I have to kill this old guy, it is unbelievable that he would be here and also more unbelievable that he made the video. How am I going to get that fucking body to the marina? I should have killed that fucker when I had the chance. How many times has El Capitan told me; "it's just business, you can't take it personal."

Jesus has been calling hotels, off-and-on, for four hours, with frequent breaks for a shot of tequila. There is no way he is going to be able to "do the deed" and get to the marina by five o'clock. As he goes to look out the window to see how much the weather has changed he catches a glimpse of the fishing contest packet he collected for El Capitan when they arrived. It gives him an idea. He looks through the packet and there is a list of the participants and the names of the hotels where they are staying. He finds Gio's name and is pretty sure he has already called them. He quickly checks and yes he did call them. He is thinking, those rotten motherfuckers, why don't they just do their fucking job, so I can do mine. He looks at his watch. It is 4 o'clock. There is no hurry. He is sure El Capitan has already left for the marina. He will deal with Gio tomorrow. Jesus finishes the bottle of tequila and falls onto the bed and is instantly sound asleep.

47

"Come to Momma"

As Ormando bears down on Los Cabos he has become a category 4 hurricane, with wind speeds surging to 150 mph and surf reaching as high as eighteen feet. Baja California Sur has not been visited by a hurricane of this magnitude since prehistory. Even cautious tourists have begun repeating to each other what the locals have told them: "they always exaggerate the power of these things. Don't worry, just stay by your bottle of tequila and everything will be fine."

Something crashes against the patio doors of Jesus' room and it wakes him. It is pitch black outside and he goes to the bathroom and washes his face and looks at his watch, it is 10 o'clock. He sits down for a moment and tries to decide what to do. El Capitan had said "no guns" when they left for Cabo "because the locals there will not know who we are." Jesus digs in his suitcase and finds his "frog sticker" stiletto and puts it in his pocket. He has the idea that if he goes to Gio now he may be able to make it appear that he was killed in the hurricane.

Jesus goes to the hotel's lobby and looks out front to see if there are any taxis there. Seeing none, he looks at his notes and asks the desk clerk how far Gio's hotel is from here. "You are in luck, señor, it is the next hotel to the east of us. It must be a fine woman waiting for you, to go out on such a night as this." Jesus smiles a silly grin and nods his head. He goes back to his room and finds the all-weather jacket he had planned to take to the boat in case of bad weather. He unzips the collar and pulls the matted-up hood from its cocoon and smoothes it out and as he puts the jacket on, he pulls the hood over his head, zips the jacket and buttons the top button and draws the string of the hood tight and ties it around his chin. I'm getting too old for this shit, he is thinking, I should have gone to college, fuck, I should have finished secundaria. He

179

takes a deep breath and opens the patio doors and heads off into the night.

48

"Jesus Saves"

As the day had gone by Gio became increasingly concerned about the impending weather. In late afternoon he had called the airport to see if they could get a flight out and was told the airport was closed, no flights in or out since noon. The hotel employees keep reassuring him that it will only be some wind and rain, not to worry. Gio and Sally have dinner in the hotel restaurant and nervously go back to their room. That wonderful room they scored right on the edge of the cliff. The weather station on their cable TV is still warning about the severity of this hurricane, although they are still uncertain if or where it will make landfall.

"If this gets really bad, here is what we are going to do."

"I'm all ears."

"We are going to run out of here and head up the hill, as far as we can go from the ocean. If I have to I'll kick the door open on one of those rooms where we were supposed to be, before we were so lucky to get this room on top of this fucking cliff."

"But everyone is still saying we can ride it out, I sure hope they are right."

"Me too!"

At around eleven o'clock Gio asks Sally, "do you think we should try to get some sleep?"

"I know I won't sleep. I keep thinking of how they always tell you to get in the bathtub in such weather, and just look at our bathtub, it's a death chamber with that huge window over it."

"Yeah, I'm quite sure I won't sleep. Let's just try to find a good movie on TV and run up our bill by drinking booze out of the little fridge here in the room." Just as Gio finishes his suggestion the power goes out.

"I noticed there are lots of candles sitting around here." Sally recalls.

"Maybe that should have told us something."

Sally feels her way to the coffee table in front of the sofa and finds a round container with a candle in it and finds a book of matches under it and lights it. She then walks around lighting all the candles she can find and says, "guess it could be romantic, if Ormando wasn't trying to join us."

Jesus can see the lights to the east and decides to walk across open land rather than use the road. It doesn't look that far, but after walking for fifteen minutes it doesn't look much closer. The wind and rain are pelting him and after ten more minutes he seeks shelter behind some kind of utility box. He then continues and now there are no lights to guide him. He trudges on figuring that he'll either find the road or fall in the ocean before he gets too far off the track.

He finally reaches the hotel grounds and can see a light shining from the hotel office. He is walking toward the light and a sudden whip of the wind causes him to stumble and fall to the ground. "Fuck! What a vacation."

Jesus finally arrives at the office door and tries to open it but the wind wrenches it from his hand and slams into the door frame each time he tries. The clerk comes to his aid and they hold the door long enough for Jesus to get inside.

"I have a fishing buddy that is staying here. Can you please tell me what room he is in?"

"His name please."

"Yes, his name is Giovanni Valducci."

"I don't think he is here fishing, he is on his honeymoon."

Jesus has to think that one over. "Yes, but he is also fishing some of the time. Here, look at the list of fishermen, here is his name right here."

"I should call him first. Sometimes the power goes out and the phones still work. Let me try." The clerk picks up the phone and pushes several buttons. "It doesn't seem to be working."

"Please, this is important, I have some information to give him about his winnings in the fishing contest. Would I walk here in this weather if it wasn't very important?"

"He is in room 23, you'll have to go back out that door and across the plaza and beyond the fountain."

"Good man, thank you, can you help me with the door?"

The two men force the door open and Jesus is on his way. He is thinking, what is this bullshit about a honeymoon? I thought he and the old lady were old married folks. Great, now I have two people to deal with. He touches his jacket pocket and reaches in and moves his stiletto in position so that he can easily pull it out.

Jesus finds 23 and knocks at the door. At first gently and then harder. Inside Gio asks Sally, "who in the hell could that be?"

Gio walks to the door and looks through the viewer but can't make out who it is. He yells into the door, "what do you want?"

"This is the hotel manager, we want to move you to a safer room."

Gio asks, "what did he say?"

"It's the manager, he wants to get us to a safer place."

"Oh, fantastic."

Gio pulls the door open and Jesus pops in. Gio doesn't recognize him in the rain gear and asks him where they will be going. Jesus takes advantage of the situation and turns toward the back of their villa. He pulls the stiletto out and turns and grabs Sally around the neck and pulls her to him and puts the stiletto to her neck.

"It was a big mistake to take that video of El Capitan and now you have to pay."

Gio freezes and feels totally helpless. "She has nothing to do with this, please let her go, you can kill me, but you have to let her go!"

"I think I am the one giving orders, sit down in that chair by the table and keep your hands where I can see them." The whole building seems to shutter as the wind increases dramatically.

Gio does as he is told. Jesus pulls Sally along with him and goes to the curtains that cover the patio doors, he pulls on the cord to open the drapes and having made it much longer grabs it with the hand around Sally and cuts it with his stiletto.

Gio knows he is planning to tie them up and he also knows that once that happens they are done and he vows to not let that happen; if I die, I die fighting.

Jesus forces Sally into a chair and starts tying her to the arms. Gio makes his move and charges across the room. Jesus runs toward him with the stiletto in hand. As the two men come together the 120 mph wind blows the bathroom window frame out and it flies through the air and hits the bathroom door frame and the glass shatters into hundreds of pieces. A long shard of glass goes end over end and plunges into Jesus' neck and severs his spinal cord. He falls to the floor, the entire back of his body riddled with shards of glass. His body has completely shielded Gio.

Gio runs to Sally, who has already freed herself from the poorly tied knot and Gio grabs her hand, she grabs her purse, and they go flying out the door and up the hill. Gio doesn't stop until he is at the next to last block of villas and then pulls Sally down the walkway toward the middle. Now they are shielded from the brunt of the wind and Gio knocks on one of the villa doors and there is no answer. He stands back to kick it open as Sally reaches down, turns the knob and opens the door.

Safe inside, Gio finds and lights a couple of candles and with Sally's aid pulls the mattress off the bed and pushes it against the patio doors. Then they take the inner springs off and block the rest of the windows. Then they move furniture against the bedding and sit down on the sofa to catch their breath. They look at each other and then embrace.

"That was a close one," Sally says.

"We're not out of the woods yet, missy, but if I have to choose between Jesus and the hurricane, I'll take the hurricane. That was a fucking miracle."

"Yes it was, but my hero made it all happen, if you hadn't rushed him, who knows what would have happened?"

The storm is raging now and they sit in silence, holding hands and relishing that they are still alive and thinking, but not saying, what a shame it will be if they now die in the hurricane.

Ormando has made a direct hit on Cabo, coming ashore in true category 4 fashion. The surf has reached twenty-two feet on the cliff holding up the block of three-story villas where Jesus lays paralyzed from the neck down and bleeding to death.

Two hours go by and Gio and Sally haven't moved, each with their own thoughts, too worrisome to share. Suddenly the whole building shakes and they think it will disintegrate with them blown out into the storm. The shaking passes and the building is still intact except that some of the windows have blown out against the bedding and Gio reinforces them with more furniture. He brings a bottle of water back to the sofa and two snickers bars and hands one to Sally.

"We need to eat."

"What do you think that was?"

"It sure felt like an earthquake."

"Could we really be that unlucky?"

"Or lucky."

"Yeah, well, that too."

"Years ago I rented a house that was not far from the Glenn Brook River. It was on a cliff high above the river and some kids were lighting fires in a hollow, huge oak tree at the edge of the cliff and probably smoking dope. Eventually the trunk got so thin from the fires that the tree fell off the cliff and plunged down fifty feet into the river, which was only a few feet wide at the time. It shook my house just like what happened here. I really thought it was an earthquake and when I found out there was none, I remembered that tree and sure enough it had fallen. I think the villas on the cliff may have been undermined by the surf and have fallen onto the rocks below."

"Oh, my, I sure hope Alsace and Marge are OK."

"Me too, I was thinking that. She couldn't be with a more able man than Alsace."

Sally touches Gio's face with her hands and says, "my man is the most able of all." She kisses him full on the mouth.

49

"An Eye For an Eye"

El Capitan and his hired boat captain have somehow survived the first half of Ormando's wrath, sequestered in between some of the islands off shore from the City of La Paz, in the Sea of Cortez. The cooler temperatures of this sea have dissipated the storm a little and they are now in the eye of the hurricane and experiencing light breezes and a starry sky overhead. There is even some moonlight peaking over the top of Ormando's eye wall. Both men are lying on the deck, having tied themselves to the rail atop the boat's gunwales. Now that the eminent danger has settled, the men realize how sick they are and begin retching, bringing up a little digested food, but mostly sea water.

Captain Hector Alvarez, a very educated man, looks at El Capitan, "Mark Twain once said -going to sea is like going to jail, with a chance of drowning." Both men manage a miserable laugh.

"Hector, how much time do we have before the other half hits us?"

"Maybe an hour, depends on how fast the storm is moving. There's not much more we can do, the sea anchors are working quite well."

"I don't want to go through this again. Do you think we can make it to shore before we are hit again?"

"We came here to save your boat!"

"Fuck the boat, I can't take any more of this."

"We might do better to head North, further into the Sea of Cortez. If we are lucky enough to stay in the eye long enough, the colder water will reduce the severity of the storm."

"And why didn't we do that in the first place?"

"We didn't know the direction of the storm. Also, I would say that being in the eye of the storm is very unusual, it is very small compared to the overall storm."

"Let's pull the sea anchors in and get started. Hector, I hope you are right!"

Captain Alvarez cranks the engines, but they refuse to start. He is beginning to feel a little intimidated with El Capitan standing over him. Finally the engines start and they are able to wench the sea anchors in and head North, the boat cruising at top speed.

Captain Alvarez shouts over the engine noise, "help me to watch, we need to stay in the middle of the eye as much as possible and when we see the storm coming back we must quickly deploy the sea anchors again."

"Hector, you keep saying "storm," Isn't this a fucking hurricane?"

"Yes, a big one!"

The men watch the towering eye wall grow closer. In the eye wall; the wind driven waves are all traveling the same direction, interacting with the erratic converging waves of the eye and they soon build into a rogue wave nearly one hundred and thirty feet high. The men grab hold of the boat's wheel and hang on. One of them shouts, "motherfucker." The boat is lifted like a cork, goes vertical and is spit out of the giant wave end-over-end.

El Capitan, a man who thought he would die in a hail of bullets, takes a deep breath of sea water, is quickly covered by the huge wave and drifts back and forth, like a leaf in crisp Autumn air, all buoyancy having been sucked from his body. His lifeless arms seem to wave at Captain Alvarez's body, as it drifts by.

50

Baja California Dreaming

As the storm subsides Gio and Sally both drift off into real sleep for the first time in about twenty-six hours. It is a fitful sleep for Gio and he dreams of walking through the doorway out into the light winds of the eye of the hurricane. The sun is shining and he sees a donkey in the distance. The donkey brays loudly and runs up to Gio and he is wild-eyed and bleeding from the many injuries on his body. The donkey seems to expect Gio to help him and he brays an awful sound. There is some sort of work saddle on the animal and there is a huge coil of rope hanging from it. Gio hears someone calling and goes toward the shouting and is soon at the cliffside and looks down below to the smashed and broken string of villas that have toppled off the cliff and he sees Jesus standing on top of the concrete heap. Jesus is covered with blood and is waving and shouting, "save me Gio, only you can save me."

Gio shouts down to Jesus, "you tried to kill us, why should I help you?"

"Because you are a good person and now I am changed by this horror and I am now good too, please Gio help me."

Gio looks at the donkey that has followed him to the cliffside and takes the coil of rope from the work saddle and ties it around the donkey's neck and throws the coil over the side of the cliff and is amazed that it is actually long enough to reach where Jesus is standing. Gio shouts, "tie the rope around your chest tightly and the donkey can pull you up."

Gio looks at the donkey and tells him, "back boy, back." The donkey moves slowly backward as Gio watches Jesus "walk" up the side of the cliff. At the top of the cliff Gio helps Jesus to struggle over the lip of the cliff. Jesus stands up and shakes Gio's hand and then hugs him around his arms and back and whispers to him, "you are such a fool" as he hurls Gio off the cliff............

Gio awakes with a start and is muttering, "I am a fool, I am a fool."

Sally wakes up and shakes Gio a bit and he pushes her away and then fully awake he grabs her and hugs her tightly.

"You must have been having a nightmare."

"Was I ever, I dreamt I rescued Jesus from the rocks below the cliff, using a donkey and a rope and then he pushed me off the cliff."

"Oh, I don't think Jesus can hurt us any more, I think he has probably bled to death by now. I hate to say it, but it served him right; he was going to kill us both."

Gio puts his head in his hands and tells Sally, "I feel like I've lived my life backwards. All those years at the bakery, all those boring years and now in retirement all these wild and exciting things are happening, things that it seems like should be a memory for me now, of when I was young. When will all this stop?"

"You want it to stop?"

"No, I don't mean meeting and marrying you, that's the best thing that's ever happened, but so many other things. I just want to go home and sit on the deck and have a simple life again."

"Well, Gio, not too many things have been simple since we met. But don't you see, if it hadn't been for the ambergris and our dogs, we probably would never have met."

"You are right of course, sorry, I guess the nightmare just overwhelmed me."

"And rightfully so."

"I wonder if the hurricane is really over, or if we are in the eye and still have many hours to suffer through this? I'm going to go outside and scout around and see what's left. You wait here and I'll be back soon."

"Not on your life buster, until we get out of this place, we are going to be like Siamese Twins!"

"I suppose you are right," Gio takes her hand and says, "shall we go see what's left?"

As they walk out and look to the north, they see a huge wall of vicious looking clouds. The wind is still whipping around and they are unsure if it is raining or they are just being pelted by water blowing off the roof. The palm trees have all been flattened and debris is whipping around in circles like the dust devils they have seen in the desert. They see a few people emerging from the villas and Gio turns to Sally and quietly says, "we can't tell what happened with Jesus, it will just cause us trouble and don't forget we are in a foreign country."

"Got it!"

A young man holding hands with a young lady walks by them and asks, "do you think it is over? I am worried we could be in the eye, but it doesn't look like it."

Everyone within earshot looks all around and all agree that it is gone, they have survived!

The small group of tourists walk down the hill, stepping over debris and walking around other building parts that are to large to step over. As they emerge from the last row of villas everyone stops suddenly; the water fountain is still in it's place but the three-story building where Gio and Sally had been staying is gone. Part of the foundation on one end is still there and a few concrete columns remain but the building is gone. Everyone cautiously picks their way through the rubble and they all stand at the edge looking down. The building landed upside-down and is broken into thousands of pieces.

The young man that had passed them before places his hands around his mouth and shouts down to the ocean, "anybody down there? Is anyone there?" Only the crashing surf answers his call. "I'll bet they are all dead."

They suddenly here a loud noise behind them and they all turn around and see a bloody, wild eyed donkey braying at them. The crowd is larger now and they all laugh, except Gio and Sally, who look at each other in amazement. Sally whispers to Gio, "weird!" Gio is wide eyed and nods his head to the affirmative.

A teenage girl approaches the donkey to consol it and gets bit on the arm and her father chases the donkey away.

An older woman tells the crowd, "I don't think there was anyone in that building, a bus was here to take them to a shelter and I think most of them went." Gio and Sally stare at each other and Gio says, "how did we miss that?" Sally replies, "beats me!"

A middle-aged man says, "I don't know about you guys but I'm tired of eating candy bars, let's raid the kitchen and see if we can find some food." Everyone follows him amid, "sounds good to me – that's a great idea."

Several of the men remove the trunk of a palm tree in front of the door and one reaches through the broken glass and unlocks the door. They are beginning to hear sirens from out on the highway. The roof to the restaurant is caved-in in places and they all work together to remove the debris and finally make their way to the kitchen and the freezer.

A middle-aged gentleman in a Panama straw hat takes the lead and Gio is his most trusted second. They run everyone out of the freezer and walk about sniffing the beef, pork and seafood. They are in agreement that all the meat is still good, at least for right now.

Panama Jack goes back to some of the seafood for a second sniff, "what do you think Gio?"

"Frozen seafood always smells suspect to me, but I think everything else is fine."

"Me too."

"Let's see how we can cook this stuff."

"I'll have Sally sniff the seafood, she'll know."

It seems the small crowd has acquiesced to Jack and Gio's leadership. The impatient ones have found a few things to munch on and all are comparing their shared experience of being survivors. Gio is thinking how he and Sally's experience could trump them all, if they only dared to share. The two men agree that there has to be charcoal here somewhere and send one of the onlookers out to the patio to see if the large concrete block barbeque grill is still there. As they move through the storage area they make a grisly discovery; a young man probably in his twenties has been crushed to death by an overturned shelf of can goods, meat slicers and other equipment. After a short discussion, the two men remove some of the debris and pull the body through the back door and agree not to mention it to the others until absolutely necessary. The deceased seems not to be of Mexican heritage, very dark complexion with African facial features.

"Gio, do you think the hurricane killed him?"

"I think he climbed up on that shelf trying to reach a bottle of tequila and down he came with the shelf on top of him."

"You are a keen observer my friend, I don't recall having seen him here at the resort. Do you?"

" Me neither, but we haven't been around here much. No one here is missing anyone, thank god, otherwise this would be a disaster. "

"No shit, that would be awful."

As they return to the kitchen the onlooker, now staff member, has returned with news that the barbecue grill was damaged.

"The good news is I found one of the grills on the edge of the roof and retrieved it and it fits on there fine, just a little wobbly." Thus the new staff member cements his place as third in line.

Jack says, "help us find some charcoal and some lighter as well."

The three men rummage through the small warehouse and finally uncover some very large bags of charcoal. The bags are soaked from an opening in the roof.

"Let's keep digging, maybe there are some dry ones on the bottom."

"We're in luck," Gio relates as he pulls a dry bag from the bottom.

The determined men are totally focused on the task at hand; "feeding the flock." The wrath of Ormando is not forgotten but has been surpassed by the crowd's eminent needs.

" Now, what about the lighter?" Jack asks.

"When I put the grill on there I noticed there was a gas line. I looked under the patio and there's a pig under there. I think the gas line is OK but why don't you guys check it to make sure?"

Jack looks at Gio, "if he knows what a "pig" is, I'll bet he's right about the gas line. Let's find some matches and get this party going."

Jack's third says, "I picked up a book of matches in the lobby.". The young man motions for Gio and Jack to move into the corner and whispers, "there's a dead woman in there, in the office, by the looks of her I'd say she was sexually assaulted and then straggled to death."

"Jesus," Gio says, "like the hurricane wasn't enough. I'll go put something in front of the door, we better stay out of there until the locals can take a look."

"I already did that, my name is Jim Bishop." He extends his hand. They all shake hands and it turns out the man in the Panama hat really is named Jack, which makes Gio smile a bit. Jack and Gio separately slip away and assess the murdered woman. The three men agree she was a Mexican maid here at the resort, reddish brown hair and freckles, a gift from an English sailor that jumped ship several generations ago.

With the aid of the gas line soon the "team" has the charcoal going and the meat sizzling, assisted by their wives locating buns, sauces, and other condiments. Someone has retrieved a few bottles of tequila and whiskey. It is amazing when not having suffered any personal loss how quickly people move on with their lives. Sally has been assigned the task of checking the phone lines every few minutes to see if they can get hold of the authorities as they listen to the various sirens flying by out on the highway. They can see black smoke billowing up over in the direction of town and some discuss the likelihood of the fire department even attempting to put the fires out.

Someone says, "I'll bet some of the boats are on fire in the harbor, fiberglass and vinyl makes black smoke like that." "So do tarpaper shacks, " adds another.

After their appetites are sated the victims of Ormando begin to speak of what is next. Sally relates that all of their possessions have been lost. Jim Bishops wife, Chris, asks, "how did that happen? Our things are fine. Did your roof blow off?"

"No, we were in the Villas that fell off the cliff, we ran out and up the hill and found an unoccupied Villa to wait out the storm."

"Was it falling off when you ran?"

"No, the bathroom window blew out and Gio grabbed me by the hand and up the hill we went. We were lucky to get out and left everything behind. I did manage to grab my purse, thank goodness. We felt a jolt later in the night and Gio thought the building may have fallen onto the rocks below. But we are alive and unhurt, so we are lucky."

"We're all lucky!"

Gio, Sally, Jim, Chris and Jack's wife Val are sitting on one corner of the patio, surrounded by the remnants of their meal. Jack walks up and quietly says, "I need to talk to you guys a minute." As they walk away Val says, "he can't ever stop being the plant manager he is, always in charge."

Sally replies, "I think we're lucky to have him," then adds, "and Gio and Jim too."

The men follow Jack into a sort of office off the kitchen and Jack addresses his concerns, "fellas, we're going to have to do something with those bodies, and soon. Do you guys think the authorities here are really going to give a shit about how they died? What do you think Gio?"

"I wish the power would come back on, we could put them in the freezer."

"Me too, but I don't see it happening, Jim, what do you think?"

"Those bodies will be stinking to high heaven by this evening, I know that from being in the Gulf War. I hate to sound racist, but I think the black guy did it."

"Me too," Gio puts in, "there was an empty bottle of tequila near her body. I think he went back for another one and wasn't so lucky the second time."

Jack replies, "sounds reasonable to me, let's give the authorities another couple of hours and if they don't show we'll have to sneak out back and bury them. I don't want to stir up a bee hive with all these nice tourists. I saw one of the yard workers put some tools away in a shed a few days ago. I'm going to see if it is still standing. Gio, see if you can find a purse or any I.D. on the woman. Jim, see if the black guy had a wallet on him. When this mess starts getting cleaned up we can at least I.D. those two. I hate to play God, but both families would be better off not knowing what happened. As far as they will know, they both were killed by the destruction of the hurricane."

Gio nods, "sounds good to me."

"Me too," adds Jim.

Gio and Jim return to the office and wait for Jack. Gio has the woman's wallet and opens it and shows Jim a picture inside, "look, isn't that a picture of that black guy?"

Jim takes the wallet and peers at the plastic picture holder, "I think it might be, let's go take a look at him again. As they walk out of the office Jack joins them, "I found a shovel, the shed was gone, but some of the tools had part of the roof on them. I tossed the shovel around back, in case we need it later."

"Jack," Gio offers him the wallet, we think they knew each other."

"What?"

"Yeah, we were just going to go compare the picture to his face."

"Holy shit, I think you may be right, let's go see."

Each of the men hold the picture up and make an attempt to make the I. D. determination.

"That's him," Jim says, "look at that scar over his left eyebrow."

Gio and Jack reply, "you're right, that's him."

Jim speculates, "rigors has set in, so I'm guessing he's been dead at least six or seven hours, she's stiff as a board, we've probably got a window of about six hours to get them in the ground."

"Guess you saw this in battle." Jack says.

"Unfortunately, yes. But I wonder what set this guy off?"

Gio responds, "seems to me the relationship wasn't going so well, pure speculation, but maybe he came to pick her up or maybe he did work here. He saw the hurricane as an opportunity to get rid of her, something he'd been thinking of for quite some time."

"True," Jack weighs in, "but why rape her?"

"Maybe it wasn't rape. Maybe she liked it rough. Maybe he just wanted to get laid one more time, then choked her to death." Gio says.

Jim smiles a little, "he probably wasn't getting any, there were times I felt like choking my first wife, but divorce worked for me."

"You didn't have a hurricane to cover your ass, " Jack smiles.

Jim rolls his eyes, "I'd like to think I wouldn't have done that."

"I doubt it," Gio puts in.

"Well fellas," asks Jack, "what are we going to do?"

Gio and Jim look at each other and Gio speaks first, "let's give them a couple of more hours. Then I say we pull her underwear up and tidy her up and bury them side-by-side."

Jim adds, "connubial bliss for eternity." They all laugh.

It is amazing how callus people become under dire circumstances, dealing with people they don't know nor care much about. However, who knows? Maybe their conclusion would be arrived at exactly by the local law enforcement. This conclusion would certainly uncomplicate their job amid such devastation.

So, it is settled: by the time authorities get around to digging the bodies up all three men will be back in the good ol' U. S. of A. Safe from any probing questions or questioning of their judgment. At least, that is what they thought would happen.

51

"I love your new look!"

"Mom, I know what Bryan is doing and I want it stopped."

"I'm not sure what you are talking about, what did he do?"

"He's been taking pictures of me. From several different angles, I might add, I think he may be looking for a plastic surgeon. I found a business card in our old van he's been using."

"What?"

"Don't you see? He wants to be "fixed" so we look exactly the same again."

"Look Ryan, he's been having a really hard time, you were inseparable your whole lives until you met Lynn. And now you've set off as if you were just ordinary brothers, striking out on your own."

"That whole experience of being tortured and disfigured changed me Mom. I don't want to play those stupid switcheroo games any more. I want to be somebody. I want to have a good career, and, as corny as it sounds, I want to help save the oceans, the coral reefs and I want.....I don't want to share Lynn. All that stuff we did seems so stupid to me now." Ryan looks at the ceiling and blows air through his lips making a horse sound, totally exasperated.

Mom sits quietly drinking her chai tea for a while. She's wearing a sweater with the sleeves hanging down onto her hands and Ryan is wondering, why do women and girls do that? Never seen a guy do that.

"Ryan, if I were you, I wouldn't worry about it. Bryan hasn't the money for such things. But I hope you know he's hurting. It's almost like someone going through a divorce after being jilted. He's hurting, he's a lost soul."

"Mom, he asked me if he could sleep with Lynn. For the first time in my life It's not like that, it's different, I want to spend the rest of my life with Lynn. We're going to get our master's degree. We plan to have adventures together, work on summer projects on remote islands and eventually have a family, after we are well established oceanographers.

"Wow Ryan, you've really thought this through and I think it's wonderful, I do, but I love your brother the same as you, doesn't mean I don't admire you more.....But I do have to help him through this difficult time. I think you can at least help us with it. He came to me for rent money, he can't afford your old apartment on his own and I think he is using drugs, he seems strung out, we don't know what to do."

They sit in silence for a while.

"I'm the happiest I've ever been in my entire life. I still care about Bryan, but I'm not going to let him drag me down."

"What will he do?"

"He could probably move in with Jordan and not even pay rent. They can stay high and play games together."

Mom gives him a cross look.

"Sorry, I'm just so frustrated right now; and, I'm not going to let this drag me down. When I'm with Lynn I forget all about Bryan, but he keeps calling me, wanting to hang out, plan a new scam to make money. It's all too much."

"Do you think he would move back home, if we asked him to?"

"There's an idea." They both sit silent for a long time, then Ryan says, "do you want me to try to talk him into that?"

"Let me talk to your Dad, he'll insist on rules and curfew I'm sure, but I need to run it past him first."

"Sounds good, I hope it works. Let me know what Dad says. I've been trying to tell Bryan what an opportunity it is that you guys are willing to pay our tuition. He needs to take advantage of that."

Ryan stands up, looks at his cell phone, "I've got a meeting with Professor Branson, I'm trying to get us in his summer program for next summer."

Mother and son embrace and Ryan says, "thanks Mom, let me know what Dad says, I gotta go, love you."

"Love you." Mom sits down and picks up her tea cup and mutters, "son-of-a-bitch, I wish those boys had not been born identical twins."

52

Best Laid Plans

"Can I have your attention please? Is everyone listening? There is no water pressure and even though this isn't a very pleasant conversation to have, we need to cover it. There are some empty villas. I've made a list of them and I'll post it next to the lobby door. If you have to go number one, and you know what I mean, then use your own villa and do not flush, you'll be able to use it for quite a while. If you have to go number two, use one of the empty villas and please do flush. If you go into an empty villa and there is no water in the commode, go on to another and do not use it. That should get us by for a day or so, after that we'll have to use other measures. Any questions?"

The teenage girl that was bitten by the donkey asks, "what will be other measures?"

"No need to worry about that now, we may have water pressure soon, we just don't know until we've made contact with the outside world. We'll keep you posted, OK?" She and others nod their heads and for the first time it hits some of the tourists that the "we survived" phase is over and the daily tasks of living are here.

A middle-aged couple walks into the middle of the small crowd and right up to Panama Jack. They walk with Jack out of earshot, followed by Jim and Gio. The middle-aged man tells them, "I think we've got a serious problem. We walked down the road toward the highway, thinking we might be able to get some help or at least find out how the government here is handling the devastation. The road is completely washed out in one spot."

"Won't four wheel drives be able to make it in?"

"No, when I say "washed out" that's what I mean; there's a crater about fifteen feet deep and there is still water

204

rushing through the crater. Some of it is going through on toward the ocean and some looks like it is going underground."

"You mean to say the concrete slabs are completely gone?"

"Oh, they are there, but they are at the bottom of the crater and the road drops off steeply on both sides. There is probably a way to walk around it, but we decided to come back. I'm afraid there may be sink holes that could collapse under our feet."

"You could be right. I know a lot of Mexico, especially the Yucatan Peninsula sits on limestone, which is prone to sink holes, but I've not heard any of the local people talking about having them here."

"My guess is the danger is with water flowing underground, just thought you should know, seems like you are the man in charge." The middle-aged man says this with just a bit of animosity, which Jack ignores.

Sally has been quietly talking with Jack's wife, Val. "Is Jack always in command?"

"Is he ever!"

"Well, someone has to do it and I can tell it's quite natural for him, did you say he's a plant manager."

"Yes, the official title is V.P. in Charge of Operations, but even he calls himself The Plant Manager."

"Who does he work for?"

"Randolph Tires, you know, "reach for the stars, Randolph Tires!"

"Oh yeah, I've seen those commercials. I'm surprised they are still making tires in the U. S."

"Well, don't hold your breath, he's talked about maybe being sent to China. This was supposed to be a pure vacation but he's been asking around here and there and talking "unofficially" to some government officials. I think he'd sure rather be here than in China and I'll second that. We were supposed to be heading up to La Paz today. They have a pretty good port there, to bring raw materials in by ship."

The pool is littered with debris and with no filtration there is little need to go near it or have any thought of rinsing off in it.

"Can I have your attention again please? Gio, Jim and I have been talking and Jim has found a stack of five gallon buckets behind the kitchen. We need to get some volunteers to dip those buckets into the pool and carry the water to villas 2305, 2618, 3110 and 3112. Those are now the designated bathrooms for doing number two. After you flush, remove the lid from the commode and pour the entire contents of the half-filled bucket into the flush box. If you don't think you can lift it, get some help. That should solve our sanitary situation for a while. We still have many cases of bottled water and some pop. The less alcohol you drink the better hydrated you'll be." Jack steps down from the fountain wall he's been using as a "soap box."

"Gio, we need to go outback and have a little discussion, you too Jim."

"I'll be there in a minute," Gio advises. He walks over to Sally and tells her she might as well relax for a while.

"Can't do it, us women are going to put the cooked meat into some plastic containers and sit them in the pool to keep them cool, since we have no ice."

"Good idea, I'll tell Jack. You know who he really reminds me of?"

"Alsace?"

"Yes, exactly. Can you imagine those two simultaneously trying to take charge?"

"It would certainly be a site to behold. I'm really worried about them."

"Yeah, me too, but it may be days or even weeks before we can find out where they are and even if they are OK."

"Well, I'm hoping Alsace is over at their hotel, right now, barking orders like Jack is here."

"Let's keep our fingers crossed, I've not known him long, but I really love that guy."

Gio leaves to join Jack and Jim behind the kitchen.

"Let's go ahead and start digging the graves."

"I think we should just dig one hole and put both of them in there." Jim suggests. "That's what we did in the Gulf War, this ground looks similar, it's not going to be easy to dig here."

The men take turns using the shovel. Soon they hit solid rock about three feet down.

"This is going to take a while, I think all we can do is make it wide enough for both of them." Gio looks at the other men for their opinion.

"Yeah, I think you are right," Jack agrees and Jim nods his approval.

A couple of hours later Jack and Jim tidy up the young woman's body and drag her and her alleged murderer/rapist out to the grave site. Gio is posted as guard to prevent anyone from going around to the back. They drag the bodies into the swallow grave and cover them with the rocky dirt.

"Let's take a break, then I think we should find some rocks and cover the earth. There are probably hungry dogs and coyotes lurking about, they'll dig them up if we don't do it." Jack and Gio nod, as Jim has been recognized as the expert on the after effects of devastation.

As the men are walking toward the patio to take some refreshment they hear the distinct sound of a jeep lugging along in second gear. One of them says, "someone's here."

Sgt. José Vasquez Ortez of the Ejército Mexicano, the Mexican Army, has driven his jeep along the edge of the cliffs from the resort where Jesus was staying.

He jumps out of his jeep and asks, "who is in charge here?"

Jack lifts his arm high and walks to Sgt. Ortez, who says in English with a very heavy accent, "you are the manager of the resort?"

"No, just a tourist, but I'm pretty much in charge here." Jim and Gio, who have followed Jack nod to the Sergeant.

"Do you know your road is washed out?"

"Yes, someone walked down the road and told us."

"OK, so you are in charge, do you have food, water, first aid supplies?"

"We cooked the food from the freezer and we have bottled water and we are using water from the pool to flush toilets."

Gio adds, "and the women have placed the cooked meat into containers and put them in the pool to stay cool, but it may not last past tomorrow sometime."

Sgt. Ortez says, "you are a good boss man, you could perhaps be a Sergeant in the Mexican Army." Gio and Jim smile a little, both thinking, maybe Colonel – but they keep silent and feed the man's ego.

"I am Sgt. First Class Ortez, and who are you?"

"I'm Jack Hanley, and this is Gio and Jim." The men put out their hands. Sgt. Ortez ignores this and walks away surveying the surroundings. He walks toward the cliff and then looks down at the string of villas now being gobbled up by the high surf still pounding the coast. "No sounds from below?"

"No, someone said a bus took those people into town, but we don't know for sure, we've not heard a thing."

"I'm sure anyone down there is not around us anymore. You have no injured or deceased?"

"Please follow me." Jack takes Sgt. Ortez around to the graves, followed by Gio and Jim, shoos away a mongoloid looking stray dog and says, "we had to bury them, we thought it might be days before anyone came and none of the other tourists know about it."

"How did they die?"

"A women was raped and strangled and the man who did it was smashed by a shelf while reaching for more tequila."

"You have made a big mistake boss man, tampering with evidence and removing a victim from the scene is a very serious offense in Mexico."

"I made the decision to do this, backed up by Jim here, and Gio. Jim was in the Gulf War and he knew the dangers and ramifications of leaving the bodies above ground."

"You were in the Army?"

"Yes."

"In the Gulf War?"

"Yes."

"And your rank?"

"Same as you, First Sergeant."

"Gentlemen, you are confined to the immediate grounds of the resort, do not leave for any reason. I will return to my unit and let the Captain decide if this is a matter for the Army or the local policía. Marshall law has been declared for a period of three months. This is a very serious matter, do you understand?"

"Really? Where would we go?"

"Don't be so smart boss man, as I said, this is a serious matter."

"Do you know when the airport will be flying planes again?"

"Soon, but no civilian flights will occur for quite some time. Your country has agreed to send supplies, food and medicine on C-130 cargo planes. You may be here for a month. Los Cabos has nearly been ripped from Baja California. I am surprised you have survived at all. I assume most of the people here took the bus to one of the schools for safety."

Sgt. Ortez does an "about face" movement and followed by the three men walks around the building and to his jeep. "Make sure you do not leave, this is a fair warning to you!"

"We'll be right here," Jack says, "wouldn't think of going anywhere."

As the Sergeant turns the jeep around, Jack says quietly, "wouldn't think of it you pompous ass." Gio and Jim laugh and Jim says, "hey, give him a break, he's bucking for master sergeant."

"No doubt about it," Jack adds. "Well, sounds like we're pretty much fucked, gentlemen, "I say we open a bottle of that tequila, since we are no longer in charge and have been designated common criminals."

"I think it helped that Jim was in the army and the Gulf War." Gio speculates.

"I was a Major during Vietnam, I should have pulled rank on him." Jack declares.

Gio and Jim smile, both surprised to have witnessed an act of modesty from "the boss man."

In spite of Jack's admonishment to others, tequila now seems like a good idea. Everyone feels a little bit better since they've been contacted by the outside world and with a little tequila, better still.

Gio is the first to bring up there new situation of suspicion. "What do you think Jack? We are in a foreign country, how much trouble do you think we are in?"

"I wouldn't worry Gio, I will take full responsibility for our actions, I'll exonerate you and Jim."

"No need to do that, we did it together."

"Yeah, Jack, we'll back you up," Jim reflects.

"I'm not sure, but we may be better off dealing with the army versus the local-yocals. I haven't found the people of Los Cabos as warm and friendly as other parts of Mexico. I almost said "the mainland," it sure as hell feels like we're on an island."

"I agree," Jim puts in.

"I was telling Sally the same thing. They remind me more of the folks in the Caribbean."

"Maybe an example of Charles Darwin's theory, "Origin of Species."

"No kidding." The men all laugh.

Everyone is well fed and those that imbibed a little tequila are very relaxed and all are bored. However, the truth is, they have enough safe meat for one more day and water for three more. There are fewer sirens speeding by on the highway now but they still serve as a reminder of the dire situation they are in.

The women are preparing the evening meal; warming up the meat that has been kept cool in the pool and throwing together instant mashed potatoes, pasta and other packaged or canned foods.

All the little clutches of family and friends are finishing their evening meal and "the top brass," Jack, Gio and Jim are dining with their wives and discussing the dilemma, when they hear the distinct sound of the army jeep lugging along the cliff edge in second gear.

"Here comes the cavalry," someone says. As the jeep comes into view they can see there are three men bumping along. Closer still and they recognize Sgt. Ortez, another army uniform and a police uniform they recognize from having been in town.

Sgt. Ortez takes the lead and walks directly to the gathering of "the brass" and says, "El Capitan, these are the men who have tampered with evidence and buried bodies without the proper paperwork."

The army officer reaches his hand out and says in near perfect English, "I am Captain Fernando Gomez." Gio is the closest and he shakes his hand and introduces himself and the others.

"You have met my First Sergeant and this is officer Mendez of the Cabo San Lucas Police Department. Can you please tell me what has happened here?"

Jack steps forward and says, "please, let's discuss this inside. The six men move into what remains of the hotel lobby.

"We've not told the rest of the tourists about finding the dead bodies, I thought it best, although I'm sure they know something is going on."

"They moved the women's body and in so doing destroyed evidence and"……..

Captain Gomez holds up his hand to silence his First Sergeant. "Sergeant Ortez, you need to go guard the jeep and make sure these tourists don't try to steal it."

"Yes sir," the First Sergeant does an about face and heads for the jeep.

"I'm so sorry but my First Sergeant is what your army troops used to call a "Doodly Dooright.""

"Dudley Dooright," someone corrects him.

"Yes, he is a good man in some ways but he also gets on my nerves."

"Mine too," Jack says.

"So, gentlemen, please tell me what you have done here."

Gio and Jim motion toward Jack.

"We first found the black man, crushed, by can goods and machinery. We think he raped a woman right in there, strangled her to death and then went back to the store room to get more tequila from the top shelf and it fell on him crushing his chest. We, I, decided we should bury them for reasons of sanitation and to prevent panic among the other tourists."

"Can you please take me to the graves?" The men file through the kitchen and walk out to the graves.

"How deep are they buried?"

"About three feet, we hit bedrock."

"I think I know you," says Jim to Captain Gomez."

"Excuse me?"

"You were in the Gulf War."

"Yes I was, I don't remember you."

"Well, I was one of thousands, you were one-of-a-kind."

Jim turns to Jack and Gio, "Captain Gomez was a Second Lieutenant then. Most people don't know it, but we regularly train Mexican officers "in country", so we can keep them on the payroll when they return to their own country, then they can keep us informed of what's going on in Mexico."

Captain Gomez lifts his right arm and pulls his pointed index finger across his neck as a signal for Jim to stop talking about it.

"Well, I'm certainly not doing that! But I do remember you now, you were the man who said that citizens of the United States shouldn't be the only people called Americans, that Mexicans, Central Americans and South Americans are all "Americans" too."

"Hmm, I don't remember telling you that, but yes, that is my philosophy, so I'm sure I did tell you that."

"It's a pleasure to see you survived, some didn't." Captain Gomez shakes Jim's hand and says, "gentlemen, Officer Mendez has looked at the pictures of this man and he is a known criminal and the other one is his ex-girlfriend that he has been harassing from time-to-time. Gentlemen, this is not Miami Vice, no one will ask about these bodies. As soon as you can, you can go home and keep quiet about this. Can I count on you?"

All the men nod yes.

"I have at least three months of pure hell ahead of me. We have no power at the morgue and we will soon have to start burning bodies, but I will make sure the relatives get their personal belongings. So, go home as soon as you can and keep quiet and you have my assurance that my First Sergeant forgets this before we get to the highway. I will add you to the list of resorts to receive food and water. You have done a good job here of cleaning up and keeping the tourists calm. It is good to see you again," he shakes Jim's hand again, then Gio and Jack.

"It is a relief that I don't have to dispatch soldiers here to keep the peace. Thank you again gentlemen. We must go."

The officials return to the jeep and are soon out of site.

"Wow," Jack says, "I wasn't expecting that, this calls for another drink."

53

The Land of Milk & Honey

&

Other Mind Altering Drugs

When Agnes returned to her condo on the Nyhavn Canal in Kobenhavn in the Capital Region of Denmark she had lots of things to do. As every professional knows, "take care of business and business will take care of you." The first few days every moment Agnes could spare was devoted to love making. Tekeysia managed to entertain herself otherwise with Agnes' large library of exotic art and photography books, as well as a bit of exploring the neighborhood. About a week after they arrived a canal barge came by, loaded with bohemians selling many "flavors" of weed. Tekeysia hung out with them for an afternoon and they told her of a place called Christiania, that she wants to visit. Tekeysia saw bicycle riders every where and asked Agnes if she could get one. It took Tekeysia an afternoon to master pedaling and steering at the same time. Agnes wasn't about to turn Tekeysia loose on a bicycle in Copenhagen and purchased a bike for herself as well. The bikes are of the "cruiser" type with fat tires and coaster brakes. The next day Agnes has an afternoon and evening free and gives in to Tekeysia's desire to explore Christiania, a place she hasn't been to in years.

The bridge to Christiania is not far away by bicycle. Christiania, an eighty-four acre commune reminds Tekeysia a lot of her little village in Jamaica. Christiania was a military installation mostly abandoned after WWII. In 1971 a few "hippies" moved into one of the large abandoned buildings where they were mostly ignored by the city officials as the property was owned by the central government. Christiania now has about eight-hundred inhabitants. It is the original Greenwich Village type of community with lots of artists, musicians, actors, and other sorts that fancy themselves marching to their own drumbeat. The main street is named

Pusher Street. Although the sale and use of marijuana is against the laws of Denmark, officials have long ignored its use and concentrated on ridding their country of hard drugs. For many years there were marijuana vendor stands at the entrance of Pusher Street and although a coincidence, it seemed a likely name for the thoroughfare.

Before flying on to France Alsace made the arrangements for Tekeysia to get a passport, making her a legal resident for the first time since leaving Jamaica. Tekeysia has been told of the cold winters they have here and of the many extra hours of darkness that comes over the land and she is already hoping to escape to a warmer climate. Tekeysia's enthusiasm for life and all the good things in it probably means she will easily be welcomed into Christiania.

Agnes hasn't frolicked on a bicycle since her days in the South of France with her friend Rene. The two women have fun passing each other and it makes Agnes feel young again, which after all is what seducing young women is all about. They head across the bridge to Christiania and turn into Pusher Street and ride it until they have passed through the commercial area and make a U-turn and stop to chat about where they will have lunch. Part of the quaintness of this bohemian near-paradise is that there are no advertising signs of any significance, just enough to give the name of the restaurant or business. They both recall a café with three bells at the entrance.

They choose the Three Bells Café, place their bikes in the bike rack and Tekeysia goes ahead while Agnes attaches the bicycle locks to her latest investment. Agnes has been enjoying the animalistic sex with Tekeysia very much but is also mindful that one day Tekeysia will wonder off and she is so relieved that she had Alsace get Tekeysia a passport and I.D. card in the hopes that she won't end up in a legal mess when the bird does decide to fly.

As they finish eating a delicious meal Tekeysia asks the waitress, "Who es this beeg-deal singer, Abou Aboubacar, that is performing tonight?"

The waitress is from Florida in the U.S.A. and tells Tekeysia and Agnes, "he's from Senegal, in Africa, I believe. He is very good, sings things like afro-pop and also he does some Bob Marley, I'm sure you know about him."

"Oh, yees, everyone in Jamaica knows Bob Marley's music, he es a national hero. I dated w'one of hees sons for a short time, th't fukker had da best dope ever!

"So when will he start playing this evening?" Agnes puts in.

"He is supposed to start at nine, but it is sometimes nine-thirty or ten before they get everyone together, they kind of just filter in."

"Are you sure hees from Senegal? Sounds like a Jamaican to me."

"Really Tekeysia, outside of the symphony hall and playhouses, I think that's pretty much the way musicians are world wide."

"Con we come bak tonight?"

"I suppose so, we'll have to take a water taxi."

"He's a very popular guy, if you ladies want to get good seating I suggest you get here by seven forty-five or eight o'clock."

The two women spend the rest of the afternoon exploring the shops of the many artisans and crafters. They place their purchases in the baskets attached to the handle bars that came with the bikes. Agnes lets Tekeysia take the lead as Tekeysia's cantilevered derriere looks sensational sitting atop the bicycle seat. Her long braided, beaded hair flies in the wind as she bounces along. Agnes "can't wait" to get inside and free Tekeysia of the expensive clothes she purchased for her in San Diego.

Now inside, naked except for a new neck scarf, Tekeysia prances around the room shaking her ass because she knows it drives Agnes crazy. At this time Agnes has near complete control of Tekeysia's life; strange country, strange language and no means of support. However, in the bedroom Tekeysia is very much in control and walking away from Agnes she stops and does a little Flamenco dance that makes her mahogany ass shake like jelly. Agnes laughs, "I love your independent rear suspension."

"Thank you Aggie, it's all for you." Tekeysia goes to the bed and lies on her tummy, licks her right hand and puts it between her legs. "Come and get it baby, I know you want it." Indeed she does, yes, indeed she does.

The water taxi drops them off near the Three Bells Café. As they walk hand-in-hand it is quite a picture; pallid white skin on glistening ebony. Let's just say no one will mistake them for mother and daughter. As they pass by a small crowd someone quietly speculates, "looks like she's found herself a sugar momma."

The stars begin to glitter as the crisp, cool air is quickly shortening the days that soon will only offer winter daylight from 8 a.m. to around three in the afternoon. The couple is all polished and draped in beautiful clothing which stands out in the ever so casual Christiania.

54

Wishing You Were Here

Back home Gio's sister Judith is in her third week of vacation. Gio and Sally are overdue on their honeymoon and she hasn't heard a word from them. News reports talk about the large number of dead tourists, although compared to the numbers of deceased local people it seems small. Some of the tourists that got out before the airport was closed have been on the evening news telling about how the local people were all saying how Ormando wouldn't live up to the weather forecasts and how lucky they were to make it home. Lynn, who is most concerned about her new love and new life wishes Gio would hurry home so she can ask if she and Ryan can rent his condo.

In the meantime it has been a full week since the day after Ormando passed over Los Cabos and Gio and Sally are getting frantic as they haven't heard a word from Alsace and Marge. Some of the men found a generator in a forgotten corner of a maintenance building and after a day of trial and error it is running, so that the emergency lighting system for the resort is on. A Red Cross truck has visited them and left adequate fresh water and some military type meals and a little fresh fruit and vegetables that they somehow have obtained locally.

"Sally," Gio calls out. "Oh, there you are. Jack is going to hitch a ride on the Red Cross truck back to town, I'd like to go with him."

"Does that mean I'm not invited?"

"Well, Jim's going and that's all they can carry. I'm going to see if I can find Alsace and Marge. The Red Cross people said there are lists posted of survivors."

"And, I suppose the dead as well?" Sally quips.

"Why would you say that? I only want to believe they are alive."

"Me too, and that's why I haven't said anything but I'm worried that Jesus or another of El Capitan's thugs killed them. Alsace was just as involved in upsetting El Capitan's apple cart as you were."

"That has been on my mind too. But I think if Jesus had done it he would have bragged to us about it. I can't see him or anyone else taking on Alsace and coming out on top. Apparently they, just like Alsace, couldn't bring guns down here or we would surely be dead."

Gio, there are thousands of people that are victims of Ormando, no matter how tough they are."

"Very true, if you don't mind, I'd like to get going. The Red Cross also said there might be a possibility of getting an email out. I think I remember Judith's email correctly, I'm sure they are worried to death about us and your nieces and nephews as well. Plus, we both could sure use a change of clothes, these borrowed ones don't look so hot."

"O.K., how will you get back?"

"That's a fair question, Jack says we'll find a way."

"Promise me you'll be back before dark."

"I will, somehow I will make that."

They embrace and Gio hurries out to hitch his ride.

Having been told that Gio and Sally left everything behind in their room, which is now in the ocean, their fellow "guests" have given them enough clothes to get their soiled ones washed. The water lines have been restored, although it is not safe for drinking, as if it was before Ormando. The large washers used for laundering sheets and other linen are getting power from the generator now and the resort is beginning to look like a remote Mexican village, with piles of junk from the hurricane and clothes and linens hanging from every railing and impromptu clothesline. The cliff top has become their

221

road and some people have said they think the busses might be running out on the highway. But so far not one of the workers or supervisors employed by the resort have shown up for work.

Jack, Gio and Jim are squeezed into the back of the Red Cross mobile response van. It is a long-bed full size van with a raised top but no windows. They are literally sitting in the hole left from the off-loaded supplies of food and water. The vehicle's heavy-duty suspension makes for a bone jarring ride along the cliff top road. A few boxes fall off the partially unpacked stack and the three men struggle to restack them in the darkness. Being unable to see where they are going, it seems like it takes forever to get there.

The back doors open and as they get out they realize they have stopped at another resort and they help the Red Cross workers to unload the rest of the boxes. As the van is underway again, Jack says, "this reminds me of being stuck in the belly of a ship, waiting to go ashore."

"No kidding," Jim quips, "I think I might be seasick." They all chuckle.

The van stops and they can hear the driver and passenger step down from the van. The back doors don't open this time and one of them says, "what the fuck?" Jim moves like a crab through the darkness and finds the inside latch to the back doors and throws them open.

The Red Cross temporary headquarters occupies the remaining half of a school building. From this elevated vantage point the men are able to survey the harbor where boats are stacked like kindling wood. There is nothing they can see that has not been affected by Ormando. However, in just a week all the desert land that was not washed away has come alive with all kinds of plants that are just beginning to bloom. Gio has seen such pictures in nature magazines of other deserts after a generous rainfall. Gio thinks how this beauty will do little to get these mostly poor people back on their feet, but surely such beauty is giving them hope.

Gio speaks first, "I need to go to the Hacienda Hotel to see if I can find our friends."

"O.K. Gio," Jack replies, "I'm going to look around and try to find some kind of transportation, Jim, you want to come with me?"

"Sure."

"O.K., let's meet back here in two hours. Gio, they may have a list posted inside of people who have survived."

"I knew that, don't know why I wanted to head to the hotel, getting old and senile I guess. And I need to see if I can get an email to the folks back home. Aren't you guys doing that?"

"He's right Jim, we should do that as well."

As the three men walk into the building they locate a "communication room" and get in line. Gio hears a familiar voice and tells Jack and Jim, "I'll be back, I'm pretty sure that is my buddy's voice." Gio walks down the hall towards Alsace's booming voice and walks into a large room that appears to be the school lunch room. Alsace is sitting at one of the large lunch tables giving some Mexican men instructions of some kind. As he looks up and sees Gio he shouts to the men, "ándele," and crosses the room to give Gio a big hug.

As the men embrace Gio asks, "where is Marge?"

"It's not good Gio, she's in the hospital, what's left of it, she's in a coma, the next few days will tell, they are saying that as the swelling goes down, she may come around."

"What happened?"

223

"I stayed with her for a few days, but I felt I'd be better off helping out with the disaster relief."

"But, how did it happen?"

Alsace pulls Gio over to the corner, "I don't want anyone else to hear this, that fucking El Capitan sent one of his henchmen over to even the score on us turning that video over to the officials. I really wasn't expecting it with the hurricane and all, but he busted into our room and had a big butcher knife. It was a hell of a struggle, we crashed through the patio doors and were battling it out on the patio when Margaret came out with a leg off a chair we broke and hit that asshole in the head and I got the knife and stabbed the fucker. Margaret was just standing there in shock and one of those big red clay tiles slid off the roof and hit her on top of the head. Damndest thing I've ever seen. All that and she gets hit by that tile. I carried her inside and put her on the bed, but the rain was blowing in, so I found an empty room two doors down and carried her in there and put the mattress from the other bed over the patio doors. I gave her a little sip of whisky hoping she would come around and she perked up for a second and called Sally's name and since then nothing. I couldn't get her any medical care until the next day. I kept putting a bag of ice on her head until the ice machine played out. It was awful, I felt so helpless. Is Sally O.K.?

"Yes, we had a similar experience," and Gio told him the whole story.

"So, you are sure no one knows about what happened to Jesus?"

"Yes, we've told no one, what did you do with the guy's body?"

"I threw him off the balcony and told the medical people all my scratches and scrapes happened when Margaret

224

got hit. As long as we keep silent about it, I don't think we have to worry; disaster has it's advantages."

Gio is able to get on a computer that is logged into the satellite dish the Red Cross set up a couple of days ago and sends his email to Judith. He only tells her to inform Marge's kin that she is hospitalized.

The two hours pass quickly and Jack and Jim are back. Jack somehow located a four wheel motorcycle and rented it for a week.

"Did they have anything else down there to rent?" Gio asks.

"They've got a Honda 150cc scooter, but Jim doesn't have a motorcycle designated driver's license. Who would guess they would give a shit down here?"

"He said because of the insurance," Jim puts in.

"I've got a motorcycle license, that's the main reason I've kept it up all these years, for trips to Mexico."

Gio introduces his friend to Jack and Jim and says, "Sally is going to want to go stay with Marge, you got room on that thing for three of us?" "It'll be cozy, but I can get us to the scooter shop." Gio gets the details on how to get to the hospital.

The Honda PCX-150 is a dandy, candy apple red with black trim. Though not required, Gio purchases two helmets as it has been a while since he last rode a scooter this size.

"I promised Sally I'd be back before dark."

"We have the same curfew," Jim responds. "Let's make one stop, I found a shop selling pulled pork barbecue sandwiches. We'll have to smuggle them in."

"Sounds good."

Gio already decided that trying to find some clothes for him and Sally can wait until tomorrow, when he can bring Sally along. He follows Jack and Jim back to the resort with great dread. Things are looking up in some ways but he has to tell Sally about her friend, and that grinds in his gut.

55

A Friend Indeed

"Oh, my goodness, I can't believe this has happened. After all we've been through and Marge gets hit on the head by a tile. Maybe she got hit during the fight."

"I never thought of that, but why would Alsace lie about that?"

"He couldn't say what really happened or he would give away him stabbing that thug."

"I think if it had happened that way Alsace would have told me and just told me not to tell anyone."

"That's true, but I don't understand why he just left her there. I've read that people in comas can hear every word that's being said and that it helps them in their recovery. Do you think you could get me to the hospital in the dark?"

"Sally, I think it would be a big risk. That cliff top road, I haven't ridden a scooter in years. I'm not sure I could find the hospital and…."

"O.K., O.K.! I know you are right, but I'm outraged at Alsace, did he even try to find us?"

"I don't know, but he is a good friend and I think you are just upset about Marge and I understand that. Here, drink this whisky, it might settle you down."

Sally takes the tiny bottle of whisky Gio has pulled from their room's tiny bar. She swallows, takes a moment to recover, then finishes the bottle. "One more bottle of that and I'll go find Alsace and kick his ass."

"Eat your sandwich, it sure beats anything we've had around here lately."

They both silently finish their pulled pork sandwiches and Gio says, "I think we should go to bed early and get up early tomorrow morning. I bought some pastry at the barbecue place. We can have that for breakfast and then head into town."

Gio is the first to wake. He is used to letting Sally sleep as long as she wants. But today he knows she too wants an early start. He makes coffee in their little two-cup coffee pot and the aroma wakes Sally. They quickly eat and climb on the red scooter parked in front of their door. Sally is impressed at how well Gio handles the scooter over the rough terrain. Once in town, it doesn't take Gio long to find the hospital.

"Sally, I know you are upset, but when we see Alsace later today please stay calm, O.K.? Gio secures the front wheel lock and stashes their helmets in the rear storage compartment and they walk to the hospital entrance hand-in-hand.

"I'm going to tell them I'm her sister. I don't know about here, but back home you can't do a thing if you're not related to the patient."

"Good idea, I hadn't thought of that."

They arrive at the reception area and ask if anyone there speaks English. They wait for about twenty minutes then a nurse walks up to them.

"Are you the folks that need an interpreter?"

"Yes, are you an American?"

"I'd say so, I'm from Canada. Decided I wanted a new life in Mexico. This is my worst week so far."

"I'm here to see my sister, I'm told she's in a coma."

"Her name?"

"Marge, or Margaret Scranton."

"Let's take a look, my name is Mary Compton, and yours?"

"I'm Sally and this is my husband Gio."

Nurse Compton goes to a nearby computer and asks, "her name again?"

"Margaret Scranton."

"I'm not finding that, let me look at the I. C. U. list, you said she's in a coma?'

"Yes."

"I don't have anyone by that name. I do see a Margaret, but the last name is Wohl….jung, or is it Wohl-young?"

"Yes, Yes, I'm so unset, I gave our family surname. That's her married name, they haven't been married long."

"Jeez," Gio tries to cover her, " I was thinking Scranton too. We've been cut off at our resort for a week so we….."

"I understand," Nurse Compton replies. She grabs a pad of paper and asks, "and what is your full name?"

"Sarah or Sally Valducci and this is Gio Valducci."

"Here, just take the elevator to the sixth floor and give this to the nurses station and they will take you to your sister."

"Thanks so much!"

"If you need more translation I put my extension on the pass I gave you. But I won't be available for a couple of hours. I'm headed for surgery. Because of the hurricane we've been working fourteen to sixteen hours a day."

On the elevator Sally tells Gio, "well, at least he's claiming he is her husband. That makes me feel a little better."

They take the "pass" to the nurses station and are led to a waiting room where they are given white gowns, latex gloves and then told to wash their hands with disinfectant foam. The I.C.U. is a large room with many patients, all of which are connected to all manner of medical devices. As they arrive at Marge's bedside neither Gio or Sally recognize her. But sitting next to her in a large chair is Alsace, who has dozed off. Gio taps Alsace on the shoulder. Alsace opens his eyes and just sits for a moment and then springs to his feet.

"Gio, Sally." The three embrace. All of Sally's animosity toward Alsace evaporates.

Sally Says, "thanks so much Alsace, for taking care of her and watching over her. Has there been any improvement?"

"The swelling seems to be going down, not that you would notice unless you saw her when they brought her here."

"Oh my, she looks awful. Damn it, I shouldn't have said that, some people think they can hear everything, even if only subconsciously."

Alsace then does a better job of bringing Sally up-to-date than he did with Gio the day before. "I volunteered down at the Red Cross, I figured it was the only way I could make some contacts to try to get her flown out of here to a state-side hospital. They are telling me that if the swelling continues going down she could be moved in a couple of days. I've got my fingers crossed. The day after tomorrow a hospital plane will be leaving for Dallas at 2 p.m. Damn, I hope she can be moved by then, because I don't have any information when the next one will be in."

Sally hugs Alsace, "thank you so much Alsace. If you need to get back down to Red Cross I'll stay with her."

Sally looks around. "This doesn't look like any I.C.U. I've ever seen."

"You're in Mexico Sally, during a disaster." Gio tells her.

"Oh, believe me, I know where I am, and it may be my last trip. It is certainly a honeymoon to remember!"

"How did you get here?" Alsace asks.

"I rented a scooter."

"Oh, good. Can you give me a lift to Red Cross?"

Gio looks at Sally, who nods her head yes.

"You sure you'll be O.K.?"

"Yes, I'm going to hold her hand and talk to her, if it doesn't help her it will at least make me feel better."

Gio takes out his wallet and gives her a handful of Mexican paper money.

"Just in case you need something."

Alsace looks at Sally, "I want to check on some things. I'm going to tell them Margaret will be ready to go and hope for the best."

231

"Will I be able to go with her?" Sally asks.

"I don't know the answer to that."

"I've told them I am her sister."

"Good move. But do you understand she will be hospitalized in Dallas? I don't know when she will be able to be moved to San Diego."

"Doesn't matter, when I get there I'll at least be able to reach her son. I will stay with her, no matter what, if I can."

"O.K., all I can do is show them my Interpol shield and hope it works."

"I'll try to be back by noon," Gio informs her.

"O.K., honey, I'll see you then."

56

Resort to Move on

As Gio exits his villa he sees Jack's wife departing her villa. She waves at him and he waves back. Gio knocks on the door and hears Jack stumbling around. Jack opens the door.

"Hey Gio, I thought Valarie forgot something. What's up?"

"I was in the resort office, went in through the kitchen and I don't think the new manager heard me. He was talking to someone about what's going to happen around here. I guess the owners must be American, he was speaking English."

"Yes, I talked to him. He attended the University of Chicago, he is the owner's son-in-law."

"Did he tell you what they are planning to do?"

"In regard to what?"

"I gather from the conversation that they are going to bill the post-hurricane guests for their room, and the food and drinks they've consumed. Also, that the guests who had all-inclusive packages will be charged the per day charge of that package. Sally and I didn't have all-inclusive and I'm not about to pay a bunch of charges when we were the ones that kept this place going. What do you think? Am I right on this?"

"I have to agree, especially after the staff pooh-poohed how serious the hurricane would be. Really, those fuckers should be paying us for our services. On the other hand, we're in a foreign country Gio. I'm not sure what we can do about it."

"Well, I can tell you, I am planning to leave early tomorrow morning. As far as they know, I might be down there in the ocean where my villa fell during the storm. Sally stayed at the hospital last night and we don't really have anything to pack. I'm going to head out early and find us some place to stay near the hospital, providing there are any places open right now."

"Hmm, we were on all-inclusive, but I say fuck'em, you are right, this place would have been totally fucked if I hadn't, rather, if we hadn't stepped up and kept it going. And, I still haven't given up on the main reason I came here. Well, it was to give Val a vacation, but I still want to check things out in La Paz for my company. The new manager said the highway to La Paz is clear, so I'm planning to go up there for a couple of days and just see what I can find out. I'll tell Jim. I don't think we should say anything to the others. Shit, I'm not sure how we'll manage this." The men sit silent for a moment and then Jack says, "o.k., here's what we'll do. I'll leave when you leave, let's say, daybreak. Providing Jim and his wife want to go, I'll take all the luggage out, on the four wheeler, when you go. Then when we find accommodations, I'll stash the luggage there and come back for the other three. Damn, we got three on when we were in town, but I'm not sure we can get four on that thing."

"We lost all our stuff in the hurricane. I can take one of the girls out on the back of my scooter."

"That'll work. When I come back for Jim and his wife, the manager won't think anything is up, since we won't have any luggage."

"Sounds like a plan."

"Thanks Gio, you could have just disappeared, thanks for thinking of us."

"You bet. I'll see you in the morning, let's just say five-thirty, o.k.?"

"See you then."

57

Amnesiac

Gio's and Jack's plan was carried out with precision, except that Gio returned to the resort with Jack so that they only had to carry one passenger each, Jim and his wife. They found a really nice bed and breakfast that had survived the hurricane with minimal damage. Gio was glad to find that the B & B was now able to process credit cards as he was running low on cash.

Gio, Sally and Alsace have had a conference with Marge's doctor, assisted by nurse Compton and decided to leave Marge here at this hospital, as the swelling has gone down considerably and they are hopeful she will soon exit the coma. Alsace went up another notch on Sally's "reason to like" scale, since she found out he had purchased a very good medical insurance policy on himself and Marge before making the trip here. She doesn't need to know that he bought the policy in case there was an accident related to him spending so much time on a tournament fishing boat and had added Marge for a small additional charge.

On the fourth day after Sally has been at Marge's bedside, relieved at times by Alsace and Gio, Marge wakes up and doesn't remember any recent happenings and wonders who the strange man is that's sleeping in the chair next to her bed. Sally and Gio come in and see Alsace sleeping and notice that Marge's eyes are open.

"Marge, Marge, thank god you are awake. Gio, please go get a nurse."

Gio scrambles out of the room and Sally grabs Marge's hand and tells her, you've had a nasty bump on the head, do you remember what happened?"

Marge just stares at Sally, while her eyes are fluttering all around the room. Marge tries to speak, but nothing much comes out, just some guttural noises. She coughs and puts her free hand up to her head to touch the excruciating pain. "Do you know who I am?"

Marge clears her throat, which sends her head pounding again.

"You....you are my friend Sally, right?"

"Yes, thank god."

Marge now puts a hand on both sides of her head as if she is holding it together.

"Every time I talk, my head just pounds."

"Then don't talk. You don't have to. Now that you are out of the coma, talking can wait."

Marge continues to hold her head and asks Sally, "was I in a car accident?"

"No, you've been hit on the head by one of those red clay roofing tiles, during the hurricane."

"Hurricane?"

"Yes, we're in Mexico, we were hit by Hurricane Ormando a couple of weeks ago."

Marge doses off. Soon she opens her eyes and asks, "how did I get to Tijuana?"

"Poor baby, you're not in Tijuana, you're in Cabo San Lucas. No more talking for now, I'm thrilled you're better, just get some rest and we can talk later."

Marge puts her hands down onto the covers and closes her eyes and is soon sleeping.

Alsace jolted awake when Sally first started talking to Marge. He's been sitting quietly, not wishing to complicate the conversation further.

"It's wonderful that she's come around. I was afraid to say anything to confuse her further."

"Thank goodness you had the foresight to purchase vacation medical insurance. Something I would never have thought of doing. This is better than being stuck in Dallas, knowing that we still had to get her home."

Alsace looks up and says, "here comes Gio."

"Where is the nurse?"

"I sent for Nurse Compton. There is no sense in trying to talk with anyone without her being here to translate."

Gio and Sally wait in the hallway. Alsace excuses himself on the premise that she won't know who he is anyway. Marge's doctor passes hurriedly by and when he returns nurse Compton is there.

"He says that he woke her. That she is doing quite well and that for now, her short term memory is shot. He's unsure if she will regain it or not. You can never tell in these situations. That when she wakes up next time, go get a nurse and she'll be helped out of bed and we'll see if she can walk."

58

The Sirens Are Calling

Gio has offered to stay with Marge so Sally can do some shopping and get out a while, but she insists on staying with Marge. Gio is relieved that Marge is better and begins to relax a bit. Without Sally by his side he finds himself missing Amber. He finds a map of Baja and decides to head up toward Todos Santos on the west coast of Baja. They were not hit as directly as the tip and eastern shores of Baja. Gio stops frequently to admire the beauty of the countryside. The hills are alive, not with the sound of music, but hundreds, perhaps thousands of acres of beautiful pink and purple flowers, a virtual carpet of blossoms. Gio's camera was lost in his villa and he wishes he had purchased another, if he could find one. Some businesses in Cabo were looted right after the hurricane, before the army was sent in to re-establish law and order.

Gio stops often to take in the contrast between the recent bounty of blooms and the starkness of the desert. Once in Todos Santos he visits art galleries and has a snack at the famed "Hotel California." Later he finds a good spot and parks his scooter and walks down the beach. The beaches here are less rocky than Cabo but there are still numerous outcroppings and stones underfoot mixed with sand. Gio walks a couple of miles, searching for sea shells and any thought of finding some ambergris is the furthest thing from his mind. Soon he sees something swirling around among the rocks as the surf pounds into the shore. After a bit of effort he grabs the object, and nearly falls into the sea. He rubs the small object between his index finger and thumb. It is waxy and then he sniffs it. How he wishes Amber was here. He would know if this was genuine ambergris. Gio asks himself, 'am I not an expert on ambergris? Surely I am. I found a whole suitcase of it. I saved the beach house with it. If I am sure this is the real thing, then isn't it truly the real thing?' Then he thinks of the big ball of grease and has to chuckle remembering Sally saying, "you really wanted your big ball of grease back." That was a good joke on him. He feels a little sad for Fred, thinking that he could have been a good contributor to society if he had tried. Never mind, he thinks, he was a killer and thief. Then he remembers the camera he "stole" from Fred. He's glad he left it at home, otherwise, it would be lost as well.

Gio purchases some fruit from a roadside stand and heads south toward Cabo. It has been a good day. The first good day since the hurricane. Some young women in an open-top jeep pass him and honk their horn and wave. They are in their swimming suits and Gio's penis jumps a little. Sally has had no interest in sex since Ormando passed through. Gio understands why but it doesn't stop his buildup of cravings. He honks his horn back, thinking how surprised the young women would be to see such an old guy under the fancy helmet he is wearing. The girls soon turn off the main road and onto a one lane private drive. Gio can see a large villa down by the ocean with blue water glistening from the pool. He passes through several desert washes, where the huge volume of the hurricane rain pooled and rushed to the sea. The paved road is gone in these areas, replaced by loose gravel, the enemy of all motorcyclists. He rides at a crawl with his feet out to protect against flipping the scooter. It had only happened to him once since he started riding scooters years ago. So he's not taking any chances. It is a strange feeling riding along in the humid desert air. Gio figures in another week the whole tip of the peninsula will finally dry out from the rain and the humidity will be gone and things back to normal. The blooming carpets of flowers will dry out and blow away, spreading the seeds into the sand where they will wait patiently until Ormando's brothers or sisters decide to pay Baja a visit, it could be decades, unless "global warming" is changing the weather patterns here forever.

Gio heads down a rocky hill and his scooter starts to go sideways, slipping on the gravel. Gio quickly applies the back brake and snaps the bike parallel to the road again and accelerates just enough so the tires can aggressively push the gravel aside. It scares him a little but a warm glow of pride and admiration comes over him that he responded so quickly to what could have been a very nasty accident. He makes the next curve in the road and slows way down as there is an old pickup truck parked in the road with the hood up and steam rising in great columns reaching for the sky.

Gio goes around the truck, kills the motor on the scooter and puts his foot on the center stand foot rest and applies all his weight to lift the bike up and stabilize it. As he walks toward the truck he sees a giant of a man hunkered over the engine, touching things and pulling his hands back to avoid a serious burn, while rapid firing Spanish curse words. The man doesn't seem to have noticed Gio and he is afraid to walk up behind the agitated mechanic. Gio moves to the middle of the road and the man's head spins around. He says something in Spanish which Gio guesses would be something like, "where in the fuck did you come from?" Gio walks over and looks in the engine compartment. The radiator cap is off and the steam is blowing out of the opening. The man points his finger and Gio peers inside a bit and sees there is busted water hose.

Gio motions toward the scooter with his finger, "¿Usted Y yo vamanous Todos Santos?"

"Sí, muchos gracias."

Giant and average man walk to the scooter. Average man grabs his helmet, puts it on and is about to step through and mount the seat when the giant grabs him by the arm and points to the passenger part of the seat.

"No, no, no, Gio nearly shouts, the insurance doesn't cover other drivers." But it's of no use, Gio can tell. Gio points to himself and says, "Gio." The giant touches his own chest and says, "Pedro Rodriguez Arturo Mendez."

Pedro mounts the bike, Gio settles in behind him and Pedro pushes the bike off it's stand, accelerates slowly to start the turn and then guns it and soon they are back in Todos Santos. Pedro speeds through the town like a maniac, Gio thinks. Pedro pulls up in front of a sort of general store. Pedro mills around and picks up a roll of friction tape and a water bag. Gio touches Pedro's arm and points to a rack of water hoses high on the wall. Pedro shakes his head, rubs his thumb and middle finger together and says, "no dinero." Gio takes the tape from Pedro's hand and puts it back on the shelf, pulls his wallet out and says, "yo." Pedro goes over to the wall and picks a hose out, not noticing the ladder there, he easily plucks the hose from it's perch. Gio walks over and points to the shiny new hose clamps. Pedro selects two. Gio pays for it on his credit card.

As they leave the store Gio notices an outdoor café just up the street, he points to It and says, "comida."

They have a quick meal of fish and rice and a couple of beers. On the way back Pedro sees a faucet on the back of a garage down an alley way and quickly fills the water bag with about three gallons of water. Gio puts the hose and clamps in the seat compartment of the scooter and they mount up. Pedro picks the water bag up and puts it on the floor and wedges it between his knees. The ride back is just as hair raising. They work together to replace the hose. The engine has cooled off and Pedro is able to fill the radiator. The truck starts right up. Pedro and Gio look at the engine to see if there are any leaks. Pedro turns to Gio, pulls a knife from his waistband and says, "Tu dinero tu vida!" Your money or your life! Gio shudders and pulls his wallet out. Pedro returns the knife to his waistband and starts laughing his head off. He points at the water hose, to the bike, to Gio's wallet and motions like he is eating. Gio thinks, oh so fucking funny to rob a guy that just helped you, but Pedro's laugh is contagious and soon both men are laughing. Pedro grabs Gio's right hand and shakes it and says many times, "muchas gracias, muchas gracias and then he points to the sky and crosses his heart. Gio lets Pedro go on ahead and follows at a distance to avoid all the dust that can be kicked up since the hurricane.

Now back in Cabo San Lucas Gio stops at a store to see if he can find a cheap camera as he wants to capture the temporary beauty of this place and take it home with him. It is an "Americanized" store, with items displayed on shelves and in locked glass cases and Gio can tell that there will be no bargaining with the owner for a better deal. Fine by me, Gio thinks, I'm not too keen on working for a better price anyway. He finds a small digital camera and is able to use one of his credit cards to purchase it. Then he thinks, 'aw, fuck, the resort has my credit card on file. What if they put charges through for the extra time we stayed there?' He, nor Jack or Jim had thought of this. Time will tell on that one.

Gio arrives at the B & B to find Sally in the shower. He quickly undresses and joins her. Gio pleasures her from the back with the water streaming and steaming down their bodies. It is the most delicious thing they've experienced in weeks. Soon they have dried and are lying on the bed.

"I have a surprise for you."

"I thought I just got it in the shower."

"Nope." Gio reaches over and pulls something from his pocket and hands it to Sally."

Her eyes bug out a little and she feels the texture and sniffs it and says, "you've got to be kidding me. Did you buy this from someone?"

"Nope, found it up by Todos Santos."

"Where is that?"

"Oh, a little town about thirty or forty miles up the west coast. You know the song, "Hotel California."

"Yes."

"I saw it and I had a snack there, and then I walked the beach for a couple of hours and I found this."

242

"Do you think there is more there?"

"Don't know. So in your expert opinion, do you think it is the real thing."

"Absolutely. Do you have any doubts."

"No, but it seems a little strange, I never dreamed I'd ever find any again, ever."

"So while I was sitting with Marge you were out exploring."

"Yep, I was restless. What made you decide to leave the hospital?"

"Well I felt really gritty and dirty and the good news is Marge is up and walking, albeit slowly, and everything seems to be working, except she hasn't a clue who Alsace is and was calling him, "that strange man." They both laugh.

"It's so good to see you smiling again."

"You too."

"So, what about me, does she remember me?"

"Yes, but only when we first met. The doctor said that she may get some more memories back but will probably never remember the hurricane and when she got bonked on the head."

"That's probably just as well. So, she doesn't remember Alsace. That's a real hoot!"

"And, they were both worried about dumping each other." They both laugh again.

"Isn't life strange?"

"It is indeed."

"I'm hungry as a horse and tired of hospital food, which is way different here than at home, but still, not so great."

"Well, me too. I could eat another horse. Shall we stop by the hospital on our way or after we eat. You're not going to believe what happened to me on the road today!"

"Let's do it after we eat, I may take some food to Marge."

"I know just the place Madam, I saw it on the way out-of-town this morning. So she doesn't remember Alsace, that's a riot, do you think she's faking it?"

"I doubt that, you know, she's not out of the woods yet. The doctor said her recovery after being out so long is amazing, but we still have to worry about blood clots and the long term results of a serious concussion."

They get dressed and share a big hug before walking out the door.

"We'd better go you dirty old man, I feel something that can only lead to trouble."

"I think I could go again."

"When we get back."

Gio puts out his hand to shake on it. Sally just laughs and out the door they go.

59

Claim Jumpers

After a day patrolling the beaches, Gio has returned to the B & B, showered and is enjoying a cup of tea. Sally comes in, gives Gio a kiss on the forehead and asks, "is there another tea bag?"

"Yes several, different kinds."

Sally loads the tiny coffee maker with a green tea bag and says, "you look tired, any luck today?"

"First, how's Marge doing?"

"She's the same. She is still ambling off course when she walks down the hall. Something on her left side isn't quite right. She's been talking about God a lot. As far as I've ever known, she was a near atheist."

"An agnostic?"

"I can't even say that for sure, yeah, I guess that could be accurate."

"That isn't that surprising. I think it is a characteristic of folks that have had serious head injuries."

"Really? How do you know that?"

"I read a book a long time ago about a guy that became a believer after a car crash. He was in a coma also and ended up founding a church. I think he was sort of a religious phenomenon in his local area."

"Well, I hope she's not headed in that direction. Although, that would be better than lying in a coma for months and then dying. Howard had a friend that did just that."

"You're not going to believe what happened today."

"Try me, I'm all ears."

"Well, you remember Ryan's brother Bryan and his friend Jordan?"

"Of course."

"Well, they are here in Cabo. I ran into them on the beach today."

"What are they doing here? Trying to score some dope or exotic animals?"

"They were looking for ambergris!"

"How did they even get here, and why would they even know to come here?"

"My thoughts exactly." Gio finishes his tea and washes the cup out and turns it upside down on the circular tray. "They told me that they drove down in that old white van the twins had. It took them three days of hard driving. They received an email from Agnes saying that the hurricane had stirred up some ambergris near Cabo and that they should consider going there. That she received word that some was being found after the big storm."

"How would she know that?"

"My thoughts exactly. I told Alsace about it the day after I found the second piece, on a beach near here. I tried to talk him into going with me. He said he had no interest in finding it, only in protecting it. He would have had to say something to Agnes about it, that's the only way she could have known."

"Wow, here I just recently warmed up to him."

"I got to thinking. After I sent that sample to her after our initial contact, there soon seemed to be lots of people looking for it. That was the reason I started pushing that stupid baby carriage, so people wouldn't question what I was doing. And, I'm also thinking; why wouldn't she? Especially if she knows it is all coming to her. As far as she is concerned, the more the merrier."

"Do you think it is possible that she has done business with someone down here before, and that's how she knew?"

"That would be great, at least then I wouldn't have to be pissed at Alsace. Right now I think he contacted her. The reason is, he told me yesterday that if the airport didn't open soon he was going to have to drive out of here. Because, Agnes is going to New Zealand and he's going to join her. She goes there a couple of times a year. Apparently a lot of ambergris comes ashore there."

"So, what are you going to do?"

"Well, I have to say something to Alsace. But I've got to tell you, I don't have the drive to go out there day-in and day-out to gather it up like I did when I was working to save the beach house. That's hard work for an old man and I've got to tell you, this hurricane and all the other shit we've been through the last few months seems to be taking a toll on me."

"You'll be fine, once we're back home and into a routine."

"I suppose you are right. I avoided wealth and contact with criminals my whole life and then in retirement."

"You met me."

"Point well made. Sorry to drone on about this. I'm just disappointed that Alsace would put his employer ahead of our friendship. I'm having lunch with Alsace tomorrow and I told Jack that if he got back from La Paz by then to join us."

"Since you are not interested in going all out for ambergris this time, maybe you should let it slide. Is it possible he told her about it, not knowing that she would contact others?"

"So now you are Alsace's protector?"

"I've certainly warmed up to him by the way he has handled this situation with Marge."

"You are right, it's not that important, but I've got to say something. Am I wrong to feel betrayed?"

"I understand your feelings, time will tell."

60

A Revealing Lunch

"I never gave it a thought Gio. I was just happy for you and told her about it. I got an email asking me to call her about going to New Zealand. That's a pretty regular trip we make. I'm sorry, I had no idea that she would tell the world about it."

"Well, in fairness, I think I tipped her off back home when I sent my first sample to her. I can see now that people I had never seen on the beach before started showing up. Live and learn, quite frankly, I don't have the drive to put much effort in it now. Before, it was all about saving the beach house."

"So, are we good Gio? I value your friendship very much. I didn't realize what I was causing by telling her."

"We're good. If I have a beef it is with Agnes."

"Say that again. If you have a cow with Agnes?" Alsace sings out with a hearty laugh.

"Another American expression Alsace."

Jack comes into the restaurant and looks around for Gio, as Gio hales him over to their table. Jack and Alsace were introduced a few days ago and seem to genuinely like each other.

"How's your friend doing, guys, is she still improving?"

"Yes, she's continuing to improve, but it's going to take a while to get back to normal."

"What's normal for us old folks?"

"Good point, I don't have that excuse when I do dumb things." Gio quips.

As he has been speaking Jack has opened his laptop computer and put a small electronic card into a slot and soon has a picture gallery pulled up.

"Here are the pictures I took in La Paz." Jack starts clicking through the pictures, stopping on certain ones to tell the men favorable things he found there in regard to Randolph Tires building a factory there.

"Whoa, back up." Gio comments. "One more, hold it there." Gio puts his face close to the screen.

"What's up Gio, what are you looking for?"

"Alsace, look at this, what do you see?"

"Let's see, a bunch of boats all destroyed and mixed up together."

"Look right here!" Gio touches the screen.

"Oh, I see it."

"O.K. gentlemen, clue me in, what are you seeing?"

"See that stern of a boat?"

"Yes, what about it?"

"It says "El Capitan.""

"You know that name?"

"Yes we do."

"It doesn't look to me like any of the rest of the boat is there, it's as if just the stern was washed in from the sea."

"Do you think that's it?" Alsace asks.

"I'm sure, and here is why." Gio points to the picture and looks at Jack and says, "can you make this bigger?"

Jack double-clicks on the image and it goes full screen. See that Dallas Cowboys' sticker under the second "A"? I remember that being on his boat, I'm sure of it."

Alsace reaches down deep in his pocket and pulls out a memory card, and says, "I've been carrying this thing around with me for weeks and I keep forgetting to give it to you Gio. It's the video you took for the contest. They copied it and gave it back to me, I apologize. He hands the card to Jack, who brushes some pocket lint off the memory card and pops it into his computer. And, sure enough, there it is, the Dallas Cowboys' sticker. They have confirmed that the El Capitan sails no more.

As Gio and Alsace high five each other Jack asks, "Am I getting this right? You guys are celebrating the sinking of a boat in the hurricane?"

"You got it! Do you really think it was sunk. Do you think there could have been any survivors?"

"The harbor chief in La Paz told me that there were lots of people from Cabo that went up into the Sea of Cortez, thinking they could save their boats. Because the water is much colder there they thought the hurricane would fizzle out. It was a big mistake, because the hurricane's eye went right up through there and some said the eye wall produced giant waves, over a hundred feet, not one person is known to have survived being out-to-sea there."

Alsace and Gio high five again and tell Jack the entire story, both looking at the other knowingly and each stopping prior to El Capitan's henchmen attacking them.

61

Reality Check

"But Ryan, I wanted to be here by the ocean, I feel like I'll be able to study better here and I love the town, the ambiance." Amazing, that is so much better than, "but Ryan, I like, like it here by like an ocean, I like could study better, I like, like the town......." And Lynn has managed this subtle change in such a short time!

"Lynn can't you tell already, this will be a nightmare. We'll be spending all of our time driving there and back and waiting for hours on campus while one of us has a late class. If you are serious about this, we have to arrange our lives for a maximum effort. Even the preparatory biology classes are really hard, we don't need the added aggravation of commuting."

"I know you are right, it's just going to take a little time for me to adjust my thinking. There is complete silence until Amber drops his leash on the floor in front of Lynn. "Guess I'll take him out."

After walking Amber Lynn tells Ryan, "O.K., I can see you're right, but how is it possible for us to find a decent and affordable place near the campus at this late date?"

"That is already resolved. Professor Branson has a third floor apartment in his house. He stopped renting to students several years ago because his wife couldn't handle the noise and commotion. She passed away a couple of years ago and he actually enjoys having "mature" students around. The rent is cheap and it will include kitchen privileges."

"Why didn't you just tell me you already had it arranged?"

"I wanted you to come to the same conclusion I did. Plus, just imagine being in the same house with the esteemed Professor Branson. I'd say he is better than Google."

"When can we move in?"

"As soon as we paint the walls and the new carpet is down."

"So we are painting? Thanks so much for volunteering me." Lynn grabs Ryan by the collars of his shirt and pulls him to her, like a bully about to threaten his prey. She kisses him and asks, what are we going to do with the mutt, if my uncle isn't back by then?"

"We'll work it out, I'm sure they will be back soon. I heard on the news that regular airline flights will resume next week. Sally's friend is still in the hospital, so I don't know how that will affect them. You'll see, by the time we finish the painting and the carpet is in, it will work out."

62

Such Sweet Sorrow

"One of the reasons I had Alsace get you a passport and I.D. was so you could go to New Zealand with me."

"But Aggie, I'm so in love wit' Abou and he wheel be gone by the time we come bak."

"And, pray tell, how would you know what love feels like?"

"A-bou A-bou- ba-car, I love to sez 'es nim. I never felt thes whay before Aggie. 'es goin' to South America and then to Jamaica. 'es manager seez he es becomin' a international singing sensation. I kin see in mi mind tha beeg lemon-zine pullin' in and how mi whole fam-ley could be so amazed at da little Tekeysia."

"So, it is more about fame and prestige than love?"

"Don' you see? It is about all deez tings. I love him and he has as-ked me to go."

"And, does he love you?"

"He seez that he does and it doesn't hurt that he ess hung like a donkey." Tekeysia gives Agnes her best mischievous grin.

The fact that Tekeysia doesn't just disappear from Agnes' life speaks volumes for the respect Tekeysia has for her, strangely, as a mother figure.

"Please Aggie, give me yo'r blessin'."

"I will be leaving in three days. I expect you to spend two of those days with me."

Tekeysia jumps up and down and kisses Agnes deeply. "Oh, tank you so much Aggie, I wheel make this next two days the very best for you!"

63

Slow Boat to San Diego

It's the fifth week since the peril of Ormando and Alsace, Jack and Gio have fallen into the habit of having breakfast together early every morning. The B & B where they are staying offers anything from omelets, slathered with hot sauce or not, to cranberry and walnut muffins. Gio gets a big breakfast with the boys and when Sally and Val come down later he nibbles at the various sweets washed down with lots more strong coffee. Sally then heads over to the hospital and Gio sometimes goes. "The boys" have shared enough of their lives so that there is a certain familiarity in their conversation akin to being old friends.

This morning Jack is relating information he obtained from some of the politicians of La Paz and has some very interesting information for Gio.

"Well, Gio, I may have some good news for you."

"I've won the Mexican lottery?"

"No, even better, I may have found you a sail boat."

"O.K., so what did Ormando do to this one?"

"That's just it. This boat was being stored in a huge warehouse on the outskirts of La Paz. It is a potential site for a small tire factory. The biggest part of the facility was not damaged to any great degree and that's where the boat has been stored. Some wealthy guy from Dallas owns it. He bought it just as she sits and has never put her in the water. The warehouse owner says the hurricane scared the shit out of him and he no longer wants to ply the waters of the Sea of Cortez and he thinks he will sell it on the cheap."

"Hmm.... sounds interesting, did he say what the guy paid for it?"

"He did, but I'm a pretty good judge of people and I think he may have exaggerated that figure in order to build in a healthy commission for himself."

"He's a boat broker?"

"Naw, just a guy trying to sell his warehouse, his land, and trying to pick up a little extra cash."

"Let me talk to Sally again about it. I've kind of given up the idea, after seeing the condition of most of the boats around here. Alsace, have you seen the captain of our fishing boat since the hurricane? Remember, he said he knew a couple of guys who could check out a sail boat if I found one."

"Haven't seen him Gio. The fishing contest just disappeared into the vapors after the hurricane. I'm going to be down that way later today. Remember that crappy bar we had drinks in that day?"

"Oh, yeah, when we went to check on the bait?"

"That's the one, I'll stop by there today and see if he turns up and I'll let you know tomorrow."

"Sounds good. Jack when can you go over to La Paz? I think if I were you I'd think about staying over there."

"Yeah, that's occurred to me, but we both really like it here and being with you guys, I'm still trying to give Val a nice vacation, so, I think I'm better off commuting. What time do you want to go over?"

"Can we do it later today?"

"Sure, I think so. I'd like to stop at the airport, I hear they are beginning to fly some commercial flights out of there. I want to see how soon we can fly out of here, I've done about all I can for this trip."

"Great," says Alsace, "I've got to get to Dallas or wherever I can connect to make it to New Zealand. I'm going to spend today doing some shopping. I'll have to pick up some heat when I get to New Zealand." Alsace pretends to reach inside a jacket where his shoulder holster would be.

After a little discussion, Jack decides to ride as a passenger on Gio's rented scooter. Gio has not mentioned talking to Sally about the boat, but has called her at the hospital to let her know he is checking things out at the airport. The men find out that they can book flights out starting next week, there are lots of stranded tourists that got there before them. Gio tells Jack they should wait until they talk to Alsace, that he may be able to use his Interpol credentials to get them out at any time.

Jack directs Gio off the main highway by reaching around and pointing a finger, and after several turns they have obviously reached the warehouse district. There are all kinds of boats stacked up around the harbor. Jack and Gio walk through the warehouse building and Jack points to the boat. The boat is a 32' catamaran, blocked up for inside storage, so that they are only able to board her with a ladder. It looks like a brand new boat. Gio thinks that at $180,000, it is a steal. The toughest part is to find out if it is in the seaworthy shape as it appears to be.

"Tell me, Pedro, what is your percentage of commission?" Jack asks.

"The owner is paying me $10,000 and he owes me another $2,000 for storage costs. Plus any repairs you may need."

"And what would they be?"

"I don't know of anything, it is up to you to determine if she is seaworthy. It would be a conflict of interest if I would do a nautical survey for you and a disservice to my customer."

Jack and Gio find a nearby restaurant for lunch.

"What do you think Gio?"

"He seems like an honest man to me. He could have said he checked the boat out and that it is in perfect condition."

"I agree, what do you think of the price?"

"That's a lot of money, I would have to sell my condo in order to do it comfortably. Who knows how long that would take. Plus, I'd have to find a crew for that size of a boat, someone that I could really count on to get me to San Diego."

"There are always complications in owning things. The boats, motored boats, have always cost me more than I could project. I am only glad because of some great family trips we made when the kids were young and liked to water ski."

In a conversation later that day it is clear to Gio that Sally had thought Gio had given up on getting a sail boat. She did make a point that the boat he was looking at was much larger than he had previously talked about.

"Isn't a boat that size something you would take a long ocean voyage on?"

"Not necessarily, we could take it on short trips and find a good anchorage in a bay somewhere and spend some time there. It would be a good way to make some new friends."

"Well, you know I love the water, but I think the beach house serves the purpose for me. It is your money Gio, you can spend it how you like."

"Please don't say that. Everything we own belongs to us. Would you consider looking at it? The airport is on the way to La Paz and we need to go there, plus you might as well see La Paz while you have the chance."

"Sure, let's do it. I can visit Marge in the morning for a short time. She is really improving rapidly. They are doing some tests tomorrow to determine if she can fly home. So let's go tomorrow."

They book a passage for Gio, Sally and Marge for the next week, in hopes that Marge will be able to go and a promise from the airline ticket office that they can change the flights with a twenty-four hour notice.

When they reach the warehouse Pedro greets them with great excitement, like a car salesman who knows no deal is complete until the spouse has come in.

As they enter the warehouse Pedro raises the overhead doors and they can feel the ocean breeze pulsing through the building.

"This thing is huge!" Sally says.

Pedro scurries up the ladder and places his hand on the hull. "This is where the water will come to when the boat is in the water, so a lot of what you see here will be hidden. It will seem much smaller in the water and then when you see some bigger boats you will soon realize that it is a medium sized boat. Has the lady sailed before?"

"Not really, I've been out a couple of times with my deceased husband's clients."

Gio adds, "other than small boats I've rented, the gentleman has not sailed too much either."

Pedro hops onto the deck of the boat and gestures, "Miss Sally, please come up and see how luxurious the accommodations are. It has a head, a galley and plenty of room for living."

Gio and Sally take the tour, which is much different than Gio's first one. Pedro does not speak too much now of the size of the engines , the square feet of the sails, the draft of the hull and other technical matters. In fact, this tour, actually further convinces Gio that it really is a good idea.

Gio tells Pedro, "we just made our airline reservations for next week on our way here today. We are interested, so I'll have to go home and check on finances and probably bring someone back with me from San Diego to check the SeaScate out and help me sail it back home."

Pedro's chest drops a little and he looks a little sad, "usually Norte Americanos do not return to purchase boats, I have others that are interested in it, I suggest you move quickly if you really want it."

"I have to move some things around and make financial arrangements, if we are to purchase the boat. I can't do those things from here."

As they scooter away, Pedro is sure he will never see them again and little does Gio realize that he isn't going anywhere, any time soon.

64

Fright, But No Flight

With just a few days before they fly home Sally and Marge are staying busy buying Marge some new clothes. Before the accident Marge was what Gio's generation would have called "pleasantly plump." She has lost so much weight that her clothes just hang on her and she has decided to give them all to her favorite nurse's aid at the hospital. Marge's illness has left her in a weak condition and the girls go out an hour or two at a time and then return to the B & B so Marge can rest. Just today the doctors have given Marge the clearance to fly.

Over dinner one evening Val and Jack, Gio and Sally and Marge say their goodbyes to Alsace and he flies out the next morning to Dallas to make a connection to eventually arrive in New Zealand. With the girls shopping Gio has lots of time to scooter around and explore new areas. Gio has learned to love this mode of transport and plans to buy a scooter when he gets home. Today he is headed toward the airport and is curious as to whether his old resort has filled in the crevasse on their entrance road. Indeed they have and Gio zips down the road and turns around in the circular court yard and sees that they are just beginning to build new villas where the old ones fell into the sea. Gio is quite sure that back home there would be a six month inquiry into why this block of villas fell into the sea and then new regulations in regard to rebuilding, but this is Mexico, and a fistful of dollars grease the wheels of progress quite well. Gio resists a temptation to stop and look over the cliff to see if any salvage work has been done or if the sea has just battered the fallen building into oblivion. He is quite sure that his old nemesis Jesus has fattened the crab population far beyond their wildest crab dreams. All of the tourist industry is working hard to be ready when the whales come south for the winter. It is their best hope to lure tourists here and put Ormando behind them.

263

Gio has enjoyed this great adventure he has been on since meeting Sally, but he also is looking forward to getting back home and settling into a routine. He is looking forward to seeing Amber and taking him for walks and maybe even occasionally showing folks Amber's tricks. Whether he buys the boat or not he will need to sell his condo and he is so glad that Lynn and Ryan have decided to move near the campus. It would have been a worry to have a relative living in his condo.

As the day of departure draws near there is a flurry of activity. It seems that in their accidental residence they have accumulated more "things" than they had packed for their honeymoon. The cleaning staff at their B & B is bestowed with many and sundry gifts, an appreciation of their services that they have seldom realized.

On the day prior to their departure Gio returns the scooter and as he is walking back to the B & B he keeps pulling the receipt out of his pocket. Jeez, he thinks, I didn't realize the insurance was going to stack up that high. Gio has plenty of money now but he often still thinks like a retiree on a limited income. "Jeez," Gio mutters to himself, "if I had a way to get it home I should have just bought one." Gio is exaggerating as the amount is only about a third of the cost to buy the Honda scooter and he would have had to purchase the expensive insurance anyway. I know, he thinks, I'll write it off on taxes. It is transportation cost in pursuit of my career, "professional ambergris gatherer." Good luck with that one Gio!

They take a cab to the airport, arriving three hours early rather than the four hours the airlines recommended. Gio gets the luggage all lined up and Marge goes first, then Sally, it's the usual routine until the clerk pulls Gio's info up on the computer screen.

"Sir, would you mind stepping over to that vacant counter? It is going to be a few minutes."

"What seems to be the problem, I'm travelling with them."

"Sir, we have an irregularity, now please step aside so I can resume clearing passengers."

Gio looks at Sally and Marge, shrugs his shoulders and turns the palm of his hands up and raises his arms.

Sally and Marge head to the waiting area followed by Gio.

"Sir," the clerk shouts, "I need you to please stand at the next counter, I'll be with you in a few minutes."

Gio rolls his eyes and and is thinking, what the fuck?

After the clerk checks all of the passengers in he wriggles his index finger at Gio to call him over. He pulls Gio's info up again and seems to be carefully reading the screens content.

"Mr. Valducci, it seems you are attempting to leave the country without settling your accommodations bill."

Gio pulls papers from several pockets and hands the clerk a yellow receipt. "I just took care of this a couple of hours ago."

"The unpaid bill is for a resort along the coastal highway, this receipt appears to be for a different time period at a Bed and Breakfast near downtown."

"You have got to be shitting me, those charges were paid for in advance."

"Let me look again. Sir, these charges are for an additional three weeks and also for food and beverages."

"I won't pay it, that time period corresponds to Hurricane Ormando, we had no water and little food and left within ten days, not three weeks."

"So, you do admit you were there and overstayed your initial booking?"

"This is bullshit, I'm not paying it!"

"Fine, but you won't be leaving Mexico until you clear this matter up."

Gio stomps off and joins Sally and Marge. "Do you believe this shit? They said that......"

"We heard darling, we'll just have to delay our return."

"We can't do that, Marge needs to get back home to get checked out by real doctors and we gave our things away. You guys go ahead. It surely won't take more than a day or two for me to clean this up, it's extortion for heaven's sake. I've always loved coming to Mexico, but these Mexicans here are different, not warm and friendly like the rest of Mexico, for Christ's sake this peninsula is more like a fucking island, the origin of a different species."

"Settle down honey, it's going to be O. K. I do think you are right, we should get Marge home and in good hands, but I do think she got excellent care at the hospital here. Just because something bad happened doesn't mean everything has turned sour."

Marge is pretending she is not here, quiet as she can be and she's thinking, oh, good, I'll have Sally to myself for a few days.

However, this is Mexico and just because it is close by and familiar belies the fact that; YOU ARE IN A FOREIGN

COUNTRY! "But, I have my rights!" Yes sir, and they'll be waiting for you when you return to San Diego.

In an hour or so the clerk comes over and tells Gio, "just sit tight Mr. Valducci, I have someone on the way here to help you, it won't be long."

The departure time arrives and goodbyes are said and Gio gets a hug and kiss from Sally, who says, "call me this evening on the land line, O.K.?"

"Sure."

Marge gives Gio a pat on the back and says, "hang in there Gio, you'll probably have this resolved and be on the next flight."

But he will not, nor the next one after that and it is lucky that the girls were way up in the air when the police came, slapped cuffs on Gio's wrists with a stern warning, "do not try to escape, it will only make things harder on you."

As Gio is led away he vows never to set foot on Mexican soil again. It is kind of like getting really ill after eating a certain kind of food and though you're sure the food was fine you just will never eat that food again.

65

Jail or Prison?

It depends on who you ask. In the United States, generally, jail is where people awaiting charges or awaiting their trial are kept. Prison is where people go after conviction to serve their time.

Mexico is different. How so? It's impossible to say. Most bastions of incarceration are like small cities run by gang bosses, where anything goes as long as your gang boss approves it. Just imagine then: a bastion of incarceration that was hit with a category 4 hurricane and every prisoner who wanted to, just ran away.

There are sexual predators of course. They hang together and share pleasures and rape men that appeal to them. Even the prisoners that on the outside were one hundred percent heterosexual may see a new young prisoner, referred to as "fresh meat," bend over to pick something up and be reminded of their daughter, niece or some female family member they have found pleasure with. Since many of the hardened criminal inmates escaped during the hurricane there are lots of petty thieves and opportunists here that may not have committed their crimes without the melee.

Gio's greatest advantage is his age. The inmates don't have a name for it, but if they did it probably be something like, "old spoiled meat."

It is Gio's fifth day of incarceration and exactly no one who could help him knows he is here. Sally has called the B & B where they stayed and found that Gio never checked back in. After two hours of internet and phone work Sally finally found the place where Gio rented the scooter and they have not seen him either.

From day one other prisoners have taken Gio's food and he has already learned to wolf down as much as possible before sitting down at the table. Gio doesn't have a gang affiliation and doesn't want one as he is sure that at any moment a guard will come get him and give him his possessions and let him walk out of the clangy door. Prisoners come in two varieties; muscular and fat or very skinny, so that Gio can see he isn't the only one surrendering food.

On this fifth day Gio is seated at a table that is unoccupied and hoping to finish his lunch when another tray flops down next to him. Gio doesn't look at his new table mate but sees his hand enter his space and pick up his plate. Gio hears some shuffling and looks over to see the man who took his plate being lifted into the air by a huge single hand around his neck. The giant hand tosses the man aside and its owner sits down in the man's chair and puts Gio's plate back on his tray.

"Buenas dias Gio."

Gio can't believe his eyes, it is Pedro Rodriguez Arturo Mendez, the man he helped with his busted water hose. This one act was not as great as being set free, but the next best thing. In Gio's mind he renames his new hero: Brutus Protectus.

Because of the language barrier, neither man is quite clear on why the other is incarcerated. But Gio feels relatively safe now and he can eat!

Pedro has commandeered a nice little corner space in the old army barracks serving as a temporary jail and not only is Gio being well nourished now but he can relax a bit. On his second day with Pedro Gio has managed to inform Pedro that if he can help him get out of this place, he will help Pedro to do the same.

Gio spends hours on end trying to remember the military officer's name who came to the resort. Martial Law is still in effect and Gio is certain that if he can get word to that captain he will at least respond and Gio will be able to tell him the whole story in English.

Gio is thinking, come on you old senile fool what was his name? Twenty years ago the name would have popped up instantly. So frustrating! On the third day of Gio's frustration an army guard came into their building and shouted, "Fernando Martinez, Fernando Martinez!" A prisoner came forward and Gio is smiling because the second time the guard said Fernando, it popped into his head, "Captain Fernando Gomez!"

"That's it Pedro, that's it!" It took a couple of days for the army sergeant that spoke a little English to show up at their building.

"Do you know Captain Fernando Gomez?"

"Yes, he is the Company Commander. How is it that you know his name?"

"I, and others helped him to distribute food after Ormando. My name is written here and I've written him a note, can you please get it to him?"

"How much will you pay for this service?"

"What do you think is fair?"

"Did you have dineros when you were arrested?"

"Yes, maybe a hundred dollars or so."

"O.K., I will get your pocket book and bring it to you, it may take a couple of days, but I will do it."

It has now been three days and Gio is beginning to wonder. He has seen the guard twice in passing, but he ignored Gio and refused to talk to him. On the fourth day the guard came to Gio, pushed him behind a door and gave him his wallet. It comes as no surprise to Gio that the money is gone, but his credit and debit card and driver's license is in there and the guard has a passport in his hand.

The guard taps the debit card with his index finger, "is good?"

"It should be."

"Follow me."

Gio follows the guard as they walk through the large army depot that has been turned into a place of incarceration.

They are soon on the street with Gio's resisting the urge to run away. After a couple of blocks they find an ATM.

"One-hundred, right?" Gio asks.

"Make it two-hundred."

"O.K. how about I make it five hundred and you give me my passport and let me go free?"

"O.K., make it a thousand."

"Sir, I don't have that much in my account, I spent most of it on this trip."

The guard mulls this over and touches his right hand to his chin. "I hope you know that it may be weeks, months, maybe even years before you see a judge."

"How about Seven-fifty?"

271

"O.K., do it. If you are arrested again I will deny that this ever happened."

As Gio enters the numbers into the machine he is praying, just imagine, an atheist is praying that Sally hasn't put a hold on his card. The ATM spits out seven crisp one hundred dollar bills and one fifty. Gio hands the guard the money.

"It has been a pleasure doing business with you."

As the guard walks away Gio is wondering how long it would take a lower ranking soldier to earn that much money. Gio is glad that he is wearing the same clothes as when he was arrested, so he can blend in, although he is sure he reeks to high heaven, having not bathed since the day he was arrested.

Gio takes some alley ways and after about forty-five minutes he has made his way to the area where the B & B is located. He goes to a nearby clothing store and buys a couple of shirts, a pair of cargo shorts, underwear and socks. He is worried about going back to the B & B, but he also trusts the owners over dealing with strangers.

Sanchez and Maria are very surprised but glad to see him and they serve him a fine cup of coffee. Gio explains what happened and they are as outraged as he. Maria soon hands him a key and says, "shower please!"

After a twenty minute hot shower Gio feels wonderful, but he is still a fugitive and his mind is in a quandary about what to do about Pedro. If he had even a clue that the army guard would let him go he would have tried to get Pedro out as well.

Gio gets a little bottle of whisky from the fridge and sits at the table just feeling like he maybe has his life back. He forgot to ask Maria and Sanchez if Jack and Val are still here. Then he remembers they were scheduled to leave the next day after Sally and Marge. Then it hit him, was Jack given the same shakedown as he was? Sally must be wild with fear. At that thought he picks up the phone and calls Sally on the land line, a number he just barely remembered. He gets a recording and starts to hang up the phone and then says, "Sally, I'm O.K., I just got out of jail, escaped actually and I'll call you this evening at 6 p.m., on this phone."

Try as he may Gio is unable to remember Sally's cell phone number as he had always just used the contact list on his "smart phone." Gio eats his evening meal in his room. At six o'clock he calls the land line and Sally answers.

"Sally?"

"Yes Gio, oh my god, what has happened to you?"

"As you know, I refused to pay that phony bill. When they came and got me I thought I might negotiate, then they took me straight to jail."

"Oh my god."

Believe me, if I had known what was really happening I would have gladly paid that bill."

"Were you beaten?"

"No, nothing like that. Inmates kept taking my food until Pedro came along and rescued me."

"Pedro?"

"Yeah, remember the guy that I bought the radiator hose for?"

"Right, just goes to show , what goes around, comes around."

"Yeah, really. Here's the deal, I talked to Sanchez and he is sure that the army or police won't even be looking for me. He said as long as I don't try to fly out of here I'll be safe."

"Sounds like you just went from the small jail to a bigger one, although I'm sure it is wonderful to get out of that hellhole."

"You are so right, now I have to figure out how I can get Pedro out of there."

"Gio, what's wrong with you? I mean, don't you think you are even-up? You helped him and he helped protect you, sounds like even-steven to me."

"I suppose, when you put it that way, I'll have to think on that. How is Marge doing?"

"They checked her out at St. Joseph's and said that the Mexican doctors did a great job. But now that we are back here I can see that she's not like she used to be. I can't even explain it. The day she got out of the hospital she started painting and remember all those paintings in her gallery?

"You mean all those fields of flowers?"

"Yes, exactly, now she is painting with this heart of darkness."

"Like what?"

"Well, the latest one shows a scene of a border crossing and there is a man hanging by the neck from a tree."

"Geezo, I hope she's not foretelling my trip home. Since I can't fly I'll have to somehow drive."

"Won't they be looking for you at the border?"

"Sanchez says not. The only way they control non-payment is by airline departures. It may be a while before I can figure out a safe way to get back home."

"Just make sure you call me every day, twice if you can."

"I will, I promise at least once a day. Give me your cell phone number, I never memorized it."

Gio gets her number and they say their devotions of love and he hangs up the phone. Having relaxed after his conversation with Sally, he realizes how exhausted he is from all the stress of being incarcerated. Gio goes to bed at 7 p.m. and sleeps for twelve hours.

The first thing Gio thinks about when he wakes up is to take a shower. It is not needed of course since he scrubbed for twenty minutes yesterday but he is as gleeful as those elephants he's seen in nature films; splashing and squirting and trumpeting with their trunks. As the water splashes over him he is thinking of Sally and gets an erection and he splashes and strokes and soon squirts from his trunk, such a pity that his trunk didn't emit a trumpet sound.

66

An Expatriate Yearns for Home

It is Gio's third day of freedom. He walks down to the harbor. The walking feels good and he realizes having the scooter had cut back on the number of long walks he would have taken. Gio reaches for a longer stride and he can feel his toes completing the step, stretching his feet out and it feels good.

He has skipped his free breakfast at the B & B in search of something different and new company. He passes a man, "buenos dias."

"Buenos dias."

Both men pause just slightly but continue on. Gio is thinking. I feel like I know that guy. But he can't come up with it.

Gio arrives at the harbor, which is enshrouded in a morning mist and he walks along checking out the boats. There are lots of empty slips as the majority of boats have been salvaged or sent away for repair. Gio finds a nice little restaurant with outdoor seating. He is thoroughly enjoying his freedom but genuinely misses his wife. All my life without her, Gio thinks, and now we're separated. However, Gio feels full of energy and soon settles down into thinking about what to do next. Then it hits him, the guy he spoke to and they both hesitated; it was the captain of the fishing boat he was on for the contest. "Damn," Gio says aloud. Gio is thinking that he didn't recognize the captain without his captain's garb on. I would loved to have had breakfast with that guy. "Damn." He was trying to place me too, yeah, he definitely hesitated even though I'm among the thousands he's taken fishing.

As Gio finishes his breakfast he orders a Bloody Mary. Drinking alcohol this early is abnormal behavior for Gio but he is still taking in the newly restored harbor as the mist has cleared out and the sun is beaming down and it's another beautiful day.

How I wish my Sally could be here at this moment. I'd put her on the back of my scooter, drive out into the desert and fuck the living piss out of her. Something between his legs is trying to stand up and Gio quickly changes the subject in his mind and starts thinking about that painting of Marge's that Sally told him about. That thought squelches the hard-on and Gio is thinking how ominous that painting seems; a man hanging from a tree at the U. S. – Mexican border. It's nearly enough to keep him here for a while. As he looks up and down the malecón he sees two familiar faces and that phenomenon occurs where vacationing people see someone from back home, someone they would never socialize with, someone who suddenly becomes a friend in this exotic setting.

It is Bryan and Jordan. They look like hell. Unshaven, scruffy, wearing misshapen clothing that needs washing. As they draw near they smile widely and wave at Gio. Gio waves back, genuinely glad to see them, perhaps because they were his adventure mates from the past.

Bryan and Jordan sit down at Gio's table and Jordan says, "can I get one of those?"

"Me too," Bryan puts in.

Gio hales the waiter over and points at his Bloody Mary and then points to his tablemates and says, "dos."

"Are you guys hungry?"

Jordan responds, "are we ever, we've got some valuable grisrock but that doesn't help us at the moment."

"I'll buy, you guys order whatever you want." Gio says with a wide smile. The table soon looks like service for

277

three at a Roman orgy and Gio is doubting that they can eat all that food. However, fifteen minutes later it is all gone and the three men are enjoying their second Bloody Mary.

"Where's your wife?" Bryan asks.

"Well, it's quite a story."

Gio tells them everything as they sit wide-eyed in near disbelief.

"You should just have paid them man."

"Well I know that now. I just couldn't stand them ripping me off."

"Typical Mexico," Bryan responds.

"Really I haven't found that until coming to Baja. Other places I've been down here; Mazatlan, Manzanilla, Cancun, Cozumel, Puerto Vallarta and I've never had a problem before."

"You were lucky and besides the hurricane fucked a lot of things up." Jordan says.

"True, so what are you up to these days? Is it time to go home?"

"Yep, we've just got to raise some cash," Bryan informs. We're flat broke. I can't ask my parents, since my brother is so righteous now, it is putting a lot of pressure on me."

"Tell me, what was the drive down here like?"

Bryan replies, "shitty roads, lots of checkpoints. You can't drive at night because a lot of the road has no shoulder, so when a guy's old rattletrap truck gives out he leaves it in the road.   While he hitches to go get parts he doesn't want someone to crash into his truck at night so he gathers boulder size rocks and stacks them behind his truck.   No flares, no reflectors, just big rocks. It makes it insane to drive at night."

"So, could we do it in three days?"

"Oh yeah, that's doable. Hey Gio, I can fly, if you can buy." Bryan suggests.

The three men pick up their bloody glasses and make a toast, the trip has been hatched.

67

Travel Makes for Strange Bedfellows

"Sally?"

"Oh, Gio, I'm so glad you called, I seem to worry about you more each day."

"Well, you'll be happy to hear, I've got a ride and should be home in the next three or four days."

"Is it safe?"

"As safe as Mexico can be these days."

"So, are you taking a bus?"

"No, I ran into Bryan and Jordan this morning. They are flat broke, except for some ambergris. I'll be coming home in the old white van."

"Oh god, Gio, aren't you taking a chance with those two?"

"I know, I know. But what is the alternative? If I try to take a bus, they probably have the same information as the airlines. I thought of just buying a scooter and riding it home, but I'd worry all the paperwork might trip me up. So right now I think this is the only way I can do it. And believe me, I'm really missing you and I'm fed-up with the Baja and ready to relax in our seaside home."

"I sure miss you too. We're still practically on our honeymoon and separated by three or four days. Just please be careful. Oh, I know you will. Will you be able to call me every day."

"I don't know the answer to that. So if I don't call you'll know I'm unable to, but I'm thinking there should be pay phones that I can use. Just give me a few days before you start to worry. I'm putting up all the money for this trip and I feel like that gives me some control over these guys. They're not really bad people, just immature and probably spoiled. I think it will be O.K. Unless you have a better idea."

"I can't think of any. I guess it's really lucky that you ran into those guys."

"That's what I've been thinking. They need me to finance it and I need them to get me there. Also, I've thought it through and I'm leery of crossing the border with those guys. I can see a possibility that there could be some dope stashed in that old van, that they might not even know is there. I'm thinking of getting out and walking before we go through the border crossing. Once I've crossed I will have no problem phoning you. If I walk over do you think you can find your way to pick me up?"

"Well, I'll have GPS and Marge, we should be able to get there if you give me an address."

"O.K., well, just sit tight and try not too worry, with all the shit we've been through this is not that big a deal. So, if I don't talk to you before, I should be on U.S. soil in three or four days and believe me I'm going to get on my knees and kiss the terra firma."

"O.K., be careful, love you with all my heart!"

"You know I feel the same, see you in a few days."

Gio goes to a nearby store and buys a twin size air mattress with a built-in air compressor that works on 12 volt power, a couple of blankets, three water bags and a cheap ice chest. After taking his purchases back to the B & B he goes to the grocery store up the street and buys an array of lunch meats, bread, condiments and lots of packages of salty snacks for his traveling buddies.

He has paid for a room at the B & B for the boys and given them enough money to buy clothes for the trip back. Fuck, Gio is thinking, I sure wish I had just paid that fucking bill. I'd be home now instead of heading off on another adventure. But I'm still glad I didn't give those bastards a red cent. It seems that outrage trumps common sense every time.

Gio went with Bryan yesterday to get Mexican insurance on the van. Bryan and Jordan made the trip down without it and Gio is not sure how they made it through the various checkpoints without being asked but somehow they did. Gio is trying his very best to think of everything. Even without his "prison escapee" status Gio knows that one always has to be wary while traveling in Mexico.

It is evening time and Gio and "the boys" are finishing their dinner. Gio is thinking that if he had married years ago, these young men could be my sons. Well, except that they wouldn't be such knuckleheads.

"O.K. guys, I've treats for breakfast in the morning, we won't have to stop for breakfast. I want to be on the road by first light. I'll take the first shift of driving and you guys can sleep if you want to. You guys drove down here, so tell me if something doesn't make sense. Looks to me like it is about a twenty hour drive and that means we'll average a measly forty-four miles per hour overall. Does that sound about right?"

"Yep."

"O.K., well, it's a little over eight hours up to Santo Rosalia, so I figure we can stay there overnight. Then the next day on to El Rasario which is a little over seven hours, where we'll stay overnight. Then the last leg on to Tijuana is only four and one-half hours plus the time to get home. How does that sound?"

Jordan and Bryan look at each other and burst out laughing.

"What's so funny?"

Jordan speaks up, still laughing, "well Gio, we just got in the van and took off. We did get a map in San Quintin, but there is only one road all the way. We got fucked up a couple of times by the signs."

"Maybe more than a couple of times," Bryan adds, "sounds like a plan Gio."

Gio's alarm wakes him the next morning. He can see daylight has come and he misjudged the time, but he is still excited about getting an early start and to know he's actually going home.

Gio brushes his teeth, combs his hair and puts deodorant under his arms. He walks down to the boys room and quietly knocks on the door. Then he knocks a little harder. No response. Gio fears if he knocks any louder he'll wake the other guests. "Lazy bastards," he says softly with disgust.

Gio walks toward the office and hears water running that takes him to the courtyard, where Sanchez is washing down the cobblestone patio.

"Buenas dias."

"Buenas dias. Getting an early start this morning I see."

"I'm trying. Those knuckleheads won't come to the door. Can I get the key por favor?"

"Sure, follow me."

Gio puts the key in the lock and opens the door. To his surprise Bryan and Jordan are up and appear to be ready to roll.

"Did you knock?" Bryan asks.

"Yes, I didn't think you heard me."

Gio looks around the room. In an ashtray he sees the remains of a roach clip and ashes. "If you guys think I'm traveling with you and taking a chance on being jailed for dope smuggling you must be crazy."

"That was the last of it Gio, we saved it for the last night in Cabo." Jordan answers.

"You're sure?"

"Absolutely, scout's honor."

"You guys ready to roll?"

"Let's do it."

Gio dumps the ashtray into the toilet and flushes it away.

68

Revelation?

The three men make light conversation about their "Mexican experience" and Jordan announces he's going to try to get some sleep and lies down on the air mattress in the back of the van.

A couple of hours into the trip Bryan asks Gio, "what's the deal on my brother? Him going back to school. Is it just that he fell in love with that...."

"Careful," Gio interjects, "she's my niece you know."

"Oh, yeah. I forgot, O.K. So was it just that he fell in love with that nice young lady or what? I take it she's something in marine biology?"

"Actually no, Bryan, she's been just as lost as you guys. She, like you, had a good upbringing but had no direction in her life. Ryan is the one with the interest in marine biology. She did have some interest when she was a kid. I don't know, I guess with them meeting and being so strongly attracted to each other. You should have seen it Bryan, Ryan walked into the wedding tent and everyone there could see that something magical was happening. Everything just seemed to come together after that. From what you've told me I'm guessing you're pissed that he doesn't want to share Lynn with you, like you've always done."

"Not true," Bryan spouts, "well, maybe a little. But it all started after those guys tortured him and we are no longer identical."

"Possibly, but I think what really brought about the change was Ryan realized that his lifestyle had put him in that situation, it wasn't a random kidnapping."

"But I rescued him before things got even worse."

"Yes, and that was admirable but still, all that wouldn't have been necessary if you hadn't put yourself in the middle of something."

"Gio, look who's talking, you patrolled that beach with that dog and baby carriage and ended up on Fred's hit list. Come to think of it, we rescued you."

"You are so right, and that is one of the reasons I have tried to be kind to you guys and help you to get back home."

"I think we are helping each other Gio, but you are the guy with the money."

"O.K., I get it, you know really you are right, but I can tell you; if I didn't already know you guys from before, I would never have agreed to this trip."

"Well, so much for how we got here, the big question is where do I go from here?"

From the back of the van, where Jordan is trying to sleep, "hey, how about you guys go straight to hell and stop jabbering bullshit so I can go to sleep?"

Bryan looks over at Gio and says, "just ignore him." And both men laugh.

After a few minutes of silence Jordan starts snoring.

Gio says, "Bryan, let me tell you a story. It's a true story, I saw it on one of those TV magazine shows, maybe something like "Ninety Minutes."

"There was a young man whose family moved into town recently and in the fall he began his second year of junior college. As he was walking across the campus a week or so after the fall semester began, another young man came up to him and said, "how's it going?"

"Fine," he answered.

"Hey, I think I've got the right combination of players to get you to trade me one of your pristine Mickey Mantles."

Then the guy that just started school there says, "how do you know I have several Mickey Mantles, and how do you even know I'm a collector? I've never set eyes on you before in my life."

Then the other kid says, "you are," I'll just call him Joe Schmoe, because I don't remember his name. Anyway, he says, aren't you Joe Schmoe that lives in Higgins Dorm, second floor?"

"Nope, I'm Ed Badgett and we just moved here, I live with my parents on Cole Street."

The other kid says, "bullshit, let me see your I.D. Ed Badgett shows him and the other kid is dumbfounded. "There was a guy named Joe Schmoe here last year and he looks just like you except for that scar over your right eyebrow, when did you get that?"

"A few years ago, got pushed into another player at a soccer game."

The other kid says, "look I'm telling you that you have a body double and you're look-alike played soccer too. So you do have at least one pristine Mickey Mantle? Are you interested in a trade?"

"Yeah, I might be interested, but tell me more about this Joe guy."

"Well, you might run into him on campus. No, hang on, I think he did tell me he was transferring out to another school."

Gio continues his narrative, "anyway, the new kid Ed tracks Joe Schmoe's family down, who still lived in the town and when he shows up at their door, they ask him what he is doing coming home in the middle of a semester. It turns out they were identical twins, separated at birth."

"Did they know they were adopted?"

"Yes, and that at least made it easier, but they did not know they had a twin brother and neither did the parents."

"So what's your point?" Bryan asks.

"Well, all their interests were nearly the same. And my point is that if Ryan has it in him to pursue a college degree, then so do you. All you need to do is make up your mind to do it. You can't chase ambergris your whole life or some other questionable endeavor."

"What about you Gio, you seem to have done well in your pursuit?"

"Bryan, honestly, if I hadn't met Sally and she been in risk of losing the beach house, none of that would have happened."

"So you seem to be saying, again, that I just need to meet the right girl."

"I never thought of that, but I guess it wouldn't hurt anything. Ryan told me your parents are paying his tuition, I'm sure they would gladly do the same for you."

"Oh yeah, believe me, I've heard plenty about that."

"In regard to 'meeting the right girl' I would say that is a part of it and here is why: you have to chose your friends carefully. Hopefully the woman of your choice can be your best friend, therefore, maybe influencing you the most. But, you have to surround yourself with friends that have similar beliefs and values." Even though Jordan is snoring away, Gio glances over his shoulder a moment. "Just tell me, what kind of future does Jordan have? He certainly isn't capable of taking over his father's business and even if he was that sort of illegal business could be shut down at any time."

"Yes, I know what you mean. Jordan overheard his father talking to his uncle not long ago and he was saying that if the politics changed in the county government so that he could no longer bribe people that he would liquidate the entire operation and head for Hawaii. Presumably he would take Jordan with him."

"You are making it sound like Jordan was born with Down syndrome."

"I don't mean it that way, but come to think of it, the only difference is he requires less maintenance. I know hanging around with Jordan is not a good thing. He's never going to be any different than now. This trip really proved that. He wasn't really working at finding ambergris and that affected me. I probably could have doubled the amount I found but he was always just wanting to get high or screw some Mexican whores."

"Bryan, I think you know that your life is not going to be good if you don't get a proper education or some type of skill. I was a baker for forty-six years and a good one and even served the Baker's Union as shop steward and I retired with enough to choose where I wanted to go and what I wanted to do."

"We used to talk about it and I have to admit I wasn't really into it. You know all the bullshit about what you want to be when you grow up; while in high school I used to say I wanted to be an architect."

"So, you don't have an interest in being a marine biologist? No? Why do you suppose that is?"

Gio concentrates on looking ahead at the road as they come to a desert dry wash that Ormando capitalized on and took the road with him, out to sea. The roadway has been filled in with rock and gravel and has many potholes from the heavy traffic.

As they reach the other side of the dry wash and start up a slight grade Bryan answers Gio's question; "there is one big difference, Ryan has always loved being outdoors more than me. There were lots of times I would have been inside except that we just accepted we would do things together, so I went along. I would say I would be interested in research, you know, like lab research."

"Have you talked to anyone about it? I think for most schools it is too late to enroll, but you could go to universities and talk to some of the professors. Find out what the future is and maybe study toward a degree to put you on the cutting edge of some new field. How about something related to forensics in criminal matters?"

"Catching the bad guys, huh? Gio, that's something I've thought of doing before. You know I basically tracked my brother down and rescued him from those thugs, they might have killed him. It was hard to go through, but also very exciting. It also gave me great satisfaction, but when it's your brother you take risks you might otherwise not."

"They do offer degrees in criminal justice." Gio really suppresses an urge to tell Bryan about Jesus being killed as he knows there is a chance he might later regret it. "I only went to one high school class reunion. But I noticed that the guys that were sort of on the fringe of always being in some kind of trouble, seems like half of them ended up being criminals and the other half became police officers. Of course I only know this because the latter half was at the reunion and told me about the former half." Gio has to chuckle at his statement. "I think all of them could have gone either way. I think it was the excitement that they craved."

"Funny you should say that Gio, I'll have to say I sort of have noticed that same phenomenon over the years as well. I guess at this point I haven't decided which side of that fence I'm on." Bryan also chuckles a little. "But, I'll give you lots of credit Gio, I haven't had a serious conversation like this in many years. I just can't do it with mom and dad, it just always blows up in my face. One thing is; you have no reason to try to influence me. I guess you are just doing this out of the kindness of your heart and I appreciate that. I know I have to do something."

Jordan is still snoring away.

69

The Prodigal Daughter Almost Returns

Finally the day has arrived. Tekeysia's mother Elizabeth and her Aunt Consuela have Tekeysia's letter and today is the day that Abou Aboubacar is arriving in Montego Bay for the music festival. The letter came from a place called Rio de Janeiro and arrived about a week ago.

Elizabeth, Consuela and a few family members are going to the hotel where they will wait for Abou Aboubacar's arrival. Big Brenda has also joined them thinking that maybe Tekeysia can get Abou to listen to her play and sing. It could be her big break.

The hotel manager sent them outside and told them to wait there, that Abou and his entourage should arrive by limousine in an hour or so.

"Our little Tekeysia coming home in a limousine. Honestly, I thought she was probably dead, until we received the letter," Elizabeth relates.

It seems to take forever but finally they see the limos coming up the entrance to the hotel. Several uniformed hotel doormen open the limo doors and many people exit. Men and women, all dressed in the latest fashions.

Tekeysia's villagers look here and there trying to see their little Tekeysia.

No one has exited the first limo yet. It becomes obvious that it is Abou's limo and soon he will step out with Tekeysia on his arm. As Abou steps clear of the limo it is obvious he is the main attraction and they know his face from the concert posters that are plastered all over Montego Bay.

When Elizabeth does not see her daughter she pushes forward to Abou and stops him by holding onto his shoulder. "Where is Tekeysia?"

Abou looks at his manager and says, "who is this?"

"I'll take care of it Abou."

Abou's manager takes Elizabeth and Consuela into the lobby and motions for them to follow him into a nearly private area.

"Did I hear you ask, where is Tekeysia?"

"Yes, where is she, we have a letter saying she was coming today, with Abou."

"Please sit down. How do you know Tekeysia?"

"She is my daughter, this is her aunt. I am Elizabeth and this is Consuela."

"I am so sorry to be telling you, but Tekeysia is no longer with us."

"What has become of her?"

"I've never had to do this before. Three days ago Tekeysia over-dosed on heroin. We found her the next morning, she had passed away."

Elizabeth looks at Consuela and says to Abou's manager. "Did you bring her body, can we take her?"

"I'm sorry, although we are pretty sure it was too much heroin they have to do an autopsy and make a report. Mr. Aboubacar told me he will bring her here when they release the body."

"I thought she was his woman."

"As you can see Mr. Aboubacar has many lady companions. I can tell you that Tekeysia was one of his favorites."

"Will he pay for the funeral?"

"If you go to your funeral home right away, and here, give them my card. Have them call me here at the hotel and I'll make the arrangements."

Elizabeth and Consuela join the other people from their village and give them the bad news.

Elizabeth says to Consuela, "I told you I thought she was dead. So many months with no word from her and now I think I'll see her and she is well off and no, now she is dead. There is nothing we can do, let's go to the funeral home and make the arrangements. She will have a decent burial. Much better than I could provide for her. She was a willful child, always doing things her own way."

70

Walk This Way

"The boys" and Gio just had a remarkable dinner in the hotel restaurant. A variety of sea food and wonderful homemade sauces. Who would imagine eating a meal like that on the road? And in the desert?

The three men head back to their rooms, which requires a short walk outside. The moon is nearly full and makes the desert seem soft and inviting. Bryan puts out his arm to stop Jordan and stands still until Gio is a few steps ahead.

"Gio, we'll see you in the morning, we're going to take a little walk in the desert."

"Gotta get up early guys, don't get lost."

"Don't worry, we won't be long."

Gio walks to his room and doesn't turn on the light and pulls open the curtain on the patio door. He looks around at the softly lit desert and the Saguaro cacti standing at attention like so many phantom soldiers. Finally he sees Bryan and Jordan walking along slowly in conversation. Gio suspects they might be smoking a joint but he is certain he doesn't see any fire or smoke. He is hoping that Bryan is giving Jordan the talk that he gave Bryan earlier in the day.

Nope.

"What's up Bry? Are you trying to romance me by the light of the moon?"

"Fuck you, man."

"Guess so then."

"Jordan, I'm getting cold feet on this whole thing and don't want to spend the next ten years of my life in prison. I just feel like we're going to get caught."

"Cut it out man, we got all our money tied up in this. We both stand to make six or seven grand. We won't get caught. We're gonna do just what we said; make sure Gio is driving when we cross the border."

"What about the sniffer dogs?"

"And when do they bring the dogs?"

"If the driver seems nervous or evasive."

"Exactly, and Gio is gonna say we went down to work on the hurricane clean up. There are hundreds, maybe thousands of cars and trucks every day. Just you and I, a good chance they would bring the dogs, but not with Gio. The pot market is really hot right now and we should double or triple our money. Just calm down, stick with the plan. Come on man, this is all we've got."

Bryan looks out across the silent desert and hears a soothing sound drifting up from the surf in the Sea of Cortez.

"Yeah, I know, I'm busted. O.K., we have to do this."

"Let's go drink a shot of tequila in our room and get some sleep, we'll be home in a couple of days makin' money."

"Promise me one thing, if we do get caught, and I know we're not, but if it happened we tell them Gio knows nothing about it."

"Really Bryan? As I recall, he doesn't know anything about it anyway."

71

Major Help Needed

Major Ferdinand Gomez is having a busy day as usual. That's right. I said Major. Shortly after being assigned as the number one military man for the duration of the martial law, he received a well deserved promotion. It's almost as if he is the mayor of a large rural town. There is always someone jockeying for some time with him. Pleading for help if they are poor. Offering bribes if they are people of means.

Having been born poor and struggling to get an education, volunteering for what some would call dangerous missions, Major Gomez, as the purveyor of martial law has his promotion and it has invigorated him. He now feels that he will make the rank of Colonel before his retirement. A wonderful achievement for someone that came from such abject poverty. His men love him. He is though but fair. They know if they perform their jobs well and are always honest with him, they too, can move up the ranking ladder.

So when Major Gomez gets a phone call from the most northern military checkpoint that he is responsible for, he is just a little irritated. The source of his angry pause is that the checkpoint supervisor has called him in regard to a certain Gio Valducci that has been sequestered for suspicion of smuggling drugs. What kind of drugs? Well, that's just it you see; the sniffer dog has located a substance in Gio's luggage that has caused a behavior the dog handler has never seen. The dog is supposed to sit once he has located illicit materials. The dog has tried to tear the backpack apart to get to a strange substance. And once the waxy cake he was seeking fell onto the floor, the dog performed that ancient ritual of canines of turning onto his back and rubbing against the waxy cake. This ritual is usually reserved for mostly rotted dead animals found upon the trail. The behavior believed to be an ancient way of masking the canines scent as an aid to stalking prey.

The checkpoint chief tells Major Gomez:

"This man says you know him and can vouch for him, is that true?"

"Is he there in the room with you?"

"Yes."

"Please put him on the phone."

"Hello."

"Hello Gio, I hope you are continuing north until you leave Mexico behind. You seem to have a knack for getting into trouble."

"Well, just that situation at the resort, after the hurricane."

"And I got you out of jail on that debt the resort said you owed."

Gio can't speak, his mind is spinning around. He has to process this; so that asshole guard was sent to release him and he parlayed it into $750.00.

"Gio, are you there?"

"Yes, and thank you so much for getting me released. Here is my problem right now. I am headed home with a couple of other guys. Because of the hurricane there is something washing up on the beaches that was familiar to us from back in San Diego. Have you heard of Ambergris?"

"Hmm, exactly what is it?"

"It comes from whales and is used to make perfume last longer on a woman's skin. It has a unique odor and dogs go crazy when they smell it."

"And what will you do with it?"

"I have a broker who might buy it, if the quality is good enough."

"Please spell it for me, I have the amber part- is it g-r-e-a-s-e?"

"No, amber and then g-r-i-s."

"O.K., I've goggled it, hang on a minute. O.K., so basically it is some form of whale shit?"

"Yes."

"Gio, if you are taking something from a Mexican beach for profit this may be a violation of Mexican law. How much of it do you have?"

"Just a couple of small cakes of it," Gio has an idea….."in fact I have a friend that is studying to be a marine biologist and I plan to turn it over to him for research purposes."

Major Gomez recognizes this is a ploy. But it actually solves his dilemma, so he can get on with the job of running a still recovering Baja.

"O.K. Gio, you know even a cat only has nine lives. Do you think you can leave Mexico without getting into any more trouble?"

"Yes, I'll be sure of it."

"I'm going to fax the checkpoint supervisor a short letter giving you permission to remove ambergris for research purposes. You can show this letter to the border guards as well. I really like you Gio, but please go home, you are wearing out your welcome in California Sur. If I ever come to the U.S. and find myself in trouble, I expect you to take care of me!"

"Absolutely, mi casa es su casa. You can come visit me with your family."

"Do you have money you can give to the checkpoint chief? Say, fifty dollars American?"

"Yes."

"O.K., put him on the line and I will explain this to him and it may take an hour or so for me to get my secretary to fax the letter. I'm very backed-up here, but I will get my secretary on it right away."

"Thank you so much Cap…. I mean Major Gomez and congratulations on your well deserved promotion. I'll put the checkpoint chief on here and thanks again."

72

The Honeymoon is Rekindled

Armed with the research letter and still unaware of a couple of bags of marijuana. Gio has decided to cross the border with Jordan and Bryan and surprise Sally. Gio can't recall the last time he felt this excited and he has had a lot of excitement in his later life. He and "the boys" stay overnight in El Rosario. The next day, the last day of their journey, they pass easily through another military checkpoint. When the border officer starts asking questions Gio just hands him the letter and he glances at it and waves them through.

Now at the border, it's all about waiting and apprehension. It takes them over an hour as late afternoon is not the best crossing time. The border guard asks Gio the standard questions and Gio decides to show him the letter. The guard reads the letter and tells Gio, I'll be back in a few. When he returns, he says, "according to the computer this guy is a captain, not a major."

"He's in charge of the Cabo recovery and martial law, that's why they promoted him."

"Sounds like you know this guy pretty well."

"Yes, I'm retired military so we have a lot in common."

"Which branch?"

"Air Force."

The guard hands Gio the letter and says, "have a good day gentlemen."

"I didn't know you retired from the air force." Bryan inquires.

"I didn't, not sure why I said that, but we got through and that's the main idea."

"Nice move Gio."

The great crescendo of the day having been played out it leaves the three men pensive. All agree to make a pit stop for fuel, restroom and beverages. Bryan and Jordan buy ice and a case of Modelo Especial beer and put it in the cheap ice chest.

As Gio pumps the gas he shakes his head from side-to-side as he watches the boys load the beer. He yells back to them, "I thought you guys were broke."

There is a festive mood in the van as they resume their journey. No one comments but all three men are grateful that the old van has made it albeit during the consumption of many quarts of oil.

"What a fucking relief." Jordan says.

"Yeah, it feels good being back on U. S. soil." Bryan puts in.

Gio says, "shit, I forgot to get on my knees and kiss the U. S. dirt. But never mind, I doubt if my knees would take it."

"We have a special reason to celebrate, right Bryan?" Jordan shares.

"Don't Jordan, just keep your fucking mouth shut." Bryan quickly angers.

"What?" Gio asks.

Jordan goes on, "well Gio, we just successfully crossed the border with enough of Mexico's finest pot to keep us in spending money for a good while."

"You fucking guys swore to me there was none in the van." Gio is quite disgusted and wants to tell them they can now share in the trip's expenses. But, he doesn't want to ruin their arrival and says, "give me a beer you assholes."

"Way to go Gio, here you go man, Mexico's finest. Jordan has more to say, "and the best news is, we now know that ambergris fucks the sniffer dogs up so much they forget to sniff out the dope. I think we can go back for more when this batch is sold."

Gio asks, "do you really believe that? That may have been an isolated incident. I wouldn't bet that it could work again."

"You might be right Gio," Jordan says, "that's why we need you to drive the next time we go down there."

"You can forget that Jordan. I hope never to set foot on Baja again. I'm not sure about the rest of Mexico, but I'm done with Baja. I spent three times what that trip should have cost. Another beer please."

"Now you're talkin'," Jordan hands Gio another beer.

Gio stops at two beers and finds his way home without any detours. He stops at the cross street and gets out to get his luggage. Jordan and Bryan are looking at each other. Bryan shrugs his shoulders at Jordan. Gio walks up to the driver's window. "I'll walk the rest of the way."

"O.K., thanks Gio, you saved our lives." Quips Bryan.

"And you mine," adds Gio. He looks at Bryan, "think about what we talked about."

"I will, I'll keep in touch."

"Be careful you guys." Gio heads up his street and walks the half-block quickly. He doesn't want Sally to see the state those guys are in or risk one of them needing to use the bathroom.

Gio walks around to the deck and up the steps and looks through the sliding patio door. Amber plunges against the glass and jumps around trying to get to Gio. Gio can see Sally and soon he's inside. Amber is jumping all over him and Gio is hugging Sally while Amber continues to jump up as high as he can. Gio hears Marge's voice nearby, "welcome home stranger."

Sally asks, "have you been drinking?"

"Just had a couple of beers with those guys to celebrate being back in the good ol' U.S. of A."

"That must have been quite an ordeal with those two."

"You are so right, I'm not sure I could have stood another day, I just kept thinking, I'll be home soon."

Amber brings his leash in and drops it at Gio's feet and runs in circles.

"He was out less than an hour ago."

"Then he can wait."

Marge says, "I've never known anyone who drove all the way from Cabo."

"That was my first and last trip. I didn't want to tell you on the phone, but we got stopped at an army checkpoint and a dog sniffed out my ambergris and I had to call that.....you remember that army officer that came to the resort."

"Gomez?"

"Yes, that's the guy. I called him to get us through the checkpoint and then found out that he also had me released from jail."

"I thought you bribed a guard."

"I did, I did, that fucker just conned me out of my money."

"Mercy," Marge comments, "I'm going to tell anyone who asks me not go to Baja. Damn place nearly killed me."

"That reminds me," Gio asks, "how are you doing, are you O.K.?"

"Yes, I guess lucky to be alive really."

They chat on and in about a half-hour Marge gets up and heads home.

"Jeez Louise, I thought she would never go."

"Me too, let's head for the bedroom."

"I need a shower really."

"O.K." Sally agrees, let's get in together."

Sally puts a still unrequited Amber in the laundry room and joins Gio in the shower. It is a tremendous emotional and sexual reunion.

Now lying on the bed Gio says, "is Marge really as well as she claims?"

"Well, you'll have to go over to her studio. She's been painting like crazy since we got back and as I said on the phone, you're not going to believe what she's painting, mainly violence."

"I thought she would never leave, I just wanted some love from my baby."

"I think she's a little jealous of us. She hasn't said anything but we spent a lot of time together before I met you."

"I saw you two holding hands the night we went to Alsace's hotel."

"What?"

"When we got there Marge had pulled the rear view mirror down to check her makeup and later when I looked in the mirror I saw you guys holding hands."

"And you're just now bringing it up?"

"I didn't know what to make of it, did you guys have something going before we met?"

"Do we really have to discuss this?"

"Well, I would like to know."

"Oh, bullshit, you're a guy and instead of being upset, you'll be asking to watch."

"Now you're talking."

"See, I knew it. If a wife discovers her man with another man it's devastating. The other way around and the man wants to watch."

"O.K., let's drop it, you can tell me if and when you are ready to. I just have one question; is it still going on?"

"No, absolutely not and I don't think it would have happened except that, well, I almost think she took advantage of me when Howard died. I've told her that I'm absolutely dedicated to you and our marriage."

"Can you please blow me."

"You bet, let's see if this cocky little guy is up for it."

"Little my ass, see, he's starting to grow already." Gio leans back in anticipation and tries to imagine Sally and Marge making out.

73

Theo

R. I. P.

Two days after Jordan and Bryan left for Cabo San Lucas Jordan's father, Theo, had a heart attack and two days later died during surgery. Theo's Last Will & Testament left his business to his brother, Abe, who has worked for Theo most of his life and to Jordan. He had only said he was going to Cabo and with all the problems associated with the hurricane, there was no way to contact Jordan. It had never crossed Jordan's mind to call home.

To those close by, Theo's funeral is history. Although Abe has been a valuable asset to the business he is not good at socializing and lobbying in local politics. Worse still for Jordan, Abe's wife, Jessica, has great disdain for Jordan and regards him as a worthless leach; actually a worthy assessment. She has wasted no time in Jordan's absence and Abe and his family have already moved into Theo's old house.

The loss of Theo and his political savvy is like a pall hanging over everyone's head. Anyone at the management level has acquiesced that the business will gradually go down hill and some day close. Uncle Abe has told Jordan that it could have been all his if he had ever showed any interest.

It being obvious to Jordan that his best buddy Bryan has lost all interest in the import business, Jordan wholesales their stash and gives Bryan his share of the profits.

Jordan's homecoming is a cold and cruel one. He has overheard more than one conversation; "who just takes off to Mexico and doesn't tell anyone where they are going and then doesn't call home their entire stay?" "Irresponsible," is the most popular description. It's a cold and steely transition from the "boss's son" to "jerk," albeit well deserved.

There was a time when Theo made Jordan wear a suit and tag along to political events and meetings. After a few days of wide eyed soul searching, Jordan begins to recall some of the many things his father taught him, before he gave up on Jordan.

Jordan's Aunt Jessica has taken over in Jordan's absence and he doesn't know how to turn back the clock. He never gave a thought to the fact his dad wouldn't always be there while he played the fool. No treasure is more valuable than treasure lost. Although Jordan initially blamed Aunt Jessica for everything, Bryan quickly set him straight, "you're the one, you fucked yourself Jordan, this could all have been yours."

It has been two weeks since Jordan returned and the shock of it all could have gone two ways: The first, he would have descended into a cloud of pot, alcohol and drugs. The second, the path he chose, was to be struck sober by the impact of reality. Thus, for the longest period since Jordan was fifteen years old, his mind is free of drugs and alcohol. He's like a blind man, suddenly sighted; he sees things differently, he thinks about his future, he worries about things, he wants to make a plan. Sounds pretty much like what a lot of people would call "normal" wouldn't you say?

Jordan realizes that first he must convince himself, then the staff and Uncle Abe and in particular he must impress Aunt Jessica. At first when Jordan showed up for work people were rolling their eyes and laughing behind his back. Some how Jordan is asking lots of questions and arrives before the staff and is still there when they go home. Someone says, "I'll give him to the end of next week." Someone else suggests, "it's just a matter of time before he shows up higher than a kite."

Uncle Abe mentions that the Sheriff is coming in the next week and he is pretty sure that they will need to make a contribution to his campaign for reelection. Jordan talks to their accountant and determines the proper amount and has the check cut.

Jordan goes to his apartment every evening exhausted from his determination and hard work. The only thing he can relate it to is having stayed out all night. Something keeps going through his brain: why didn't I do this when Dad was alive? It would have meant so much to him. And, no matter how many times he asks himself, no answer comes. When he runs into a few of his "druggy" friends he tells them he's running the business now and has no time for partying. These friends mirror the employees at the salvage yard; "I'll give him three weeks and he'll be hanging with us again."

74

The Art of a Bump on the Head

Supposedly Van Gogh cut his ear off in a fit of depression and anxiety. Although that may have helped to cement his place in history it probably didn't much change his style of painting. However, Marge's concussion has produced a drastic change in how she paints and what she paints. Gio liked her "before the bump" paintings very much. Mostly bucolic scenes with lots of flowers and maybe an old half tumbled down building somewhere in the background. She certainly never fit in the category of an artist with "something to say" in her paintings. Marge is on fire with creativity and tells anyone who will listen, "I can't believe I painted that shit," in reference to her "before bump" canvasses.

It has been about a week since Gio arrived and with some loose ends, such as listing his condo for sale done, Sally and Gio go to visit Marge's studio. The first thing Gio notices is that the parking lot is nearly full.

"Wow, what are all these cars here for? There must be something going on across the street at the golf course."

"Nope, it's been like this for a couple of weeks now. They printed an article in that free newspaper we get in the mail, I meant to show it to you, but there is a copy on the bulletin board inside."

As Gio's eyes scan the room he can see what Sally meant as all the paintings contain violence and chaos. Sally takes Gio's hand and leads him to a door mounted on the wall. The door has many panes of glass and it looks as if someone has broken a few of the panes and reached through and unlocked the deadbolt. One pane in particular is dripping blood where the usurper has cut his hand and there is a partial bloody palm print near the dead bolt. Sally has directed Gio to stand on a red X that is painted on the floor. "This is where you stand."

As Gio looks at the painted door he sees a reflection in the window panes that makes him turn around in search of the two bludgeoned bodies reflected in the panes of glass. Marge has painted the images transparent and Gio can't help but look around again marveling that Marge was able to capture a murder scene so perfectly. It makes the hair on Gio's neck stand up. The victim's faces are bludgeoned beyond recognition with teeth missing, eyes misplaced and blood everywhere, giving them a sort of Picassoesque cubist look.

Marge whispers in Gio's ear, "she's been offered twenty-five grand for it."

"Holy shit." Gio says just a little too loud. Then he realizes there is a queue of people behind him waiting to stand on the red X painted on the floor. The next patron steps up and says to Gio, "Holy Shit, indeed, I've never seen anything like this and I've collected paintings most of my adult life. I hear she turned down a hundred grand for this. She had better have it put in a vault somewhere before it is stolen. Not that I would ever do anything like that," he smiles.

When they return to the beach house Gio gets on the internet and does a little research. He has told Sally that he is sure he has read more than once about people who have had severe head injuries frequently becoming very religious to the point it antagonizes those around them. Gio does find just what he remembered, but nothing is said about the effect on Marge. He supposes that had she not been an artist she would have just been haunted by the images in her mind, not knowing why it was happening. Instead, she is quickly becoming a local celeb and has asked Sally if she can work at the gallery again so she can keep painting the unending horrific images in her head. Sally has declined saying she can't take so much standing anymore with the gallery being so busy. Her real reason is that she is freaked out by what is spilling out

312

of her friend's paintbrush. The door painting will eventually sell for $37,400.00 to a Mexican art collector rumored to be part of a drug cartel. There seems to be no end to how a Category Four hurricane can mangle and change people's lives.

Where in the World is Jordan?

Uncle Abe, "I'm not sure if I should report him missing or not."

Aunt Jessica, "I can't see why. Everyone thought this would happen."

"I know, no one expected him to follow through. But damn, he sure had me fooled. He was really a pretty smart guy without the drugs."

"He just fell off the wagon. It happens to people every day. Let's give it at least a couple more weeks, there are plenty of witnesses to him having disappeared before Theo died. We do need to file a report. It will take seven years if he doesn't show up or his body isn't found. We have to think of our future."

"I guess you're right. I had such hope for him. I always felt so bad for him, you know, losing his mother during his birth."

"I think that's why Theo was such an enabler. He was tough with every one else, but not Jordan. I think he was largely responsible for Jordan being such a loser."

"Yeah, I know. What a mess. O.K., lets give him another week." Abe looks at the calendar and puts a circle around the next Thursday. "I'll go into town and make a report. I'll take Tucker with me for support on how Jordan was, or is, I suppose."

"Sounds like a plan, let's get back to work. I have a feeling that in time, this place will be all ours."

Retirement Begins Again

Gio is walking Amber on the beach. When they left this morning Sally was heading out the door to buy groceries, one of the things they seldom do together.

Gio and Amber have been up on the boardwalk putting on a "show" of Amber's tricks, to the delight of all. As they walk along the sand feels so good on Gio's feet. The bright sunshine is cascading off the ocean in rivulets of brightness. The air smells so good. A storm far out to sea has created a pounding surf and it thunders into his ears and through his head. What a wonderful moment, life is good.

As Gio looks up the beach he sees Sally has returned from shopping and is sipping from a tea cup. She's watching them and squints enough to recognize Amber pulling her lover along. She puts down the cup and waves. Gio waves his free arm over his head.

The mood is broken as Gio's cell phone rings and he stops, still a little out of voice range from Sally. Amber is soon tugging at the leash, wanting to greet Sally. Gio bends down and unhooks the leash and Amber runs on ahead. Gio is on the phone for about fifteen minutes. As he walks onto the deck he bends over and kisses Sally on her left ear. "Cut it out, you'll have me all wet. Who was that on the phone?"

"Just an international friend of mine."

"Well, let's see, would his first name be Alsace?"

"Good Guess."

"So what's he up to?"

"He's going to be going to Mozambique in a couple of weeks."

"Isn't that in Africa?"

"Yes, apparently they had a terrible civil war there that supposedly ended a few years ago. He says the C. I. A. is wanting to overthrow the president there. They've discovered oil there and the U. S. wants in on it."

"What does Alsace have to do with it?"

"He's brokering a deal to sell the latest weapons to the rebels. He says he'll make at least a million bucks on it and he wants me to go with him."

Sally sits silent for a while and sips her tea. "What did you tell him?"

"That I'll think about it."

"Gio, are you craving that kind of excitement? You could get killed in a place like that."

"Still, a million dollars."

Both remain silent for a while. Gio stands up and walks over to Sally and kisses her deeply and holds her ever so tight. He nuzzles her ear and whispers, "I not only told him no, I told him hell no." Gio grabs both of Sally's hands and pulls her up from her chair.

"Now madam, do you think we can continue that honeymoon, you know, the one that got so botched-up in Cabo?"

"Well, I don't see why not."

The newlyweds discard their clothing as they walk down the hallway. The surf is thundering through the open windows. One of the many gifts from the sea.

The End

72344270R00192

Made in the USA
Columbia, SC
16 June 2017